THE WORLD OF
SHERLOCK

ABOUT THE AUTHOR

 PROFESSOR B. J. RAHN teaches English Literature at Hunter College in New York. She has been teaching, researching and writing about crime fiction for over two decades. She has published articles in journals and reference books such as *The Armchair Detective*, *The Dictionary of Literary Biography* and the *Oxford Companion to Crime and Mystery Writing*. She also leads detective walking tours in the UK, which visit sites in the lives and fiction of authors such as Arthur Conan Doyle, Dorothy L. Sayers, Agatha Christie and Margery Allingham.

THE REAL WORLD OF SHERLOCK

B. J. RAHN

AMBERLEY

First published in 2014
This edition published 2015

Amberley Publishing
The Hill, Stroud
Gloucestershire, GL5 4EP

www.amberley-books.com

ISBN 978-1-4456-5055-5 (paperback)
ISBN 978-1-4456-3777-8 (ebook)

British Library Cataloguing in Publication Data.
A catalogue record for this book is available from the British Library.

Typesetting and Origination by Amberley Publishing
Printed in the UK.

In homage to a good-natured man
Paul Robert Rahn
20 June 1938 – 7 February 2014

CONTENTS

ACKNOWLEDGEMENTS

I owe thanks to several friends in the Sherlockian world who have filled gaps in my knowledge and my memory and made suggestions of where to look for elusive information. First among them is Roger Johnson, seemingly the fount of all knowledge, whose patience is exceeded only by his goodwill. On the other side of the pond Susan Rice and Mickie Fromkin fulfil this role. Catherine Cooke and Shirley Purves have also been generous in answering queries. Joan Lock shared books and cuttings from her valuable archive on the Metropolitan Police, and Trish Morris supplied a crucial reference on cocaine. To William Harlowe goes a special thanks for his tenacious search for obscure items in the nineteenth-century periodical press and for being my first reader.

Like Blanche Dubois in *A Streetcar Named Desire* I have also relied on the kindness of strangers in finding sources for this book. Many of them apply their arcane skills of information retrieval in libraries and archives. My admiration and appreciation go to the resourceful and unstinting staff members at the British Library, Senate House Library of the University of London, the Library of the Royal College of Surgeons of Edinburgh, the Metropolitan Police Heritage Centre in the UK, as well as the New York Society Library and Butler Library at Columbia University.

Special *abbracci e baci* go to Nicole, Lucca, et al. at Gastronomie for a thousand cups of coffee delivered with sunny Mediterranean smiles and panache to their most enthusiastic Wi-Fi user, and to Dawn and Maureen et al. at Manhattan Mail Room for internet assistance and photocopying.

Finally, to members of my personal support system – Thom Taylor, the man who cannot say 'No' and is always there to help, and Carmela Farella, who always lends a sympathetic ear and offers psychological support.

INTRODUCTION: THE STORY BEHIND THE STORIES

Almost from his first appearance in *The Strand Magazine* in 1891, Sherlock Holmes has enjoyed a remarkable cult of celebrity, which extended through his last investigation in 1927 on into his 'afterlife' in the present day. For over a century his popularity has transcended all geographical boundaries and time zones. He appeared in only fifty-six short stories and four novellas in the periodical press, but they have never gone out of print. There is hardly another character in all of English literature as well known or as well liked, as respected and revered. His fame has eclipsed that of his creator – not an easy feat. The vital energy usually lies with the creator rather than his progeny. Arthur Conan Doyle was, indeed, an extraordinary individual.

To paraphrase Proteus when contemplating the charms of Silvia in *The Two Gentlemen of Verona*, one might ask, 'Who is Sherlock, what is he, that all the world commends him?' This book attempts to answer those two questions by investigating the real-life sources of Arthur Conan Doyle's inspiration for his iconic hero Sherlock Holmes, as well as the individuals, contemporary events and social issues that inform the context of Holmes' adventures. It will provide an accurate historical insight into the ideas and circumstances which produced the world's first consulting detective.

Conan Doyle's chief sources for his detective hero and his

adventures were his own character and experience. Conan Doyle was very much a man of his time, shaped by events and in turn helping to shape them. He was the quintessential Victorian, exemplifying the thrusting spirit of the age – energetic, inquiring, resourceful and independent. Endowed with robust physical health, he was an avid sportsman and world traveller. Early reading of medieval tales of chivalry, valour and derring-do stirred his imagination and inculcated an idealistic code of honour. He was open to fresh ideas and eager to investigate ingenious original theories. His medical training instilled in him a great respect for using scientific method to establish truth, and his Jesuit schooling engendered a deep sense of right and wrong. His well-developed social conscience led him to champion the cause of individuals wrongly convicted of criminal offences, like Alfred Dreyfus as well as Nicolo Sacco and Bartolomeo Vanzetti. It also prompted him to run for Parliament twice. He was intensely loyal to queen and country, volunteering to serve as a doctor in the Boer War and writing a much-lauded book defending Britain's policies. His equitable treatment elicited respect from friend and foe. Conan Doyle's inquiring mind, intellectual rigour and determination are embodied in his fictional hero. Sherlock Holmes displays his dedication to social justice and commitment to national welfare, as well as sharing his personal tastes in tobacco and passion for music.

Nonetheless, Holmes is not a clone of Conan Doyle. He lacks his creator's breadth of vision and *joie de vivre*. Holmes is a focused, obsessed manic depressive with eccentric habits and an intermittent drug dependency. However, his custom of resorting to cocaine and opium when he is bored wanes as he becomes more successful. This self-indulgence is mentioned in only five stories, so it is not really accurate to consider him a confirmed addict. He shows his anxiety by curling up in a chair with his chin on his knees and his arms hugging his shins, and boasting to Watson about his superiority. An infantile streak is revealed in his love of playing mischievous practical jokes. Unlike the gregarious Conan Doyle, who was a devoted family man and had a wide circle of friends and acquaintances, Holmes shuns society to prevent personal relationships clouding his objective judgment. He is certainly not a misanthrope. As time goes by, he does display concern and compassion for a great many female clients and other women. He altruistically fights crime to preserve the social welfare of his fellow citizens. Although he is a recluse, he can interact easily with people in all social circles. His well-spoken, polite, confident manner is disarming and encourages even the most reticent to cooperate during interviews. His intuitive insight into human nature guides him to vary his approach from gently compassionate to harsh and hectoring when seeking information. This paradoxical combination of strengths and weaknesses has won homage from fans around the world.

Holmes is most famous for his brilliant logical deductions, for his ability to draw inferences from close observation of material evidence and human behaviour. His character was based on both fictional and human models. He combines features of the first literary detective, Chevalier Auguste Dupin, and Dr Joseph Bell, a brilliant diagnostician and Conan Doyle's medical mentor at Edinburgh University. Conan Doyle became a devotee of Edgar Allan Poe's short stories as a young man, while he was studying mathematics and chemistry in Austria before matriculating in medical school. While he was acting as Bell's outpatient clerk during his weekly clinics at the Royal Infirmary, Conan Doyle had ample opportunity to observe Bell's astonishing diagnostic methods. To Poe, Conan Doyle is indebted for the odd-couple detective partnership and some plot devices; to Poe's detective hero Holmes owes his 'Bi-Part Soul' and manic-depressive personality, his mind-reading gift, clever disguises and personal eccentricities. Both Poe and Bell inspired Sherlock's method of logical deduction based on close observation of often trifling details, such as the dog who did not bark in 'Silver Blaze'. Negative evidence is also important in 'The Naval Treaty' and 'The Second Stain'. When no repercussions occur following the theft of vital documents, Holmes concludes that they have not been sold abroad and deduces their whereabouts.

What especially distinguishes Holmes from other sleuths of the era, even Poe's Dupin, is his scientific approach to solving crimes, his insistence on treating criminal investigation as a science. In reality, the significant advances in crime solving during the past two centuries, sometimes quite dramatic, are the result of the brilliant insight and diligent application of scientific researchers. The detectives in the laboratories are real-life heroes. Some of them were celebrated in their own day, like Bernard Henry Spilsbury, and some posthumously. Holmes' success as a private consulting detective depended in great measure on the disorganisation, mismanagement and lack of expertise of the police. Throughout the twentieth century the police became more effective as they began to rely more on scientific methods and proofs and less on routine surveillance, informers and the occasional 'lucky breaks' of individual police officers. Centralisation of offenders' records with photographs, introduction of a system for classifying fingerprints, reliable blood tests, improved methods for gathering trace evidence – all played a role in improving police results.

Conan Doyle had a life-long interest in crime and its detection. He avidly followed newspaper accounts of criminal cases, cross-referencing press cuttings in scrapbooks, and he studied new forensic techniques. He conducted his own criminal investigations and successfully challenged two jury verdicts. Ever *au courant*, he introduced details from Scotland Yard's investigation of the first railway murder into his story 'The Bruce Partington Plans'. As an early member of the exclusive Crimes Club, he interacted with prominent criminal lawyers and police officials. At their meetings, papers on intriguing crimes were followed by discussion in which members disclosed 'insider' views and even displayed pieces of trial evidence.

Conan Doyle never missed an opportunity for first-hand observation. For example, he took a tour of Scotland Yard's famous Black Museum, visited the crime scenes of Jack the Ripper's victims, and attended important trials like that of Dr Hawley Harvey Crippen. Many of the villains Holmes confronted, together with their crimes, were drawn from real life. For example, the bank robbery in 'The Red-Headed League' was modelled on Adam Worth's bold tunnelling into Boston's Boylston National Bank.

Conan Doyle earned the right to be considered a consulting detective when he investigated the George Edalji case following Holmesian methods, and gathered enough scientific evidence, based on ophthalmology and chirography, to prove Edalji's innocence. He also marshalled logical arguments to undermine the police case. In effect, Conan Doyle became Sherlock Holmes. Working in the face of police hostility to countermand an unjust verdict, he turned to the press as his court of appeal. The pressure of public opinion forced the Home Office to appoint a Committee of Inquiry, which reluctantly recommended a pardon. So, like one of the knights in the medieval tales of chivalry he had loved in his youth, Conan Doyle had the satisfaction of defending an innocent victim and righting a serious wrong. Unwilling to abandon the matter without full reparation, however, he also collected material evidence and verbal testimony to build a convincing dossier against the true culprit. What could be more Sherlockian?

PART I

THE REAL SHERLOCK HOLMES:
A PERSONAL PROFILE

1

EDGAR ALLAN POE: GENERIC CONVENTIONS

Edgar Allan Poe is credited with having invented the detective story, introducing its principal conventions in three tales featuring his reclusive investigator Chevalier C. Auguste Dupin: 'The Mystery in the Rue Morgue' (1841), 'The Mystery of Marie Rogêt' (1843) and 'The Purloined Letter' (1844). Poe referred to these stories as tales of ratiocination, that is, exercises in logical analysis. The word 'detective' was not in general use at the time of Poe's writing.[1] In fact, it was first applied to a special department of the Metropolitan Police in London created in 1843 to detect crimes instead of trying to prevent them by a protective show of power and vigilance.[2] Matthew Pearl notes that 'the first American bureau of detectives ... was established in Boston in 1845'.[3]

Sherlock Holmes is most often compared to Edgar Allan Poe's Chevalier C. Auguste Dupin, whose feats of ratiocination Conan Doyle read with relish as a schoolboy. He later acknowledged Poe as the writer who had had the most influence on him: 'Poe's masterful detective, M Dupin, had from boyhood been one of my heroes.'[4] He confided in a fellow student at Edinburgh, Dr George Hamilton, 'that he had the idea of writing detective fiction according to the system of Poe, but greatly simplified and brought down to the level of ordinary people'.[5] Years later, when asked by a journalist in America whether he was influenced by Poe when he created Sherlock Holmes, he replied, 'Oh, immensely! ... His detective is the best in fiction ... Dupin is unrivalled ... It was Poe who taught the possibility of making a detective story a work of literature.'[6]

To 'The Murders in the Rue Morgue' (hereafter 'Rue Morgue') can be traced the two most important features of the classical detective story: the puzzle plot embodying principles of logical deduction, and the character of the eccentric cerebral sleuth. During the nearly 175 years of the genre's history, Poe's six-step plot formula has at times been modified somewhat but has remained largely unchanged:

1) A crime occurs within a closed or isolated environment.
2) The police are called in but are stymied, though they may think they have solved the case and even arrest an innocent suspect.
3) A gifted but eccentric amateur detective with encyclopedic knowledge, intuitive insight and great skill at deductive reasoning volunteers or is invited to investigate. He is sometimes assisted by a trusted but less able friend, who performs minor tasks, keeps a record of the case and later publishes it.
4) The sleuth observes the crime scene, examines the physical evidence, interviews witnesses and suspects and conducts research. He analyses the data collected and forms a hypothesis explaining the means, motive and opportunity of the crime.
5) He tests his theory by reconstructing the crime and/or confronting the villain – often the least likely suspect – in a dramatic climax.

6) The denouement includes a full explanation of any unanswered questions or obscure points of the puzzle.

Dupin's first case is easily summarised.

1) Neighbours and the police were drawn to the premises of Madame L'Espanaye and her daughter in Paris's Rue Morgue by the women's shrill screams and the deep, guttural menaces of a foreigner. After forced entry into the wildly disordered fourth-floor bedroom with its door and window locked from the inside, neighbours and police found the body of the throttled daughter wedged feet first up the chimney. The mother's bruised and nearly decapitated corpse lay below the bedroom windows in a courtyard directly behind the building.

2) The police were faced with a seemingly impossible crime because they could not understand how the culprit got in and out of the building. A thorough search uncovered no hidden passages or secret rooms, and they had passed no one as they ascended the only staircase leading to the crime scene. Because of public pressure in the media, the police arrested Adolphe Le Bon, a bank clerk who had helped Madame L'Espanaye carry home a sum of 4,000 gold francs three days earlier. Yet they had no direct proof to link him with the crime. The money was still in the bedroom, so robbery was not the motive for the murders.

3) Dupin and his anonymous friend read newspaper accounts of the brutal murders and the questionable police investigation. Because he believes that the police have erred and because M. Le Bon once did him a service, Dupin proposes that he and his crony make their own investigation. He lacks faith in the police because they want method and confuse the unusual with the abstruse.[7] Actually, he claims, the more outré a crime is, the easier it is to solve.[8] When the police fail, it is because they have no imagination. They achieve best results by simple diligence.[9]

4) Having been granted permission to inspect the crime scene, Dupin walks around the house and observes the rear courtyard before subjecting the bedroom and the victims' bodies to thorough examination, noticing several details unremarked by the police both outside and inside the building. He takes samples of the physical evidence, makes measurements, draws sketches and conducts trial-and-error experiments with the windows before leaving. Peter Costello writes that 'to the Chevalier Dupin, no detail was too trivial to be without significance'.[10]

En route back to their apartment, Dupin stops at a newspaper office to insert an adroitly worded notice to entice his suspect to call on him. Relying on interviews from eyewitnesses reported in the press plus his own personal observations, Dupin has formed his hypothesis before leaving the crime scene. At home he briefly consults a zoological reference book, Jean Leopold Nicolas Cuvier's *Le Regne Animal* (1817), merely to confirm his theory.

The next day he shares his reasoning with his companion. Dupin asks him whether he noticed anything peculiar about the murder scene. When he receives a negative reply, Dupin reviews the details of the case and invites his comrade at four stages in his explication to draw logical inferences from the facts, but like the police, he lacks the imagination to connect disparate elements to form a coherent solution. In solving the most difficult part of the puzzle – how the culprit got in and out of the locked room – Dupin invokes the cardinal rule of logical deduction: when all impossibilities have been eliminated, that which remains must be the truth.[11] He finishes his exegesis and presents his solution just as a knock on the door heralds the arrival of the individual whom Dupin summoned, after imagining his thoughts and feelings via the newspaper advertisement.[12]

5) Their interview is really a confrontation in which the visitor confirms Dupin's hypothesis and supplies the few details which Dupin had not deduced.

6) A very brief denouement follows in which Le Bon is

released and the true culprit detained. Clearly this seminal story contributed the template for the most common plot structure in detective fiction – the whodunnit.

The other two tales of ratiocination featuring Dupin and his anonymous associate also introduce important generic conventions. 'The Mystery of Marie Rogêt' (hereafter 'Marie Rogêt') is a tour de force in which Dupin deduces a solution to the murder of a beautiful young Parisian shop assistant by analysing the information presented in newspaper accounts and collected in official police reports of her death, that is, merely by doing research. The narrative is based on the actual murder of Mary Cecelia Rogers in New York City in 1841. Poe simply transferred the locale of the crime to Paris, keeping the essential details of the murder intact. Dupin again rings the changes on the principle that the more outré a crime appears, the simpler its solution will be. He asserts that, although atrocious, this crime is ordinary and therefore more intricate because there is nothing peculiarly outré about it. Its very ordinariness makes it difficult.[13] Dupin analyses the facts to form a hypothesis using logical deduction based on circumstantial evidence and common sense; moreover, he imagines the thoughts and actions of both victim and villain in order to interpret the evidence and reach a conclusion.[14] However, in the final pages Dupin does not confront his suspect and present a solution to the crime but rather suggests a series of steps which he is confident will lead to a completion of the case. His hypothesis is based exclusively on written records rather than first-hand observation of the crime scene and personally conducted interviews; thus, Poe established the prototype of the armchair detective.

In 'The Purloined Letter' Dupin again demonstrates that the simpler a crime appears, the more difficult it will be to solve. This story is not a murder mystery. The question is not who-done-it, but rather where-is-it? Again Poe sets his tale in France. The villain is a court minister whose identity is known from the outset, and the problem is to recover a compromising letter he has stolen by sleight of hand from the queen in the presence of the king. He has used it to blackmail her to use her influence for his own political advantage and thereby endangered her. The police have searched his home and office and even his person to no avail. When the prefect confesses to being baffled by this simple affair, Dupin suggests that its very simplicity puts him at fault, once again invoking the principle that the simplest mysteries are always the most difficult to solve. Dupin explains to his colleague that he must put himself in the mind of his adversary, in order to discover where he hid the letter.[15] Success depends upon how accurate one's insight is. The police assume that everyone thinks as they do and cannot imagine otherwise. Dupin's analysis of the cunning minister leads him to the conclusion that the wily thief would anticipate the strategies of the police and decide that the best place to hide something is out in the open[16] where it will be ignored. A visit to the minister confirms his theory when he spies a cheap pasteboard card rack dangling by a dirty blue ribbon containing a soiled document of the right size which had been turned inside out, readdressed and resealed. During a second visit on the pretext of collecting his forgotten snuffbox, Dupin retrieves the document and substitutes a replica.

Readers owe a great debt to Poe, who in merely three short stories created the major conventions of the classical detective genre: both the who-dun-it and the where-is-it puzzle plot formulas, the gifted amateur sleuth in both active and passive modes and the principles of ratiocination.

Conan Doyle and Poe's Plot Structure

Conan Doyle not only adopted Poe's classical whodunit plot formula in many stories, but he also modified it and devised new templates. For example, in some tales the second step may be omitted because the police have failed to achieve satisfactory results or because the matter is too delicate or scandalous to involve them. 'The Beryl Coronet', 'Charles Augustus Milverton', 'The Dancing Men', 'The Second Stain', 'A Scandal in Bohemia' and 'The Three Students' exemplify this group. Holmes' cases often begin when a prospective client calls at his lodgings in Baker Street seeking help. Thus Conan Doyle alters Poe's pattern by beginning with the third step, in which the gifted freelance detective is invited to investigate a problem. Sometimes the client informs Holmes of a crime, but often he is consulted about puzzling or frightening circumstances that may or may not involve crime, as in 'The Blanched Soldier', 'The Solitary Cyclist' or 'The Speckled Band'. Occasionally there are just disturbing odd incidents. As Holmes remarks to Watson in 'The Copper Beeches', 'You can hardly be open to a charge of sensationalism, for out of these cases ... a fair proportion do not treat of crime, in its legal sense, at all.'[17] 'The Creeping Man', 'The Crooked Man', 'A Case of Identity', 'The Lion's Mane', 'The Missing Three Quarter', 'The Noble Bachelor' and 'The Yellow Face' all fall into this category.

As in Poe's stories, however, the fourth step – the investigation itself – forms the balance of the tale. Deviation may occur in the sequence of methods employed, but Holmes, like Dupin, relies on observation, interviews and research to gather information, then he analyses the data to form a hypothesis. Regarding the fifth step, Holmes does not always confront his chief suspect in a dramatic climax. At times, following Poe's lead in 'The Mystery of Marie Rogêt', Holmes may turn his evidence over to the police and leave them to arrest the villain, as he did in 'The Cardboard Box' and 'The Priory School'. Contrary to the popular conception that Holmes always triumphs, in a few cases Holmes is outwitted and the malefactor escapes before Holmes can confront him/her, as happens in 'The Engineer's Thumb', 'The Five Orange Pips', 'The Greek Interpreter', 'The Resident Patient', 'A Scandal in Bohemia' and 'Wisteria

Lodge'. He admits in 'The Five Orange Pips' (1891) that he has only been beaten four times – three times by men and once by a woman[18] – but this story was published in advance of 'The Greek Interpreter' (1893) and 'Wisteria Lodge' (1908), so ultimately the total is higher.

Even more surprising, Holmes may decide to exercise personal discretion and withhold his solution from the police because he is not acting in an official role and because he feels that justice will be better served by withholding the culprit's identity than by legal prosecution. This occurs in 'The Abbey Grange', 'The Blue Carbuncle', 'The Boscombe Valley Mystery', 'Charles Augustus Milverton', 'The Devil's Foot', 'The Second Stain', 'The Sussex Vampire', 'The Three Gables', 'The Three Students' and 'The Veiled Lodger'. In two murders among these cases Holmes refrains from notifying the police because the villains are in ill health and would not outlive a trial. Two other murders he judges to be justifiable homicides. He refuses to investigate the murder of the blackmailer Charles Augustus Milverton because he believes that when crimes are beyond the reach of the law, private revenge is justified. To avert ruinous scandal, Holmes is guilty of compounding a felony in 'The Beryl Coronet', 'The Second Stain' and 'The Three Gables'. To give two young men a second chance in life, he withholds information from the police and pardons a thief for the same reason. In 'The Man with the Twisted Lip' and 'Shoscombe Old Place' he colludes with the police in dismissing and/or reducing charges because the offences committed were minor. Conan Doyle always includes the sixth step, the denouement, in which Holmes answers all questions asked by the client, the police, or Watson, who serves as the readers' surrogate.

As well as adopting Poe's plot structures, Conan Doyle also invented new devices, such as the decoy plot, in which a character is employed on a fool's errand or fraudulent task in order to remove him from an intended crime scene. In 'The Red Headed League', Jabez Wilson is given the chore of copying the *Encyclopaedia Britannica* for the sum of four gold sovereigns per week between the hours of ten in the morning and two in the afternoon in order to guarantee his absence from his pawn shop, where his assistant is surreptitiously digging a tunnel in the cellar. In 'The Stock-Broker's Clerk', Hall Pycroft, who has recently secured a post at the highly respected London stock-brokerage firm of Mawson & Williams, is lured away to Birmingham before his first day at the job by a more tempting offer from a firm called the Franco-Midland Hardware Company, where he is asked to compile potential client lists of hardware and furniture companies in France. This make-work activity has been devised so that his bogus employer's brother can plan a robbery at Mawson's while impersonating him. In 'The Three Garridebs', Nathan Garrideb, a reclusive collector of bones, butterflies, coins, flints, fossils and a wealth of other arcana, goes to Birmingham to meet a man with the same surname in order to claim an inheritance. He is sent by James Winter alias 'Killer' Evans so he can search Garrideb's cellar for counterfeiting equipment and bogus currency owned by the previous tenant, Rodger Prescott, a master forger.

Other plot patterns original to Conan Doyle include stories with puzzles but no crimes. They contain deaths that appear criminal but are really accidents, as in 'The Lion's Mane', 'Silver Blaze' and 'The Crooked Man'. He also invented prevention scenarios which attempt to ward off some dreadful event, such as the marriage of Violet de Merville to Baron Adelbert Gruner in 'The Illustrious Client', the wrongful prosecution and conviction of John Hector McFarlane in 'The Norwood Builder' and that of Grace Dunbar in 'The Problem of Thor Bridge'. Abduction plots, as in 'The Greek Interpreter' or 'The Disappearance of Lady Frances Carfax', are merely a variation on the seek-and-find search for stolen objects introduced by Poe.

Both Poe and Conan Doyle use details from real-life crimes reported in newspapers. For example, Poe combined facts from several incidents in New York City in constructing the horrific details of 'Rue Morgue'. In his monograph *Edgar*

Allan Poe and the Philadelphia Saturday News, Richard Kopley cites several unrelated articles from contemporary newspapers whose details match many of those in Poe's tale.[19] For example, in 1838 a news item appeared in Philadelphia's *Saturday News* featuring an orang-utan in the London Zoo that emphasised its prodigious strength and unusual activity when excited, including dragging a heavy piece of furniture across the floor.[20] Yet another story concerning another primate appeared on 15 September under the headline 'Mischievous Ape'. It tells of the escape from a stable in New York of a baboon that opened the window of a house, entered the parlour and terrified the occupants. After being chased from the premises, the ape took hold of the hair of a child and nearly took his scalp off. He also bit and scratched another boy.[21] Finally, on 29 December a bizarre episode was related in the *Saturday News* describing a mentally disturbed man holding on to the window shutters outside a house and peering into the room where a Thanksgiving dance was being held, swinging on the shutters and 'grinning like a yellow monkey'.[22]

Another story in the *Saturday News* told of a gory murder on Broadway in New York City by Edward Coleman, who slit his wife's throat with a razor, nearly severing her head from her body, before dropping her to the pavement.[23] The razor was smeared with blood. On 18 August 1838 the *Saturday News* published an item about a French woman, whose former servant robbed her and then returned, intending to stab her to death to gain access to her jewellery that was kept in an iron box, much like the scene in 'Rue Morgue'.[24] The *Saturday News* for 1 December gives an account of two women (aged forty and seventeen) living in New York in a small upper room, who both died of suffocation from smoke fumes issuing from a charcoal furnace in the centre of the room. The door had to be broken in to reach them.

In addition to parallels in circumstance, Kopley notes the frequent similarities in phrasing between the newspaper reportage and the 'Rue Morgue' text to validate his argument concerning Poe's sources. He concludes by quoting a passage Poe wrote in June 1845 describing his creative process: 'To originate is carefully, patiently, and understandingly to combine.'[25] As he suggested previously in January 1840, '"a *creation* of intellect" is akin to a griffin – both seem new but are made up of already-existing parts'.[26] So, '"Rue Morgue" may be one of the finest specimens of a griffin that Poe ever imagined'.[27] Of course Poe elevated this technique into a tour de force when he analysed information about the murder of Mary Cecelia Rogers taken directly from newspapers to form his theory of her death.

Similarly, Conan Doyle often interwove circumstances and events into Holmes' cases that were culled from actual crimes. He 'owned a criminological library and was widely read in the criminal history of several countries'.[28] He kept more than fifty notebooks and scrapbooks of notes for literary projects and manuscripts, hobbies, anecdotes, general reflections on the human condition, etc. Scattered among them are press cuttings about crimes and criminals and notes of his own criminal investigations.[29] Much as Poe combined information from several news stories in 'Rue Morgue', so Conan Doyle melded details from two widely publicised railway murders into 'The Bruce Partington Plans'. In July 1864 the nation was appalled at the robbery and brutal murder of Mr Thomas Briggs, whose battered body was found beside the tracks in East London twenty minutes after two clerks discovered a blood-soaked carriage. His hat, watch and chain were missing. When the killer was traced, Briggs' missing property was found among his things.[30] Forty years later, in 1905, Maria Sophia Money was violently assaulted and her body was ejected from a railway carriage and found on the tracks in the Merstham tunnel on the London–Brighton line. Medical evidence indicated that some injuries had been inflicted inside the train. A signal man at Purley Oaks testified to seeing a couple struggling in the carriage. Miss Money's murder was never solved. These two cases obviously inspired the disposal of the body in 'The Bruce Partington Plans' (1908).[31]

The theft of the Irish Crown Jewels in July 1907 was also a source of details for the same story. When his mother's second cousin Sir Arthur Vickers, Ulster King-at-Arms, wrote to Conan Doyle asking for advice, he communicated the facts of the break-in, regarding times, dates and the keys needed to open the doors. Many of these details turn up in 'The Bruce Partington Plans'.[32] For example, three keys were needed to steal the plans for the Woolwich Arsenal: outer door, inner door and safe.[33]

Conan Doyle focused on Francis Shackleton, Vickers' deputy, but failed to find sufficient evidence. Shackleton was later jailed for fraud, and Vickers was shot dead in 1921 at his home, purportedly by the IRA.[34]

Despite the undeniable originality, variety and profusion of Conan Doyle's literary talent, Poe's influence was profound. In addition to assimilating generic plot formulas from Poe and sharing Poe's penchant for culling and combining details of crimes from newspapers, Conan Doyle's early stories reveal that he reworked scenarios and themes from Poe's tales. For example, in 'The Sign of Four' he creates a locked-room puzzle in which the Andaman Island pygmy, Tonga, scales the physically challenging wall as the orang-utan did in 'Rue Morgue', commits robbery and murder and escapes by the same route. (The plot in this novella, involving the reclamation of stolen Indian treasure, is also reminiscent of Wilkie Collins' *The Moonstone*.) The first of the *Strand Magazine* short stories, 'A Scandal in Bohemia', resembles 'The Purloined Letter'. Holmes is set the task of retrieving a compromising photograph rather than a letter, but he uses the same kind of external public distraction to trick Irene Adler into disclosing its location.[35]

Much of Holmes' popularity has been attributed to Conan Doyle's marketing strategy of featuring the same character in a series of short stories. This format ensured success because it maintained continuity of the central figure and yet offered closure, since each instalment presented a complete adventure. The sequence of linked tales had all the advantages of monthly serials without any of their disadvantages. The reader enjoyed the pleasure of ongoing acquaintance with an interesting personality without the frustration of having to wait for the next episode to find out what happened. This system also reveals Poe's influence, for Conan Doyle merely elaborated upon and improved the design of the recurring sleuth that was first employed in the three Dupin stories.

Character and Lifestyle

Poe's influence on Conan Doyle extended to the character and lifestyle of his protagonist. Conan Doyle adopted Poe's odd-couple detective partnership, with the brilliant, eccentric logician admired and assisted by a less gifted friend, but he enhanced each individual's personality considerably and changed some traits. Although Dupin's genius is not as fully developed as that of Holmes, clearly he served as a model for the super sleuth. Moreover, Conan Doyle described Holmes and Watson's lodgings in detail, as well as their habits and lifestyle.

M. Dupin receives a small pension generated by the remains of his patrimony. Preferring the life of the mind and too poor to indulge in material luxuries or the social round, Dupin shares accommodation with a fellow scholar, whom he met in an obscure library in the Rue Montmartre. They live in a decrepit mansion at 33 Rue Dunôt in a desolate section of the Faubourg St Germain in Paris. Beyond creating a Gothic ambience, Poe provides no description of Dupin's apartment or the furnishings except for mention of some candles, a couple of chairs and an escritoire. He offers no insight into housekeeping arrangements.[36] Presumably his antisocial pair fended for themselves.

In contrast to this Gothic Parisian setting, 221b Baker Street is located in a respectable middle-class neighbourhood near Regent's Park, with easy access to London's fashionable West End shops and theatres. Holmes and Watson share a capacious sitting room with two windows overlooking the street plus separate bedrooms and lumber rooms upstairs.[37] Their landlady Mrs Hudson provides meals, which she serves in their sitting room. Presumably, she tidies the premises regularly and looks after their bed linen and personal laundry. So while preserving the bachelor household, Conan Doyle improved the domestic comfort of his characters and gave them a less isolated, more normal lifestyle.

In addition to Mrs Hudson, other characters appearing regularly include detective officers Lestrade, Hopkins and Gregson from Scotland Yard, Holmes' clients, and a band of street urchins known as the Baker Street Irregulars, who run errands for Holmes.[38] Holmes receives his clients at Baker Street, so his home is also his office. His callers are his professional contacts. Although they have visitors, and even offer them hospitality in the form of a drink or cigar occasionally, Holmes and Watson do not have a social circle. However, they attend concerts, dine in fashionable restaurants, indulge in the Turkish bath and travel.[39] Satisfied with each other's company, they 'keep themselves to themselves'. After Watson marries, Holmes does not seek anyone else to join him but becomes more withdrawn, telling Watson, when he visits for a few days, that he does not 'encourage visitors'.[40]

Dupin and his partner are even more solitary; they deliberately seclude themselves. 'We admitted no visitors.'[41] 'The locality of our retirement had been carefully kept secret …'[42] Sharing a morose temperament as well as their tenement, Dupin and his crony lead a reclusive, eccentric life. Dupin's eccentricity is revealed by his habits – his withdrawal from society and his preference for night over day. At dawn they close the shutters and spend the day reading, writing and conversing in a twilight gloom produced by scented tapers. Like the scholar in John Milton's 'Il Penseroso' who avoided 'Day's garish eie', Dupin shuns daylight and prefers to spend his time in recondite study behind closed shutters where guttering candles create a twilight gloom.[43] 'We then busied ourselves in dreams – reading, writing, or conversing, until warned by the clock of the advent of true Darkness.'[44] The narrator in 'Rue Morgue' suggests that the candles may have been impregnated with incense, or a stronger drug which heightened consciousness and permitted escape into a fantasy world and/or which stimulated rigorous intellectual endeavour. After sunset when darkness engulfs the streets of Paris and most men are abed, Dupin explores the backstreets with his associate, discussing further topics of interest and taking pleasure from observing the city's vast diversity. Dupin is regarded as a boon companion by his colleague as he alternates discourse with meditation and then roams the streets for recreation.

Holmes and Watson's rambles through London where they watch 'the ever-changing kaleidoscope of life as it ebbs and flows through Fleet Street and the Strand', evidently modelled on those of Poe's characters, endorse the idea of compatible, self-sufficient male companionship.[45]

Although Dupin's scented tapers may hint of drugs, his indulgence pales by comparison with Holmes' practices. However, his intermittent indulgence hardly qualifies him as an addict. Mention of his reliance on drugs occurs in only five of the sixty tales.[46] *In extremis* between cases early in his career, he injects himself with a 7 per cent solution of cocaine and resorts to morphine as well. A 7 per cent solution of cocaine is only 1 per cent stronger than the cocaine being peddled on the New York black market in 1970 for contemporary recreational use.[47] The most descriptive passages occur in 'Sign of Four'. Holmes' drug of choice was first isolated in pure form in 1844. It became commercially available in Britain in 1883, four years before 'Study in Scarlet' was published.

It is interesting that throughout the 1870s several articles appeared in *The British Medical Journal* discussing experimental trials conducted by medical doctors in Edinburgh of the effects of consuming *cuca*, or coca. In 1874 Joseph Bell, Conan Doyle's mentor at Edinburgh, submitted a brief account of its uses for treating various diseases giving recommended doses. He described the effects produced by small, medium and large doses and offered to supply colleagues with small quantities should anyone desire to use it in his practice.

> In large doses, it is said to cause delirium, and finally cerebral congestion. In small doses, it acts as a stimulant, increasing the temperature of the body, as well as the respiration and frequency of the pulse. In moderate doses, it excites the nervous system ... as to render the performance of muscular exertion much easier, and producing a sensation of calmness.[48]

Another of Conan Doyle's professors at Edinburgh, Dr Robert Christison, noting that it was not commercially available in Scotland, reported at length on his experiments with *cuca* in 1876.[49] His results agree with those reported by Bell. In fact, Christison was one of several doctors participating in a lively exchange of information on similar experiments at the time. Conan Doyle entered medical school in Edinburgh two years later. As a conscientious student he may have become interested in what was obviously an important topic of the day.

A decade later Sigmund Freud began using cocaine to treat himself and his patients, with doses of thirty to fifty milligrams, approximately one-twentieth of a gram. He published an essay praising its effects in July 1884. He was enthusiastic about its ability to alleviate depression without eliminating energy for exercise or work and delighted that it produced no unpleasant aftereffects. Nor did his patients develop a craving for it. Freud's findings were confirmed at first but soon came under attack from other professionals, who reported addiction and physical symptoms like delirium tremens among their patients. Many people became addicted because a solution of between

2 and 4 per cent was used to treat catarrh. It reduces mucous and opens nasal passages, easing breathing.

So Dr Watson was well advised to caution Holmes about the physical and mental defects of cocaine and wean him from it. Watson merely suspects Holmes of taking drugs in 'A Study in Scarlet', which takes place in 1881 but was not published until 1887. In 'Yellow Face' Watson states: 'Save for the occasional use of cocaine, he had no vices, he only turned to the drugs as a protest against the monotony of existence when cases were scanty and the papers were uninteresting'.[50] Although 'Yellow Face' was published in 1893, its action purports to occur in 1884, a year after cocaine became commercially available in the UK. Watson assures the reader that 'under ordinary conditions [Holmes] no longer craved for this artificial stimulus'.[51] Nonetheless, in 'Sign of Four' he lectures Holmes on the deleterious consequences to his health of prolonged indulgence. 'Sign of Four' is set four years later in 1888 but did not appear until 1890. By 1890 the addictive and psychosis-inducing effects of cocaine were well documented (though no laws were passed to control its use until 1914). So, in the latter, through Watson, Conan Doyle reveals his knowledge of the latest research findings.

In addition to eschewing human contact, reversing the activities of day and night and courting his muse in a drug-induced elevated state of consciousness, other signs of Dupin's eccentricity include wearing green eyeglasses and smoking heavily. To put this eccentricity in perspective, one should consider that through the ages many men have sequestered themselves and devoted their lives to intellectual pursuits in monasteries and universities without being considered eccentric. In many circles today, the wearing of tinted eyeglasses and the inhaling of hallucinogenic fumes hardly qualify as eccentric behaviour, nor does withdrawing into bouts of abstraction. But his behaviour would have seemed more aberrant when measured against nineteenth-century codes of respectability. Poe obviously intends Dupin to seem eccentric.

On the other hand, the sitting room overlooking Baker Street manifested undeniable evidence of Holmes' eccentricity. His correspondence was skewered to the mantelpiece by a jack knife; his cigars were kept in a coal scuttle and his tobacco in a Persian slipper.[52] Chemical apparatus occupied one corner where he conducted experiments.[53] Pictures of notorious criminals created a rogues' gallery on one wall,[54] while another held proof of Holmes' marksmanship as well as his loyalty to the Crown in a pattern of bullet holes forming VR for Victoria Regina. Holmes has a more complex personality than Dupin and more wide-ranging interests, including playing the violin and going to concerts.[55] He organises scrapbooks of press cuttings and his untidy files overflow another corner.[56]

Readers learn little of Dupin's family except that it was illustrious, whereas information about Holmes' family tree, education and professional training is provided, as well as his values, attitudes, tastes, interests, hobbies and recreations. Holmes was born on 6 January 1854, the second son of Siger Holmes, a gentleman farmer in Yorkshire, and his wife Violet. Holmes' mother, daughter of Sir Edward Sherrinford, traced her lineage to the Vernet family of French artists.[57] Mycroft, Sherlock's elder brother by seven years and the more brilliant of the two boys, was given the same name as the family estate. Both boys were probably tutored at home before entering university. Already independent and reserved from a young age, Sherlock made few friends at university, concentrating on his studies and developing expertise at boxing and fencing.[58] Holmes augmented his skill in boxing, along with dexterity in single stick and baritsu wrestling, which come in handy on several occasions.[59]

Having decided to develop his skills at observation and inference into a scientific method of investigating crimes and to become the first independent consulting detective, Holmes left university before taking a degree and occupied rooms in Montague Street near the British Museum, where he continued his studies of arcane fields of knowledge such as criminal history, law, sensational literature plus anatomy, biology and chemistry.[60]

Hardly anything at all is known about Dupin's confrere apart from the fact that he is so eager to enjoy Dupin's acquaintance that he is happy to defray the expenses of renting and furnishing their apartment. He shares Dupin's intellectual pursuits as well as his morose temperament and penchant for pipe smoking.[61] From his reference to Dupin as 'the Frenchman', it is clear that he is a foreigner visiting Paris during the spring and part of the summer. He states that his purpose in relating the events in the Rue Morgue case was 'to depict some very remarkable features in the mental character of my friend Chevalier C. Auguste Dupin'.[62]

Holmes and Watson are brought together on New Year's Day in 1881 by Stamford, a mutual friend from St Bartholomew's Hospital who is trying to do both of them a good turn.[63] After he set up as the first independent consulting detective in London, Holmes needed larger premises for his practice than those in Montague Street, but also required someone to share expenses. Enter John H. Watson, a convalescent veteran of the Second Afghan War (1878–80), trying to make ends meet on a half-pay pension. Born in 1852, he was two years Holmes' senior. Also a second son, Watson had to rely on his army pension as his sole source of income because his spendthrift brother had ruined the family estate and died in debt.

Watson had taken a degree in Medicine at the University of London in 1878, served briefly as staff surgeon at St Bartholomew's Hospital, and then had gone to the Royal Victoria Hospital at Netley near Southampton to undergo training as a surgeon before joining the Army Medical Corps. Watson served with the Fifth Northumberland Fusiliers and the Berkshires at the Battle of Maiwand, where he received a shoulder wound (which somehow migrated to his leg) in 1880, developed enteric (typhus or typhoid) fever, and was invalided home.[64] Lonely and disgusted with his straitened circumstances and idle existence, Watson was only too happy to accept an offer to share lodgings with Holmes. Watson later married (twice) and set up his own home and medical practice.

Although parallels with the Poe partnership are clear from the outset, departures also exist. Holmes and Watson are not kindred spirits drawn together by common intellectual interests, nor is the master sleuth's companion happy to pay living expenses for the privilege of sharing his company. Instead, Holmes and Watson join together for practical reasons in a mutually convenient living arrangement. Both men hail from middle-class families and have professional training and accomplishments. Similar backgrounds often foster compatibility. Their friendship developed gradually as Watson became interested in Holmes' cases and began recording and publishing them to supplement his income. His altruistic motivation, similar to that of Dupin's chronicler, is professed in the introduction to many of the cases, as the desire to 'select the cases which are most interesting in themselves, and at the same time most conducive to a display of those peculiar powers for which my friend was famous'.[65] Owing to Watson's medical training and military experience, he often plays a practical physical role in Holmes' investigations and even saves his life on more than one occasion.[66] Watson worked with Holmes for seventeen years of his twenty-three-year career as a consulting detective.[67]

Dupin's anonymous friend is drawn to him because of his vast knowledge, the freshness of his imagination, and their common interest in esoterica. Dupin's studies yield encyclopedic knowledge of myriad topics such as nautical lore (sailors' knots), zoology (primates), astronomy (nebula of Orion), Greek philosophy (Epicurus) and French classical drama (*Xerxes*).

Holmes, too, has an academic bent and spends hours researching obscure topics, often far into the night. Richard Lancelyn Green, editor of *The Uncollected Sherlock Holmes*, points out that 'where Holmes differs from Dupin [is] that he [has] an immense fund of exact knowledge to draw upon in consequence of his previous scientific education',[68] and James O'Brien argues that 'Sherlock Holmes' [understanding] of science ... lends credibility to his impressive powers of reasoning'.[69] Holmes' extensive learning is usually, but not exclusively, concentrated on his professional interests. He shocks Watson with his utilitarian approach to the acquisition of knowledge, claiming that the human brain has a limited capacity and that a sensible person will fill it only with useful facts. He wants to know nothing of contemporary literature, astronomy, philosophy, or politics because they are not relevant to his pursuits. When Watson explains the solar system, Holmes says he will attempt to forget about it because he does not want useless facts replacing useful ones.[70]

He prefers to be an authority on 140 different varieties of pipe, cigar and cigarette tobaccos[71] as well as 160 ciphers[72] and most typewriters.[73] He has authored a monograph on the 'tracing of footsteps, with some remarks upon the uses of plaster of Paris as a preserver of impresses'.[74] He has published two articles about the anatomical features of ears in *The Anthropological Journal*,[75] plus *A Study of the Influence of Trade Upon the Form of the Hand*.[76] Less obviously related to crime solving are his monographs on esoteric subjects in music, such as *The Polyphonic Motets of Lassus*;[77] philology, *A Study of the Chaldean Roots in the Ancient Cornish Language*;[78] and entomology, *A Practical Handbook of Bee Culture with Some Observations on the Segregation of the Queen*.[79] His projected four-volume work *The Whole Art of Detection* was eagerly anticipated.

In addition to a shared predilection for intellectual pursuits, a close congruence exists in the psychological profiles of Dupin and Holmes. Parallel behavioural traits shared by the detectives include a penchant for deep abstraction while analysing a problem. According to the narrator in 'Rue Morgue,' Dupin retreats into profound silence prior to elucidating his hypothesis, refusing to discuss the case until the next day, and then plunging into a trance-like state while articulating his reasoning.[80] Dupin's moods display such a contrast that his companion is reminded of the theory of the 'Bi-Part Soul', and entertains the notion of a double Dupin – 'a duality of the creative and the resolvent', that is intuitive and analytical.[81] Dupin lapses into 'his old habits of moody reverie' at the conclusion of the 'Rue Morgue' case.[82] His comrade attributes his behaviour to an 'excited' or 'diseased' intelligence.

Conan Doyle exaggerated Poe's model of the 'Bi-Part Soul' in constructing Holmes' personality, alternating mentally and physically active behaviour with passive withdrawal to the degree that he could be considered as suffering from manic-depressive disorder. Watson comments frequently on Holmes' extreme mood shifts – from nervous excitement when employed in an investigation to deep depression and physical torpor when unemployed and bored.[83]

Both men are heavy smokers, especially when contemplating a serious problem. The narrator describes 'the twofold delight of meditation and meerschaum' in 'The Purloined Letter' while 'the curling eddies of smoke … oppressed the atmosphere of the chamber'.[84] Later Dupin converses with the prefect 'amid a perfect whirlwind of smoke'.[85] Holmes defines an especially challenging puzzle as a three-pipe problem in 'The Red Headed League'[86] and puffs away while debating with Watson in 'The Copper Beeches'.[87] While occupied in trying to solve a case, as in 'Man with the Twisted Lip' and 'Devil's Foot', Holmes was given to long, uncommunicative fits of reverie, during which he smoked constantly, filling the room with a thick haze.[88]

Like Dupin, Holmes is capable of complete mental detachment, preferring to discuss another subject altogether rather than waste time and energy in futile speculation. 'Meanwhile, we shall put the case aside until more accurate data are available, and devote the rest of our morning to the pursuit of Neolithic man … for two hours he discoursed upon Celts, arrowheads, and shards, as lightly as if no sinister mystery were waiting for his solution.'[89] An even more stunning example occurs in 'The Bruce Partington Plans', when at a time of intense national crisis Holmes switches his attention to a monograph on the Polyphonic Motets of Lassus.[90]

On one of Dupin's nocturnal excursions, he displays his 'peculiar analytic ability' when after fifteen minutes of silence he interrupts his companion's train of thought with an apposite remark that seems like mind-reading or intuition. When his friend demands an explanation of how Dupin was able to 'fathom his soul', Dupin traces step-by-step the changes in facial expression, muttered words, glances and altered posture that had accompanied the sequence of his partner's meditation. Although his insight is comprised of logical inferences drawn from keen observation and recollection of prior conversations, it has the appearance of being clairvoyant. Dupin states that acute observation had lately become 'a species of necessity', and he boasts that 'most men, in respect to himself, wore windows in their bosoms'.[91]

Similar incidents occur in 'The Cardboard Box', 'The Dancing Men', and some editions of 'The Resident Patient' when, like Dupin, Holmes reads Watson's thoughts and acquiesces with his judgment. Watson, of course, is astonished. In 'The Cardboard Box', Holmes reminds him that when they had discussed Poe's *jeu d'esprit* Watson had scoffed at the exercise as implausible and dismissed it as a meretricious tour de force. He objects that Dupin reached his conclusions by following his companion's actions, but that he himself had remained stationary in his chair and hence Holmes' intervention is more amazing. Holmes explains that his own analysis was just as dependent on observation and inference as that of Dupin. It was based on the movements of Watson's eyes between his portraits of General Gordon and Henry Ward Beecher, which prompted changes in his countenance, especially as he considered the actions of the latter during the American Civil War. He then shook his head, touched his old wound, and smiled while considering the absurdity of war. Watson continued to believe Holmes' feat to be extraordinary.[92] The final echo of this phenomenon occurs in 'The Mazarin Stone' as Holmes repeats Dupin's claim about seeing through people when he tells Count Sylvius, 'You are absolute plate-glass. I see to the very back of your mind.'[93]

Neither Dupin nor Holmes ever evinced any interest in female companionship, although for Holmes it was a deliberate professional policy. 'But love is an emotional thing, and whatever is emotional is opposed to that true cold reason which I place above all things. I should never marry myself, lest I bias my judgment.'[94] Early in their acquaintance when Holmes fails to appreciate Mary Morstan's feminine charms, Watson admonishes him: 'You really are an automaton – a calculating machine.'[95] In a letter to Joe Bell dated 16 June 1892, Conan Doyle writes, 'Holmes is as inhuman as a Babbage's Calculating Machine, and just about as likely to fall in love.'[96] But when Ronald Knox published a mock-academic satiric study of the Holmes canon (1912) in the Oxford *Blue Book*, Conan Doyle acknowledged his amusement and amazement at the feat and admitted that 'Holmes changed entirely as the stories went on. In the first one, *The Study in Scarlet*, he was a mere calculating machine, but I had to make him more of an educated human being as I went on with him. He never shows heart.'[97]

Although both Dupin and Holmes are attracted to criminal investigation because they enjoy rational analysis,[98] Holmes reveals a moral commitment to general social welfare far beyond Dupin's self-indulgent interest in solving crimes as an amusing and profitable mental exercise. In 'Rue Morgue' Dupin does express an unselfish motive to help M. Le Bon, but it is a matter of personal honour rather than abstract justice because Le Bon had once done him a good turn. In 'Marie Rogêt' Dupin accepts the prefect's liberal proposition to unmask the murdered girl's assassin(s), but is careful at the outset to identify the body as hers lest he not only fail to fulfil the prefect's provisions and thereby lose his labour, but also defeat the ends of justice. His priorities are clear. In 'The Purloined Letter' Dupin tells his confidant that he acts as a partisan for the French queen but nonetheless delays handing over the incriminating letter until the prefect pays him a fee of 50,000 francs. However, Holmes always volunteers his services in cases of national security, as in 'The Naval Treaty', 'The Bruce Partington Plans', 'The Second Stain' and 'His Last Bow'. Furthermore, Holmes was a far more heroic character than Dupin, functioning ultimately on an allegorical plane in his conflict with the master criminal Professor Moriarty. Holmes envisions the broad scale of damage to individuals and social institutions which would ensue if Moriarty is not foiled, and he is prepared to dedicate his efforts and risk his life to destroy the Napoleon of Crime and his criminal empire. Their struggle at the Reichenbach Falls symbolises the classical antipathy of the forces of good and evil; the engagement is violent, ruthless and (apparently) fatal.

Clearly, although Conan Doyle borrowed a great deal from Poe, he also broadened both generic conventions of plot and the character of the detective hero.

2

JOSEPH BELL: INVESTIGATOR OF DISEASE AND CRIME

Joseph Bell was an ornament to his family's escutcheon and a bright star in the medical establishment in Edinburgh. He gained respect and admiration in his profession from an early age and laboured in its service all his life. He became a renowned surgeon and teacher and introduced innovative changes of great benefit to patients and colleagues at the Royal Infirmary, the Medical School and University Hospital. He also wrote a handbook for surgeons and edited a major medical journal. In addition to teaching medical students, he was the first to provide systematic institutional lectures for nurses. Many students came under his mesmeric spell, including Arthur Conan Doyle. When forced into early retirement, Bell acted as consultant to several professional organisations and filled many honorary posts. In addition, he set a precedent when he became the first surgeon at the Royal Children's Hospital, and he wrote monographs tracing the history of two venerable institutions, the Royal Children's Hospital and the Royal Infirmary. What are less well documented are his many years assisting the police medical examiner as a forensic investigator of crime scenes and expert witness in the court room at criminal trials.

As Edgar Allan Poe provided a model for literary conventions of plot and character, so Bell was the primary source of Holmes' famous method of incisive deduction following close observation. Although M. Dupin's powers of observation were acute and formed the foundation of his hypotheses in the 'Rue Morgue' and 'The Purloined Letter', they were confined principally to property and physical objects. Those observations made by the Man in the Crowd were only 'skin deep' and had little psychological depth. Holmes not only demonstrates his ability to observe the physical details of a crime scene and interpret them accurately, but he also excels at observing the far more challenging subject of the human countenance and interpreting myriad nuances of expression and behaviour. No oblique glance or change of demeanour, hesitation in speech or shift in voice tone escapes his notice. No habitual gesture or mannerism eludes him. His keen scrutiny leads to a psychological insight into character, and he is able to predict the likely actions – that is, possible motivations – of the individuals he meets. In 'The Purloined Letter' Dupin assesses the court minister's personality and predicts his behaviour correctly, but the minister is a public figure whose character is well known to him. Holmes, on the other hand, must often make instantaneous assessments of witnesses and suspects on a case – as Joe Bell did week after week and year after year in his medical practice.

Having studied and assimilated what literary pioneers in the genre had achieved, Conan Doyle felt the need to contribute something original.

I felt now that I was capable of something fresher and crisper and more workmanlike. But could I bring an addition of my own? I thought of my old teacher Joe Bell, of his eagle face, of his curious ways, and his eerie trick of spotting details. If he were a detective he would surely reduce this fascinating but unorganized business to something nearer an exact science. I would try if I could get this effect. It was surely possible in

46

real life, so why should I not make it plausible in fiction? It is all very well to say that a man is clever, but the reader wants to see examples of it – such examples as Bell gave us every day in the wards.[1]

With the brilliant models of Poe and Gaboriau (and others) fresh in his mind, one might well ask why Conan Doyle would turn to Joe Bell, his former mentor at Edinburgh University, and the unlikely field of medicine for inspiration to develop the genre of detective fiction. The answer is not far to seek. Joe Bell was a legend in his own time, and Conan Doyle came to revere him as a man and respect his professional skills while serving as his outpatient clerk. Literary critics and scholars agree that Poe had great influence on Conan Doyle and also acknowledge that Sherlock Holmes' scientific approach is attributable to Conan Doyle's medical training, but most are more interested in the literary roots of the canon than the scientific origins. They pay lip service to Holmes' scientific method and his chemical experiments, but underestimate the role of Joseph Bell in shaping both Holmes' character and methods of investigation as well as Bell's personal involvement in the composition of the stories. In order to discover the *real* Sherlock one must assess Bell's contribution.

From the time that the first Benjamin Bell (1749–1806) went to Edinburgh to study medicine and helped the university to become the best medical centre in Europe, the Bell family produced four generations of distinguished doctors. Young Joe Bell was proud to carry on the family tradition. He qualified for his medical degree at the age of twenty-one, with distinction in Classics and surgical courses. He became the protégé of James Syme, the Napoleon of surgery. In his biography of Joe Bell, Ely Liebow notes that 'impressed by Joe Bell's natural curiosity, his keen interest in The Method (acute clinical and common-sense observation), the celebrated Dr Syme chose Joe Bell to be his dresser [at the Royal Infirmary]'.[2] He later appointed Bell as his house surgeon and assistant. Concurrently, Dr Goodsir selected him as demonstrator of anatomy in the university.[3]

From the outset of his professional career, Bell earned respect for his special method of observation, taught to him by Syme, and his teaching ability. Sir William Turner wrote commending Bell: 'Whilst discharging his duties he acted as my junior, and acquired a well-deserved popularity amongst the students for his powers of observation, his clearness of exposition, his capacity for taking trouble to help them in their difficulties, and by his words of encouragement.'[4] Obviously, Joe Bell was no ordinary lecturer purveying conventional ideas. He was stimulating and innovative, and he insisted on a high standard of observation, integrity and professionalism.[5]

In 1858 Bell was admitted to the Royal Medical Society, and for the ensuing decade of the 1860s steadily advanced in his profession. In January 1863 he passed the examination for Fellowship of the Royal College of Surgeons and was duly admitted. In the same month he was also appointed assistant surgeon to his father and Dr Patrick Heron Watson. Later that year in December he became surgeon to the High Constables, a para-police force usually referred to as the Special Constables, which was created by James VI. He subsequently was elected Deputy Superintendent of the Special Constables.[6] In 1864 he began lecturing as an extracurricular instructor in the Medical School.[7]

Two years later in 1866, as Florence Nightingale initiated a program for nurses' training in London, Bell began teaching classes for nurses in Edinburgh.[8] During the course of that year, Bell also published his celebrated *Manual of Operations of Surgery for the Use of Senior Students and Junior Practitioners*, which ran to a sixth edition in 1888.[9] Three years later in 1869, Bell was designated assistant surgeon to the infirmary in recognition of his great skill at the operating table and efficiency in the wards, and the following week he became examiner to the Royal College of Surgeons.[10] Hence, in the course of a decade he had steadily received recognition as a surgeon and been appointed to prestigious posts at the infirmary and the Medical School; moreover, he validated his command of the field by embodying his expertise in a textbook for the profession. In addition, Bell demonstrated his dedication to his profession and ability as a teacher by introducing lectures for nurses.

The decade of the 1870s presented further challenges and honours. In 1871 Bell was appointed full surgeon at the Royal Infirmary.[11] Perhaps encouraged by the success of his *Manual*, Bell became editor of the *Edinburgh Medical Journal* in 1873 and served for twenty-three years until 1896.[12] In 1878, having taught extra-curricular courses in systematic and operative surgery from the age of twenty-six, Joe Bell became recognised by the university as a qualified instructor of clinical surgery when he was appointed senior surgeon at the Royal Infirmary.[13] Until this time he had practised as an extramural instructor and surgeon.

Although only forty-nine, Bell was forced to retire in 1886 as senior acting surgeon for the Infirmary, after thirty-one years there in various roles. But as one door closed at the Royal Infirmary, another opened, so he accepted the post of Consulting Surgeon.[14] Concurrently, the Royal Hospital for Sick Children convinced him to be their first surgeon in the children's ward.[15] A similar change in office occurred at the Royal College of Surgeons where, having served for eleven years as secretary-treasurer, he was elected president.[16] In 1891 he became president of the Medico-Chirurgical Society.[17] In effect, as many semi-retired people do, he launched a second career, while simultaneously maintaining his editorship of the *Journal* and his busy private practice. At the behest of his colleagues, Bell published monographs relating the history of two of Edinburgh's revered hospitals: *Five Years Surgery in the Royal Hospital for Sick Children* and *The Surgical Side of the Royal Infirmary, 1854–1892*; half of the latter chronicled the history of nursing in Edinburgh.[18]

Apart from his ordinary duties, during the 1870s Bell was

actively involved in forensic medicine when his assistance was requested by his colleague Dr Henry Littlejohn, Professor of Medical Jurisprudence and Chief Surgeon to the City Police. Sir Henry, a toxicologist, was one of the truly remarkable forensic experts of his time, and was equally well known as a dedicated early commissioner for sanitation.[19] Without any official status, Bell worked with Sir Henry on a number of cases and gave evidence as an expert witness for the Crown.[20] On the basis of this experience, Bell can be considered one of the country's first consulting medical detectives.[21] At the time of Bell's death, 'the *Boston Medical and Surgical Journal* implied that many people knew of his forensic activities, but stated positively that "Bell served as assistant to Dr Littlewood [*sic*] as official advisor to the British Crown in crises of medical jurisprudence"'.[22]

Although Bell was extremely reticent about his work as a forensic investigator for the police, he did occasionally acknowledge his role. In press interviews in 1892–93, while being inundated with requests for comments about his kinship to Sherlock Holmes, he told a reporter from *The Pall Mall Gazette*, 'For twenty years or more, I have been engaged in the practice of medical jurisprudence for the Crown, but there is little I can tell you about it. It would not be fair to mention that which is the private knowledge of the Crown and those associated therewith, and the cases which have been made public would not bear repetition.'[23] Bell also clarified his relationship with Littlejohn: 'Dr Littlejohn is the medical adviser, and he likes to have a second man with him … and it so happens that for more than twenty years we have done a great deal together, and it has come to be the regular thing for him to take me into cases with him. But I have no official connection with the Crown.'[24] Although Bell was discreet about his work as a medical crime-scene investigator, a notice in *The Times* when he died alluded to this facet of his career, stating that because of his good judgment, acumen, and probity he was frequently consulted by professional colleagues. 'He was an ideal witness, cool, collected, accurate, and concise, and there were few cases, whether criminal or civil, in which his expert knowledge was not called for either by the Crown or the opposite side.'[25]

Over the years Bell must have acted in scores of cases transcribed in court proceedings, not all of which would have received press coverage, but the cases which Bell is most often associated with due to his important investigative role are the much-publicised Chantrelle poisoning case of 1877–78 and the Monson/Hambrough shooting murder in 1893, also referred to as the Ardlamont mystery.

In December 1877, Bell accompanied Littlejohn when, as a matter of professional courtesy, he was notified about a case of coal-gas poisoning by the attending physician. Mme Chantrelle had been discovered unconscious by her maid, who noticed a half-empty glass of lemonade, some orange segments and some grapes on the bedside table before calling her master and fetching a local doctor. After Littlejohn and Bell examined the patient and observed the sickroom, Littlejohn took samples of some brown and green spots of vomit on Mme Chantrelle's pillow and nightgown. Suspecting narcotic poisoning, Littlejohn sent the comatose woman to the Royal Infirmary, where she died within a few hours.

When M. Chantrelle was told that his wife's demise was probably caused by narcotic poisoning, he insisted that a gas leak in the bedroom was responsible. However, analysis revealed that the vomit samples contained opium and traces of grape-seed fragments. An autopsy disclosed the same elements in her digestive tract. Extending his investigative activities beyond pathological analysis, Bell canvassed the neighbourhood and found pharmacists had sold thirty doses of opium to M. Chantrelle, who nonetheless insisted that a gas leak was to blame. The maid swore that she only smelled gas after her return from fetching the doctor. The gas company did find a broken gas pipe, but accused M. Chantrelle of ripping it loose. He denied knowing of its existence. Again Bell investigated, and located a gasfitter who had repaired the pipe the previous year and recalled Chantrelle's keen interest in the matter. In addition to witness testimony of spousal abuse, further discovery of a recent insurance policy on Mme Chantrelle's life and Chantrelle's dire financial state were enough evidence to bring him to trial. He was convicted after only an hour and ten minutes.[26]

On the scaffold three weeks later, Chantrelle bade farewell to Littlejohn and sent his compliments to Bell for performing their investigation so well.[27] Although Bell's name does not appear in the official record of this case, because he acted as Littlejohn's assistant rather than serving the Crown directly, contemporary witnesses affirm his participation. Apparently, 'he is known to have suppressed knowledge of his involvement in a number of forensic cases, evidently fearing that it might damage his reputation as a gentleman'.[28]

In August 1893 Joe Bell figured in the investigation of the death of Cecil Hambrough, son of a wealthy London financier, who was killed in what appeared to be a shooting accident while on holiday in Scotland. After insuring the young man's life, his tutor Alfred Monson first tried to drown young Cecil in a boating accident, and then the next day took him out shooting, but returned alone with the news that Cecil had been killed when his gun had fired accidentally while he was climbing over a fence. His explanation was accepted by Cecil's family, but when he tried to claim the insurance, the company became suspicious and notified the authorities.

After the body was exhumed and examined by Littlejohn and Bell, Monson was tried for murder. The testimony of the medical investigators was supported by that of the forensic expert Dr Patrick Heron Watson. All three doctors agreed that Hambrough could not have caused his own wounds accidentally, and that the gun was fired by an assailant standing behind him. Littlejohn demonstrated that the shot was fired from at least eight feet away. Watson noted that the triangular wound was made by stray pellets from a cartridge, many of which missed the skull. Bell focused on the wound also, pointing out that the shot must have come from at least ten feet away because of the lack of powder burns on the skull and because only part of the skull had been shot away. If Hambrough had killed himself, the shot would have come from only two or three feet away and would have shattered and scorched his skull. Therefore, unless Hambrough had had abnormally long arms, he could not have shot himself. Despite the wealth of evidence, Lord Kinsburgh (who was judging his first case) cautioned the jury not to be swayed from justice by Monson's bad character, so they delivered a verdict of 'not proven', much to the disappointment of the forensic pathologists.[29] Throughout the trial Bell was referred to as 'Sherlock Holmes' in *The Morning Leader* and *The Morning Ledger*, and the real Dr Watson was referred to as 'Sherlock Holmes' friend'.[30]

Bell had already become senior surgeon at the Royal Infirmary in October of 1878 and was functioning as a crime-scene investigator when Conan Doyle enrolled in Bell's Extra Mural Clinical Surgery Class as a second-year student.[31] The university medical students were allowed to take 50 per cent of their courses extramurally. Liebow writes, 'The large classes which Dr Bell attracted testified to his capacity as a systematic teacher, but it was as a clinical teacher that Bell was in his element, and his theatre and his wards were always crowded.'[32] According to Dr Clement Gunn, 'We used to attend the Friday clinics held by Joseph Bell (the original of Sherlock Holmes) in the Royal Infirmary, in order to become acquainted with as many cases as possible ... It was here that Conan Doyle, then an ordinary student like ourselves, observed, studied and took notes, which he utilized thereafter in his stories.'[33] On the pretext of familiarising students with the taste and smell of a strong drug, but actually to test their powers of observation, Bell would dip a finger in a test tube of bitter amber liquid and grimace while sucking a different finger before passing the vial around the class. He would then laugh at them for allowing themselves to be duped.[34]

Joe Bell chose Conan Doyle to assist him in his outpatient clinic while the latter was a student. In his autobiography, *Memories and Adventures*, Conan Doyle remarks, 'For some reason which I have never understood he singled me out from the drove of students who frequented his wards and made me his outpatient clerk, which meant that I had to array his patients, make simple notes of their cases, and then show them in one by one.'[35] Bell's explanation for his choice of Conan Doyle is recorded by Hesketh Pearson in a manuscript version of a 1959 BBC talk that was cancelled: 'Doyle was always making notes. He seemed to want to copy down every word I said. Many times after the patient departed my office, he would ask me to repeat my observations so that he would be certain he had them correctly.'[36] Bell said essentially the same thing to a reporter from the *Pall Mall Gazette*: 'I always regarded him as one of the best students I ever had. He was exceedingly interested always upon anything connected with diagnosis, and was never tired of trying to discover those little details which one looks for.'[37]

Conan Doyle Names Bell as the Model for Holmes

Five years after 'A Study in Scarlet' was published and nearly a decade after taking his medical degree in 1881, Conan Doyle first publicly confided in an interview in the *The Bookman* of May 1892 that one of his mentors in the Medical School at Edinburgh University had inspired the character of Sherlock Holmes. In answer to the query concerning how he had conceived such an extraordinary individual as Sherlock Holmes, Conan Doyle denied that his detective investigator had evolved out of his own inner consciousness.

Sherlock Holmes is the embodiment, if I may so express it, of my memory of a professor of medicine at Edinburgh University, who would sit in the patients' waiting-room with a face like a Red Indian and diagnose the people as they came in, before even they had opened their mouths. He would tell them their symptoms, he would give them details of their lives, and he would hardly ever make a mistake ... So I got the idea for Sherlock Holmes. Sherlock is utterly inhuman, no heart, but with a beautifully logical intellect. I know nothing about detective work, but theoretically it has always had a great charm for me.[38]

This statement elicited a letter from Joe Bell inquiring whether he had been that mentor. Given their former working relationship, he had every right to wonder. His question generated a cordial exchange of letters in which they renewed their acquaintance. Unfortunately, Bell's side of the correspondence is no longer available, but its content can be inferred from Conan Doyle's replies. Conan Doyle freely admitted to Bell that he was the inspiration for Holmes.

Many thanks for your most kind and genial letter. It is most certainly to you that I owe Sherlock Holmes, and although in the stories I have the advantage of being able to place him in all sorts of dramatic positions, I do not think that his analytical work is in the least an exaggeration of some effects which I have seen you produce in the out-patient ward. Round the centre of deduction and inference and observation which I have heard you inculcate I have tried to build up a man who pushed the thing as far as it would go – and occasionally further – and I am glad that the result has satisfied you, who are the critic with the most right to be severe.[39]

In response to these compliments, Bell sent his photograph, which was given pride of place on the mantelpiece in Conan Doyle's study for years. He thanked Bell in a letter of 16 June 1892 and within days proudly showed it to Harry How, a

55

reporter who interviewed him for a *Strand Magazine* feature article. Conan Doyle again named Joe Bell as 'the man who suggested Sherlock Holmes to me'. He explained that as clerk on Bell's ward, his duty was to register the patients and usher them in for consultation. He described Bell's intuitive powers as 'simply marvellous'. He also confessed, 'All this impressed me very much ... his sharp piercing grey eyes, eagle nose, and striking features. There he would sit in his chair with fingers together ... and just look at the man or woman before him.'⁴⁰ This description of Bell was faithfully duplicated when Holmes made his first appearance: 'His eyes were sharp and piercing ... and his thin, hawk-like nose gave his whole expression an air of alertness and decision. His chin, too, had the prominence which marks the man of distinction.'⁴¹ In several stories Holmes habitually assumes Bell's characteristic pose with steepled hands while he listens to clients relate their difficulties. Watson describes him in 'Red-Headed League' as 'relapsing into his armchair and putting his fingertips together' (p. 176), and in 'Norwood Builder' he 'listened with closed eyes and fingertips together' (p. 499). His manner is quite academic in 'Dancing Men' as he explains a theoretical point to Watson, speaking 'with the air of a professor addressing a class' (p. 511), and in 'Yellow Face' he examines Grant Munro's pipe 'as a professor might who was lecturing on a bone' (p. 354).

Years later, in his autobiography, Conan Doyle summed up Bell's talent: 'He was a very skilful surgeon, but his strong point was diagnosis, not only of disease but of occupation and character ... I had ample chance of studying his methods and of noticing that he often learned more of the patient by a few quick glances than I had done by my questions ... '⁴²

Not only did Joseph Bell inculcate the method of drawing inferences from rapid close observation, but he also cautioned his students to corroborate them with proper medical procedures: 'From close observation and deduction, gentlemen, it is possible to make a diagnosis that will be correct in any and every case. However, you must not neglect to ratify your deductions, to substantiate your diagnoses, with the stethoscope and by all other recognized and every-day methods.'[43]

At the time of the *Strand* interview in the summer of 1892, Conan Doyle jovially warned Bell that he might be inundated with lunatic letters from constant readers who would request his assistance because 'their neighbours are starving maiden aunts to death in hermetically sealed attics' and because others 'burn to know who Jack the Ripper is'. Ironically, he suggests that Bell will 'bless' him and his yarns when the post arrives.[44]

Directly following his meeting with Conan Doyle, the *Strand* reporter Harry How wrote to Bell, who courteously answered his questions so that How was able to append Bell's letter to the text of his article, 'A Day with Dr Conan Doyle', when it appeared in the magazine in August. Bell modestly deprecates his contribution to the 'ideal' character of Sherlock Holmes and attributes Conan Doyle's praise to his 'warm remembrance' of an old teacher. But he goes on to discuss the importance of the method of instruction which impressed his former student.

> In teaching the treatment of disease and accident, all careful teachers have first to show the student how to recognise accurately the case. The recognition depends in great measure on the accurate rapid appreciation of *small points* in which the diseased differs from the healthy state [emphasis added]. In fact, the student must be taught to observe. To interest him in this kind of work we teachers find it useful to show the student how much a trained use of the observation can discover in ordinary matters such as the previous history, nationality, and occupation of a patient … For instance, physiognomy helps you to nationality, accent to district, and, to an educated ear, almost to county. Nearly every handicraft writes its sign manual on the hands. The scars of the miner differ from those of the quarryman. The carpenter's callosities are not those of the mason. The shoemaker and the tailor are

quite different ... the tattoo marks on hand and arm will tell their own tale as to voyages.[45]

Bell reiterated this theme in another contemporary interview, 'The great majority of people, of incidents, and of cases resemble each other in the main and larger features ... Most men have ... a head, two arms, a nose, a mouth, and a certain number of teeth. It is the little differences, themselves trifles, such as the droop of an eyelid, or what not, which differentiates man.'[46]

Bell was not the only medical instructor to focus on detail. Douglas Guthrie compares other near contemporaries of Conan Doyle in his article on medicine and detection:

> The importance of small things has been emphasized by great physicians as well as great detectives. Sir William Gull, one of the most eminent London physicians of the last century, insisted that 'Nothing which concerns the patient's well being should be too minute for the doctor's attention'; and Lord Lister himself was fond of stating that 'Success depends upon attention to minute detail.'[47]

As Handasyde comments, 'In no branch of life is the detective instinct of such service to man as in the art of healing ... [when] the possession of such a faculty is a matter of life or death.'[48]

As a homage to his mentor, Conan Doyle dedicated to Bell the first edition of the collected stories from *The Strand*, which appeared under the title *The Adventures of Sherlock Holmes*. 'The book will come out about September and I should much like to inscribe your name upon the flyleaf, if the dedication will not be an intrusion. I am sure that no other name has as good a right in the place.'[49] In response Bell reviewed *The Adventures* for the *Bookman* in December 1892. His essay was later used as the preface when '[A] Study in Scarlet was published as a book in 1893'.[50]

Their correspondence during this period reveals that Bell also sent some suggestions for plots, which Conan Doyle welcomed. On 4 May 1892 Conan Doyle thanks him and asks for more:

> I think that a fine thing might be done about a bacteriological criminal, but the only fear is lest you get beyond the average man, whose interest must be held from the first, and who will not be interested unless he thoroughly understands. Still even so I think that something might be done along these lines. I should be so glad if you should find yourself with ten minutes to spare if you would give me an idea of the case.[51]

He adds that he would be very grateful for any 'spotting of trade' tips or 'anything else of a Sherlock Holmesy nature'.

Bell must have responded immediately because three days later on 7 May Conan Doyle writes again:

> Your letters are really of great value to me and I am exceedingly obliged to you for the details which you so kindly furnished. The deserter-cobbler is admirable. I wish I had a dozen more such cases. I am going to do 12 more Sherlock Holmes sketches next year so that I am insatiable for material ... Your sketch of the crime is capital. It wants a sort of second plot to run parallel with the first, and to drag some other red herring across the scent besides the ex-soldier. But there is ... much more than a nucleus of something very good. I shall certainly – with your kind permission – avail myself of the idea.[52]

The letter ends with profuse thanks for Bell's 'tips'.

Oddly enough, the character of the deserter-cobbler, who had been undressed under protest to prove Bell's identification of him as a soldier, does not figure in any of the stories. In a press interview Bell gives an account of this incident, which took place in his outpatient clinic when Bell, using his famous intuition, claimed that his patient had been a soldier only to have the man deny it.

> being absolutely certain I was right ... I told two of the strongest clerks, or dressers, to remove the man to a side room, and to detain him ... I went and had him stripped ... [and] under the left breast I instantly detected a little blue 'D' branded on his skin. He was a deserter. That was how they used to mark them in the Crimean days ... Of course the reason of his evasion was at once clear.[53]

Lying to cover military desertion might not figure in the canon of Conan Doyle's fiction, but Holmes does penetrate various people's impersonations and expose them, as in the case of Neville St Clair in 'The Man with the Twisted Lip' (p. 242). Although he originally rejected Bell's idea of a killer using a bacteriological murder weapon, he does employ it in 'The Dying Detective', but without a subplot as a red herring (pp. 932–41). In his autobiography, Conan Doyle states, 'Bell took a keen interest in these detective tales and even made suggestions.'[54] So a kind of collaboration occurred.

As the following remarks disclose, in Bell's mind a diagnostician is a medical detective.

> Conan Doyle created a shrewd, quick-sighted, inquisitive man, half doctor [*sic*], half virtuoso, with plenty of spare time, a retentive memory, and perhaps with the best gift of all – the power of unloading the mind of all burden of trying to remember unnecessary details ... He makes him explain to the good Watson the trivial, or apparently trivial, links in his chain of evidence. These are at once so obvious, when explained, and so easy, once you know them, that the ingenious reader at once feels, and says to himself, I could also do this; life is not so dull after all; I will keep my eyes open, and find out things ... Sherlock Holmes has the acute senses, and the special education and information that make these valuable; and he can afford to let us into the secrets of his method. But in addition to the creation of his

hero, Dr Conan Doyle ... has proved himself a born story-teller. He has the wit to devise excellent plots, interesting complications; he tells them in honest Saxon-English with directness and pith; and, above all his other merits, his stories are absolutely free from padding.[55]

A year later, Bell told a journalist from *Harper's Weekly Magazine*,

I should just like to say this about my friend Doyle's stories, that I believe they have inculcated in the general public a new source of interest. They make many a fellow who has before felt very little interest in his life and daily surroundings think that, after all, there may be much more in life if he keeps his eyes open than he had ever dreamed of in his philosophy.[56]

Bell's biographer, Ely Liebow, sums up Bell's influence on Conan Doyle succinctly:

Joe Bell gave Doyle the scientific method, the voice, the stoic face, but most of all the true touchstone, the aspect of Holmes that instantly and forever raised him above all other detectives and made him more recognizable than almost any other literary creation: the ingenious, insouciant, lightning deduction based on a thread, a wisp of smoke, a scratch that most mortals overlook, but to Bell and Holmes was everything.[57]

Conan Doyle imported more than Bell's plot ideas and his method into Holmes' adventures. In addition to similarities in physique, mannerisms, tone of voice, terse style of expression and workaholic lifestyle, Sherlock Holmes shared many of Bell's hobbies and pastimes. Bell was as keen a chemist as Holmes and conducted 'little experiments' and lab tests in a small anteroom outside his Ward XI. He also had a small laboratory at home, and when he retired was delighted to be able to spend more time on chemistry.[58]

Both Bell and Holmes dabbled in graphology, that is,

in interpreting character from handwriting. Saxby, Bell's interviewer, writes, 'He was at one time much interested in the reading of character through hand-writing and composition, and he used to send me letters for the purpose of testing my fancied talent in that line. Everything that could lead to the identity of the writers was carefully erased.'[59] Holmes' ability to distinguish between scripts and to interpret a writer's age from his penmanship is instrumental in unravelling the crime in 'The Reigate Puzzle' (pp. 401, 410).

Bell was also a model for Holmes' role as counsellor. 'All kinds of people came to Dr Bell when they were in trouble … He inspired confidence, he was a soother.'[60] Bell's patients and Holmes' clients are impelled by the same need for help. Holmes demonstrates great ability to calm and reassure distraught callers of both genders. For example, John Scott Eccles in 'Wisteria Lodge', perplexed by the strange disappearance of his host (pp. 870–71); Alexander Holder in 'The Beryl Coronet', distraught over the theft of the precious jewel (pp. 301–02); and John Garrideb (aka Killer Evans), angry that Holmes had been brought into a private matter (pp. 1045–46); as well as Helen Stoner in 'The Speckled Band', terrified by her sister's death (pp. 258–59); and Mrs Warren in 'The Red Circle', upset by the mysterious behaviour of her lodger and the kidnapping of her husband (pp. 901–02).

Details from Bell's lectures and outpatient clinics, duly transcribed in Conan Doyle's notebooks, were introduced into his stories. For example, when Bell interviewed a patient with a thick Irish brogue, he asked whether the man had walked over the golf links en route to the south side of town. After the patient had gone, Conan Doyle asked how Bell knew the man's route. Bell explained that on showery days the reddish clay on bare parts of the links would adhere to the boots of anyone who walked across them, and this clay could not be found anywhere else in the town. Conan Doyle transcribed Bell's explanation in his notebook and the details turned up years later in 'The Sign of Four', when Sherlock

Holmes surmised that Watson had been to the Wigmore Street post office in London because of the reddish mould adhering to Watson's boots from the excavation nearby (p. 91). In 'The Five Orange Pips', Holmes remarked to John Openshaw that the mixture of chalk and clay on his toe caps, indigenous to the region, indicated he had travelled to London from the south-west (pp. 218–19).

Joseph Bell is not the only source of this technique. Like so much else, it can also be traced to Poe. From a scrap of ribbon with an exotic sailor's knot and a wisp of hair, Dupin deduces the identity of the villain in 'Rue Morgue'. Surely this process of inference from meticulous observation parallels Bell's procedure. The difference seems to be that in Poe's detective tales he applies the Method to objects and premises, while Bell also includes people. However, to be fair, in Poe's story *The Man in the Crowd* (1840), which precedes the tales of ratiocination, the narrator surmises the social class and trades of people who pass in the street by observing their physical traits and behaviour, but he does not use these deductions to adduce character or to solve crimes. He does notice the inner anguish of a particular individual, whom he follows because of his erratic behaviour, but he does not speculate about its cause. In 'The Purloined Letter', Dupin makes his own assessment of the thief's *mentalité*, but he is already well acquainted with the minister. In this example, the observation of the premises follows psychological analysis, which is crucial to solving the problem. He is not surprised to find the letter placed with other tattered correspondence out in the open in a rather soiled card rack.

In the character of Sherlock Holmes, the techniques of Dupin and Bell are melded; Holmes applies the Method universally to embrace premises, landscape, objects and human beings as he practises his profession. The cases in which Holmes draws inferences from minute observation of premises to reach a solution begin with 'A Study in Scarlet':

As he spoke, he whipped a tape measure and a large round magnifying-glass from his pocket. With these two implements he trotted noiselessly about the room, sometimes stopping, occasionally kneeling, and once lying flat upon his face. So engrossed was he with his occupation that he appeared to have forgotten our presence, for he chattered away to himself under his breath the whole time, keeping up a running fire of exclamations, groans, whistles, and little cries suggestive of encouragement and of hope. As I watched him I was irresistibly reminded of a pure-blooded, well-trained foxhound, as it dashes backward and forward through the covert, whining in its eagerness, until it comes across the lost scent. For twenty minutes or more he continued his researches, measuring with the most exact care the distance between marks which were entirely invisible to me, and occasionally applying his tape to the walls in an equally incomprehensible manner. In one place he gathered up very carefully a little pile of grey dust from the floor, and packed it away in an envelope. Finally he examined with his glass the word upon the wall, going over every letter of it with the most minute exactness. This done, he appeared to be satisfied, for he replaced his tape and his glass in his pocket.[61]

His survey of 3 Lauriston Gardens enables Holmes to determine what crime had occurred and to give Lestrade a description of the killer:

There has been murder done, and the murderer was a man. He was more than six feet high, was in the prime of life, had small feet for his height, wore coarse, square-toed boots and smoked a Trichinopoly cigar. He came here with his victim in a four-wheeled cab, which was drawn by a horse with three old shoes and one new one on his off fore-leg. In all probability the murderer had a florid face, and the fingernails of his right hand were remarkable long.[62]

In 'The Norwood Builder' (p. 509) as well as 'The Musgrave Ritual', Holmes combines observation of premises with his knowledge of geometry to deduce the existence of hidden rooms. Holmes employs a similar procedure to interior crime scenes and again produces an equally astonishingly detailed description of the villains' movements derived from his observations in 'The Abbey Grange' (p. 644) and 'The Golden Pince-Nez' (p. 618). His methods work equally well on open terrain in 'The Boscombe Valley Mystery' (pp. 212–13) and on the heath in 'Silver Blaze' (pp. 342–4) and 'The Priory School' (p. 547).

Holmes' use of the method to study ordinary objects results in even more stunning revelations when he scrutinises Watson's watch in 'The Sign of Four' (pp. 92–93), Mr Baker's hat in 'The Blue Carbuncle' (p. 246), the box wrapping and severed ears in 'The Cardboard Box' (pp. 891–92, 895–96), Dr Mortimer's walking stick in 'The Hound of the Baskervilles' (pp. 670–71) and Grant Munro's pipe in 'The Yellow Face' (350–51). Examination of the killer's eyeglasses in 'The Golden Pince-Nez' yielded this description of their owner:

> Wanted, a woman of good address, attired like a lady. She has a remarkably thick nose, with eyes which are set close upon either side of it. She has a puckered forehead, a peering expression, and probably rounded shoulders. There are indications that she has recourse to an optician at least twice during the last few months. (p. 612)

Holmes' rapid deductions about people after a quick glance are both baffling and breathtaking: Holmes sums up Jabez Wilson in 'The Red-Headed League' as a man who has done manual labour, takes snuff, is a Freemason, has travelled to China and has done a considerable amount of writing lately (p. 177). On the basis of his appraisal of Hector McFarlane in 'The Norwood Builder', Holmes concludes that he is a bachelor, a solicitor, a Freemason and an asthmatic (p. 497). Neither of these profiles contains psychological insight. However, merely by looking out of the window at a woman hovering on the opposite pavement in 'A Case of Identity', he intuits Mary Sutherland's mental anguish and decides she has come to consult him about a love affair (p. 192), and he infers from a similar survey of John Garrideb in 'The Three Garridebs' that he is telling a rigmarole of lies and is a rascal (pp. 1045, 1047). Professor Prestbury's erratic behaviour in 'The Creeping Man', plus his physical symptoms, lead Holmes' to uncover emotional desires behind his secret. The most dramatic example of 'reading' a person occurs in 'The Greek Interpreter' when Sherlock and Mycroft subject a recently discharged soldier to their joint surveillance and determine that he is a non-commissioned officer in the Royal Artillery and a widower with two children (p. 437).

Conclusion

Joseph Bell's influence on Conan Doyle was not merely a matter of literary convention derived from the printed page, as with Poe, but one of direct personal interaction. Conan Doyle publicly acknowledged Bell as the source for Sherlock Holmes. Not only did he serve as a model for the super sleuth's physical appearance and mannerisms, but also for his scientific detective methods. Bell contributed ideas for stories and characters, for which Conan Doyle thanked him and begged for more, confessing that he was desperate for material. So Bell became a collaborator in a sense. His introduction to the first hardcover edition of 'A Study in Scarlet' reveals him to have a wide-ranging acquaintance with the detective genre and to be a competent critic of its practitioners. Furthermore, Bell himself practised as a medical crime-scene investigator and testified as an expert witness in criminal prosecutions for the Crown. Nor were his activities confined only to scientific analysis but, as in the Chantrelle case, included gathering evidence through interviews with witnesses. How much Conan Doyle knew about Bell's second career is debatable. It could have been an 'open secret' at the Medical School, but if it were not, Conan Doyle might very well have known because he worked so closely with Bell in his clinic. Conan Doyle followed Bell's lead in this field as well, conducting successful investigations which changed legal history. As has been demonstrated, Bell was a profound source of inspiration for Conan Doyle and even contributed personally to some of the stories.

3

ARTHUR CONAN DOYLE: SHERLOCK HOLMES DETECTS IN THE REAL WORLD

Fons et origo

Although the origins and inspiration for the Sherlock Holmes stories have been debated for over a century, actually Arthur Conan Doyle's chief sources for his detective hero were his own character and experience – his personal abhorrence of injustice, his delight in imaginative literature, his inquiring mind and his practical professional training.[1] Drawing upon his admiration of Edgar Allan Poe's mystery fiction and his knowledge of Dr Joseph Bell's scientific methods, filtered through the fulcrum of his own intellect and imagination, he created the first scientific detective. He publicly acknowledged both artistic and scientific debts, but often modestly omitted to mention the *sine qua non* of his own talent – the intellect, imagination and ingenuity it took to combine and transmute his inspiration into the inimitable Sherlock Holmes.

Many candidates have been suggested as models for the 'real' Sherlock Holmes, but there is no perfect fit. He is not an exact replica of any single literary or human progenitor. Like most human beings, Holmes derives his identity from multiple forbears. His is a rich heritage.

Adrian Conan Doyle, Sir Arthur's son by his second wife, Jean Leckie, insisted that his father was the model for the real Sherlock Holmes and would countenance no other candidates. He denied claims that Joe Bell inspired Holmes' character and contributed ideas for plots, despite his father's published acknowledgements of Bell's role. He claimed that placing the credit for Sherlock Holmes on Bell's shoulders was analogous to giving the praise earned by a violin virtuoso to the teacher who first gave him lessons. He insisted that Bell's lectures merely brought to fruition Conan Doyle's inherent deductive abilities. 'They did that, and they did no more ... my father himself had those very gifts, probably to an even greater degree than Dr Bell, a conclusion proved by the fact that those attributes were not only expressed in his stories, but put into practice by my father on numberless occasions.'[2]

Adrian also documented his assertion with accounts of his father's withdrawal into his study, sometimes for days, to ponder some problem submitted to him in a *cri de coeur*. 'It was not a question of affectation but complete mental absorption that checked and counter-checked, pondered, dissected and sought the clue to some mystery that had been hurried to him as the last court of appeal.'[3] He supported his assertion with accounts of his father's ability to 'read' people as Holmes did, and cited examples from family holidays abroad when his father's deductions about strangers encountered in public places were confirmed by local people.[4]

Writing in *Pearson's Magazine* in December 1934, Lady Conan Doyle echoed his view: 'The public does not realize that my husband had the Sherlock Holmes' brain, and sometimes he privately solved mysteries that had nonplussed the police. He was able through his remarkable powers of deduction and inference, to locate missing people whose relatives had given them up as lost or murdered.'[5]

The case of the Danish sailor exemplifies her argument. In 1909, a young woman who had met and become engaged to a Danish man five weeks earlier appealed to Conan

70

Doyle for help when he disappeared. Inquiries by the English and Danish police had failed to trace him. Moved by her desperate helplessness, rather like Holmes in 'A Case of Identity' (1891), Conan Doyle applied to real life the general lines of reasoning employed by his sleuth. 'I was able, by a similar process of deduction, to show her very clearly both whither he had gone, and how unworthy he was of her affections.'[6] Using information gained from the young woman, Conan Doyle made contact with the sailor's cousin in Copenhagen, an employee of the Danish East Asia Company, who divulged details of the man's real character. When Conan Doyle shared them with his correspondent, she realised that she had had a lucky escape.

Who is qualified to judge this debate to determine the *real* Sherlock Holmes? Surely, Conan Doyle himself should have the last word in the controversy. After all, he declared himself in print more than once on the subject. While still studying at Edinburgh he told a fellow student of his desire to do something along the lines of Poe in a more ordinary way.[7] When on his first American tour in 1894, he praised Edgar Allan Poe for having transformed crime fiction into a literary genre and cited Dupin as the best detective.[8] In his autobiography thirty years later he reiterated that Poe had been his hero since boyhood.[9] His statements are supported by the analysis herein (Chapter 1), which demonstrates manifold parallels in plot, setting and characterisation between Poe and Conan Doyle. Although Holmes disparages Poe's Dupin and Gaboriau's Lecoq, Conan Doyle admired them.[10]

However, in correspondence and press interviews as early as 1892, as well as in his autobiography in 1924, Conan Doyle also acknowledged Joseph Bell as the immediate inspiration for his famous sleuth's scientific methods. It would seem that, while not being 'the troops' child', Holmes had a mixed heritage, owing many of the generic literary features of his adventures and several of his personal idiosyncrasies to Poe but more of his working habits, physical appearance and mannerisms to Bell. Conan Doyle uses the same image to describe both Bell and Sherlock Holmes, that of the beaky-nosed, hawk-faced, stoical Red Indian with piercing eyes and fingertips steepled under his chin.[11]

Certainly Conan Doyle publicly attributed a closer relationship between Bell and Holmes than between Dupin and Holmes. While full of admiration, he nonetheless referred to Poe and Dupin in more general terms than when expressing the kinship between Bell and Holmes. While analysis reveals parallels between Dupin and Bell's methods, Conan Doyle does not refer to Dupin as scientific or cite him as a direct source in interviews. Both sleuths used logical deduction, but Conan Doyle directly ascribed the scientific method of which Holmes is so proud to Bell rather than to Dupin.

> Then I began to think, suppose my old professor at Edinburgh were in the place of one of these ... detectives, he would have worked out the process of effect from cause just as logically as he would have diagnosed a disease, instead of having something given him by mere luck ... For fun, therefore, I started constructing a story and giving my detective a scientific system, so as to make him reason everything out. Intellectually, that had been done by Edgar Allan Poe with M Dupin, but where Holmes was different from Dupin was that he had an immense fund of exact knowledge to draw upon in consequence of his previous scientific education.[12]

He endorses the same viewpoint twenty-four years later in his autobiography: 'It is no wonder that after the study of such a character [Bell] I used and amplified his methods when in later life I tried to build up a scientific detective who solved cases on his own merits and not through the folly of the criminal.'[13]

In addition Conan Doyle finds affinities to Holmes within his own nature. An American journalist, Hayden Coffin, quoted his remark in an interview in 1918: 'If anyone is Holmes, then

I must confess it is I.'[14] Conan Doyle, though admitting that he was not very observant, also declared that 'a man cannot spin a character out of his own inner consciousness and make it really life-like unless he has some possibilities of that character within him ...'[15] He went on to say that in order to get into the Sherlockian frame of mind in real life he had to be completely alone and concentrate intensely. 'Then I get results and have several times solved problems by Holmes' methods after the police have been baffled.'[16]

Parallels Between Conan Doyle and Sherlock Holmes

In *Conan Doyle Detective* Peter Costello contends that Conan Doyle's own personality is the source for both Watson and Holmes: he combines the ordinary and the extraordinary. Conan Doyle and Watson were both

> medical men of approximately the same age with sporting interests. Both have a bluff, hearty appearance. Both seem conventional, imperialist in politics, non-intellectual men of action. Dr Watson even shares Conan Doyle's ... literary tastes, such as a liking for the sea-stories of William Clark Russell ... And he marries conventionally, like Dr. Doyle, a girl that he meets in the course of a professional case ... They were both men in their late twenties.[17]

Conan Doyle shared Holmes' interest in chemistry and owned the same kind of chemical apparatus that Holmes used to conduct his experiments. While living with his brother Innes in Southsea before marriage, his bachelor quarters at Southsea, like those at 221b Baker Street, were cluttered with memorabilia, books of cuttings and criminal records. Conan Doyle referred to his untidy bachelor lifestyle as 'Bohemian'.

This unconventional lifestyle can be explained by the

presence of artists in their families. In 'Greek Interpreter' Holmes attributes his quirky talents to his grandmother, who was the sister of the French artist Vernet. 'Art in the blood is liable to take the strangest forms' (p. 435). Similarly, Conan Doyle's grandfather was a painter, and his uncle Richard 'Dicky' Doyle was a leading artist for *Punch*. His father, Charles Altamont Doyle, who worked as an architectural draughtsman, was also a gifted illustrator.

Costello claims Conan Doyle actually owned a purple dressing gown and smoked shag in his pipe. Moreover, he took drugs to test their effects, as an early publication in the *British Medical Journal* reveals. 'Gelseminum as a Poison' describes his own reactions to the drug.[18] In the 1870s the pages of the *British Medical Journal* hosted a lively discussion of the use of coca, which Conan Doyle would have been privy to because two of his professors, Robert Christison and Joe Bell, contributed to it. So Holmes' use of cocaine would not have shocked him. Holmes' moody hours of introspection were not unknown to Conan Doyle either, as his son notes above. And he conferred on Holmes his skill at boxing and admiration for William Winwood Reade's *The Martyrdom of Man*, which played a part in his rejection of Roman Catholicism in his youth.[19]

Conan Doyle's Interest in Crime

Conan Doyle became interested in crime at an early age. For example, letters to his mother from his Jesuit preparatory school, Stonyhurst, in 1872 contain a very enthusiastic teenage review of *The Courier of Lyons, or The Attack on the Mail* – 'a jolly play (5 murders)'. It was based on the 1796 robbery of the Lyons stagecoach in which four highwaymen stole over £3,000 and killed the coachman and courier. A man named Joseph Lesurques was convicted and guillotined, but subsequently Jean-Guillaume Dubosq, who bore a striking resemblance to Lesurques, was caught and executed. The case became a cause célèbre because of the confused identification and the play endured as a theatrical thriller which enthralled audiences for decades.[20]

Two years later, when on holiday in London with family relations, Conan Doyle found a high point to be a visit to the Chamber of Horrors at Madame Tussaud's waxworks; 'I was delighted with the room of Horrors and with the images of the murderers.'[21] Twenty-five years later, in March 1901, Conan Doyle wrote accounts of three of the murderers whose effigies appeared in the exhibit in a series for *The Strand*, which he titled 'Strange Studies from Life'.[22] In a speech to celebrate the centenary anniversary of Madame Tussaud's, he recalled his reaction to this grotesquerie: 'I was alternately thrilled and horrified.'[23]

Between his schooling at Stonyhurst and his medical studies in Edinburgh, Conan Doyle spent a gap year improving his chemistry and mathematics at an Austrian Jesuit school in Feldkirch. Among the books he was sent during this period were the tales of Edgar Allan Poe, which instilled in him a life-long allegiance.[24]

Not only did Conan Doyle evince a teenage attraction to representations of crimes and criminals in museums, drama and fiction, but he also shared Holmes' penchant for collecting books on crime, and created over the years sixty scrapbooks of press cuttings, although not all about crime. Both Conan Doyle and Holmes owned a large criminological library and were widely read in the criminal history of several countries. Conan Doyle acquired a great many books from the sale of W. S. Gilbert's collection in 1911.[25] Holmes says in 'Sign of Four', 'You will find a parallel case in Riga in '54' (p. 90). In 'A Case of Identity' Holmes tells Watson that Mary Sutherland's problem reminds him of similar cases in Andover and The Hague (p. 196).

Like Joe Bell, he took an interest in crime in the real world. In adult life he never missed an opportunity to inspect crime scenes, attend important trials or listen to lectures by experts in law enforcement and forensic medicine. And, like Bell, he personally investigated crime scenes with the police and on his own.

Activities and Field Trips: Crime in the Real World

On 2 December 1892 Conan Doyle visited the notorious Black Museum at New Scotland Yard, along with Dr Gilbert, the medical officer at Newgate (prison), his brother-in-law E. W. Hornung (creator of Raffles, the ace cracksman), and Jerome K. Jerome, editor of *The Idler*.[26] On display were macabre relics culled by police investigators from notorious crime scenes over several decades. Conan Doyle took particular notice of a fading photograph of the disembowelled corpse of the last victim, Mary Kelly, and of a letter and postcard written in red ink and signed by the Ripper. This was one of the first instances in which his interest in graphology was applied to crime. Conan Doyle proceeded as Holmes did in 'Scandal in Bohemia', analysing the quality of the stationery and the style of the script, as well as some American phrases, to infer that the writer was an educated man who had travelled in America. Holmes would reason that there must exist other examples of his writing and that to apprehend him, the police should reproduce the letters in prominent newspapers, noting unique aspects of the handwriting, and offer a reward for other samples of the same script.[27] Robert Anderson, assistant commissioner at Scotland Yard, believed that the letters were a hoax created by a journalist, but withheld his name. However, internal evidence indicated that they really were written by the murderer.

Because he was the creator of the greatest detective in literature, and a well-known student of criminology, Conan Doyle was invited in 1903 to become one of the first twelve members of a very exclusive dining club called by the rather precious name of 'Our Society' (it was changed in 1904 to the 'Crimes Club').[28] The idea of the club was proposed the previous year by actor and amateur criminologist Henry Brodribb Irving. At the first dinner, held on 17 July 1904 at the Great Central Hotel in Russell Square, London, the six founding members – Irving; Arthur Lambton; James Beresford Atlay, historian; Lord Albert Edward Godolphin Osborne; John Churton Collins, scholar/professor; and Samuel Ingleby Oddie, lawyer and London Coroner – were joined by A. E. W. Mason, novelist; Max Pemberton, novelist and editor of *Cassell's Magazine*; George R. Sims, journalist; C. A. Pearson of *Pearson's Weekly*; Bertram Fletcher Robinson, editor of *Vanity Fair*; Dr Herbert Crosse; and Sir Arthur Conan Doyle. Its membership comprised both professional and amateur criminologists, including investigative reporters like Sims. In later years both Sir Edward Marshall Hall and Sir Bernard Spilsbury added lustre to its roster. The plan was to hold three or four dinners annually after which a talk would be given on a celebrated crime, followed by discussion. Often lawyers who had participated in the case would offer unique insights into the proceedings. These dinners were of great value to the creator of Sherlock Holmes because of the content of the talks and the people he met. 'It was always interesting … to examine and handle exhibits from celebrated trials, to see photographs, and to learn what had become of famous persons tried and acquitted.'[29] 'These exhibits included a box of strychnine pills found on Dr Thomas Neill Cream, the multiple poisoner, when he was arrested in South London in June 1892.'[30]

Jack the Ripper's five killings in 1888 earned him the status of the most horrific serial murderer in British history. On 19 April 1905 Ingleby Oddie arranged for a few members of the Crimes Club (including Churton Collins, H. B. Irving, Dr Herbert Crosse and Conan Doyle) to be taken on a guided tour of the nine scenes of the Ripper's crimes by Dr Frederick Gordon Brown, City of London Police surgeon, and City Police detectives familiar with the case details.[31] Dr Brown had examined the body and performed the autopsy on Catherine Eddowes, the fourth victim. Brown told the coroner (Oddie) that the killer displayed some anatomical knowledge, either from medical training or slaughtering animals. Brown's notes and the mortuary photographs, which still survive, convey a grim sense of the reality of the carnage.[32]

Through his friendship with Edward Marshall Hall, the renowned barrister and member of the Crimes Club, on 18 October 1910 Conan Doyle got a seat at Dr Hawley Harvey Crippen's trial for the murder of his wife (Cora Turner, *née* Kunigunde Mackamotski), who performed in music halls as Belle Elmore.[33] American by birth, Crippen received his medical training in the United States before moving to England. Costello notes that 'this was a case which had seized upon Conan Doyle's imagination, not only because of the macabre details, but because all the resources of modern technology had been brought into play in the pursuit and capture of the accused'.[34] For the first time in history, the detective investigating the case, Chief Inspector Walter Dew, was notified by telegraph from a transatlantic liner that Crippen and Ethel Le Neve were en route to Canada, travelling as father and son. The captain had identified them from newspaper photographs. He became suspicious when he noticed that Le Neve's boyish clothing did not fit very well and that the couple behaved more affectionately than most fathers and sons.

Because the head and limbs of the victim were never recovered, identification of the torso of the corpse as that of Crippen's wife depended heavily on the forensic analysis of Dr Bernard Spilsbury, who was able to prove identity by means of an appendectomy scar. He also found hyoscine in the body. This was the first of many high-profile cases that helped to establish his unassailable reputation. The prosecution also proved that Crippen had purchased the pyjama jacket used to wrap the remains, and had bought a lethal number of grains of hyoscine. Nonetheless, Marshall

Hall argued in a talk to the Crimes Club that a successful defence could have been mounted.[35]

Conan Doyle as Criminal Investigator

Conan Doyle was himself a distinguished criminologist and frequently acted as a consulting detective. Like Joe Bell, he investigated crimes with the police and on his own. In this respect Conan Doyle follows in Holmes' footsteps, for he did not actively engage in criminal investigation until Holmes disappeared at the Reichenbach Falls, almost as if he felt Holmes' loss and was prompted to exchange imaginary detective adventures for the real thing. In the 1890s, when Sherlock Holmes became popular, Conan Doyle began receiving letters reporting crimes and asking for help in solving mysteries, some of which were addressed to Holmes and forwarded by the Post Office from 221b Baker Street.

After he revealed in interviews with *The Bookman* and *The Strand* in 1892 that Joe Bell was the inspiration for Holmes, Conan Doyle jokingly warned Bell that he would probably receive some of these 'lunatic' missives. He found them amusing and scoffed at the ridiculous idea that his readers would confuse him with his hero.[36]

In *Cassell's Saturday Journal* in February 1893 he commented on the subject: 'Both Dr Bell and myself are constantly receiving letters from persons in distress, inviting us to unravel some mystery or other in connection with the family, to use our best endeavours to trace some missing relative, or to bring to justice some delinquent whom the police have failed to capture.'[37] He expressed similar views in a speech at the Authors' Club Banquet three years later in 1896, complaining that readers worldwide – from San Francisco to Moscow – persisted in imploring him to sort out inexplicable conundrums. Although he claimed his own powers were limited, people were undeterred.[38]

He was not exaggerating, for while he was in South Africa during the Boer War he was deluged with similar letters. Perhaps his attitude changed because of his wartime experiences, for after his return from South Africa in 1901 he regarded them more seriously.[39] At this time he spoke in the *Candid Friend* about them and admitted that he had referred one of them to Scotland Yard.[40] For the rest of his life and thereafter to the present date letters continued to arrive at 221b Baker Street for Holmes. A selection of them was edited by Richard Lancelyn Green in *Letters to Sherlock Holmes* (1985).

Although most appeals arrived in the post, in September 1901 Conan Doyle received a direct personal request from Henry Paget, 5th Marquess of Anglesey. While he was attending the opening-night performance of a new play written by and starring William Gillette as Sherlock Holmes, his hotel bedroom was burgled. Jewels from the Anglesey Collection valued at £50,000 were stolen by his valet, Julian Gault, and a female accomplice whom he had known previously in France. Working in close cooperation with Detective Inspector Walter Dew of Scotland Yard, Conan Doyle not only helped in tracing some of the jewels in London but also inferred the identity of the fence.[41] Gault was arrested trying to escape at Dover, but his partner got away. At trial, Gault confessed, blaming his accomplice, and was sentenced to five years in prison.[42]

When he was young, Conan Doyle's mother (*née* Mary Foley) told him stories of medieval chivalry and romantic adventure with gallant heroes. She also regaled him with tales of their distinguished family heritage. His mother's influence coupled with a Roman Catholic education developed his imagination and produced a highly idealistic, moral character. He had a keen sense of right and wrong and was always ready to combat injustice. His values are reflected in his fiction and in his interest in crime and detection. He was quick to pick up his pen on behalf of the vulnerable, the victimised, the persecuted, the falsely accused and the hapless. From shoplifting to murder to treason, Conan Doyle defended those he felt were unjustly treated and exerted his influence on behalf of the defendant in cases of weak or suspect evidence.

In a letter to *The Times*, Conan Doyle advocated clemency on medical grounds for Mrs Ella Castle, an American tourist, who had been tried and convicted on charges of shoplifting (1896). Pleading that no sane person would steal multiple items of the same kind which could never be used, he argued that she was not mentally responsible and should be given medical treatment, not incarcerated. Chivalrously, he urged that the benefit of the doubt should be given to 'one whose sex and whose position as a visitor amongst us give her a double claim upon our consideration'. After consulting with the police and the prison doctor the next day, the Home Secretary ordered her release.[43]

At times, his role of criminologist blended with those of public defender and/or social crusader. Risking intense social disapproval and damage to his own reputation, in 1916 Conan Doyle cited Sir Roger Casement's long diplomatic service to the nation in the Congo crisis in Africa and the Putumayo atrocities in Brazil, as well as his impaired health incurred while on duty, to advocate a reprieve from the death sentence when he was convicted of treason because he supported the Irish bid for independence during the Easter uprising. Casement had raised support in America and even tried to recruit Irish soldiers for Sinn Fein from among the German prisoner of war camps. But Conan Doyle felt that his long years of loyal service to the Crown should weigh against Casement's recent rash defection, which had surely occurred while the balance of his mind had been impaired.[44]

Complaining of weak or dubious evidence, in 1925 he defended Norman Thorne, a chicken farmer accused of murdering his mistress. The forensic evidence at the trial was so muddled the *Law Journal* declared that

Thorne 'had been condemned by a tribunal which was not capable of forming a first hand judgment'.[45] Conan Doyle examined the crime scene and did not feel that Thorne had been proven guilty beyond a reasonable doubt. In an interview with the *Morning Post* he joined with those who unsuccessfully advocated a reprieve from the death penalty.[46] He was opposed to capital punishment and felt it should only be invoked in cases of incontrovertible evidence. When reasonable doubt existed, it is better to err on the side of clemency.

The desire for truth and justice which motivated Conan Doyle in these cases, lest an innocent person be falsely convicted, is reflected in Holmes' scrupulous analysis of the crime scenes in 'The Boscombe Valley Mystery' and 'The Problem at Thor Bridge'; in his righteous anger against Mr Windibanks and Dr Roylott for exploiting their stepdaughters in 'A Case of Identity' and 'The Speckled Band'; in his altruistic concern for Violet Hunter and Violet Smith in 'The Copper Beeches' and 'The Solitary Cyclist'; as well as his compassion in his determined search for the ruthlessly victimised and sadly unprotected Lady Frances Carfax. These behavioural parallels support the argument of Conan Doyle's close kinship with his character.

In addition, he wrote a series of articles on true-crime cases under the umbrella title 'Strange Studies from Life', based on three cases from the 1860s. They were published in *The Strand* between March and May 1901. All three were notorious murder cases. In all of them, Conan Doyle focuses on the psychology of the villain. In 'The Holocaust of Manor Place', he warns that the inordinately selfish man is one of the most dangerous types because he has lost all sense of proportion. 'The Love Affair of George Vincent Parker' shows the devastation wrought by lust for money and the black resentment of disappointed love. The third tale, 'The Debatable Case of Mrs Emsley', deals with the issue of doubt in reaching a verdict. Conan Doyle pleads for clemency in the face of incomplete evidence, for it is better that a guilty man go free than an innocent one be condemned.[47]

Conan Doyle became involved in many criminal cases, several of which have been documented only in his correspondence and notebooks, presumably for the same reason that some of Holmes' exploits remained in Watson's tin box – to protect the privacy of the individuals involved. As with Joseph Bell, though Conan Doyle participated in many inquiries, usually his name is associated with only a few sensational trials. Two of the best-known and most successful cases were the investigations he initiated on behalf of George Edalji and Oscar Slater, in which he was instrumental in overturning jury verdicts. In a third one, known as the 'Brides in the Bath' case, he advised Scotland Yard. In these inquiries Conan Doyle used Sherlockian methods to investigate and solve cases in the real world. In so doing he employed his scientific training as well as logical analysis. *In effect*, Conan Doyle became Sherlock Holmes. Fiction crossed the boundary into reality. Sherlock Holmes functioned in the real world.

Edalji Case: Sherlock Holmes in the Real World

The Edalji case opened for Conan Doyle in December 1906 when he chanced to read an article entitled 'Edalji Protests His Innocence' in an obscure sporting journal published in Manchester called *The Umpire*. The article gave an account of the wrongful imprisonment and recent release without pardon of a young man convicted of maiming livestock. Coincidentally among the welter of correspondence on his desk appeared a letter of appeal from the young man himself.[48] Conan Doyle states in his autobiography, 'As I read, I realized that I was in the presence of an appalling tragedy, and that I was called upon to do what I could to set it right.'[49] Always the champion of the underdog and of victims of injustice, Conan Doyle devoted the next nine months to investigating the case of George Edalji. Putting his own work aside and personally defraying all costs, he strove to right the wrongs inflicted on Edalji by social prejudice and incompetent police work.[50]

> What aroused my indignation and gave me the driving force to carry the thing through was the utter helplessness of this forlorn little group of people, the coloured clergyman in his strange position, the brave blue-eyed, grey-haired wife, the young daughter, baited by brutal boors and having the police, who should have been their natural protectors, adopting from the beginning a harsh tone towards them and accusing them, beyond all reason, of being the cause of their own troubles and of persecuting and maligning themselves.[51]

During the course of the Edalji investigation, Conan Doyle was compared with Sherlock Holmes in the press. A *Daily Chronicle* editorial stated, 'It is a tribute to the force with which he has impressed the personality of his hero upon the reader's mind that one instinctively merges the creator in his creation, and thinks of this special investigation as the work of the great Sherlock. So far as the story goes at present, nobody who makes this identification will be disappointed.'[52] Several other newspapers made similar comments. The *New York Times* trumpeted, 'Creator of "Sherlock Holmes" Turns Detective Himself.'[53] Although Conan Doyle asserted in the *Daily Telegraph* that there was a great deal of difference between fact and fiction, he also insisted that, unlike the police, he had endeavoured to get the facts before coming to any conclusions: 'I have examined a very large number of documents and tested a long series of real and alleged facts. During all that time I have kept my mind open.'[54] What could be more Sherlockian? As Holmes tells Watson, 'It is a capital mistake to theorize before you have all of the evidence.'[55]

The Edalji family lived in the small community of Great Wyrley, part of a rural mining district north-west of Birmingham in south Staffordshire, where the Reverend Shapurji Edalji was vicar. Born and educated in Bombay, Shapurji Edalji was a Parsee, who had converted to Anglicanism before emigrating to England and training as a clergyman. There in 1874 he met and married the daughter of a Shropshire vicar, Charlotte Stoneman, and took over the Church of England parish from his wife's uncle. They had three children, of whom George was the eldest.[56]

According to John Cuming Walters of the *Manchester City News*, Wyrley was a small, insular community composed largely of clannish old families. The mixed-race family was an anomaly in the provincial community. As Conan Doyle remarked in his autobiography, 'the appearance of a coloured clergyman with a half-caste son in a rude, unrefined parish was bound to cause some regrettable situation'.[57] This situation flew in the face of the commonly accepted belief throughout the empire that it was the 'duty of the English to evangelize the Blacks, not the Blacks to preach to the English'.[58]

The prejudice that fuelled George's arrest and conviction for animal mutilation was not the first expression of hostility directed toward the Edalji family. They lived peacefully enough from 1876 till 1888, when, in the first of these episodes, obscene graffiti was scribbled on village walls by a former female servant, who was charged with libel but released for lack of evidence.[59]

After that incident, between 1892 and 1895, they became the butt of various forms of harassment, such as verbal abuse, practical jokes and poison-pen letters.[60] Rubbish was strewn on their lawn. Bogus orders were sent to tradesmen who became angry when the Edaljis rejected the goods. Controversial notices attributed to the Reverend Edalji appeared in newspapers. Insulting letters and postcards were sent to fellow clergymen, solicitors, detectives, newspaper editors and tradesmen in his name.[61] The vicar was driven to write an open letter to *The Times* complaining of this three-year campaign of hoaxes and warning the public against responding to requests signed with his name without checking first.[62]

Venomous letters also vilified all the members of the family, especially the reverend's elder son, George.[63] The three-year reign of terror ended with a final fake advertisement in the Blackpool press in December 1895.[64] Peace prevailed for seven years. In a classic case of blaming the victim, the Chief Constable Captain George Anson and the local constabulary concluded, against common sense, that teenage George, then an excellent student at Rugeley Grammar School, had written the letters persecuting his family. Even though his parents insisted that he had been with them when the malicious screeds had been pushed under their door, the police persisted in believing him guilty of the mischief.[65]

Then, between February and June of 1903, a spate of livestock mutilations occurred in which the stomachs of a good number of horses, cows and sheep were slashed with a razor or sharp knife and the animals left to bleed to death. The police had no leads to follow until July, when a series of disturbing letters arrived that discussed the crimes with relish and predicted future attacks on young girls. The writer claimed to be a member of a gang which enjoyed attacking animals and supplied a few names of local men including that of 'one Broell', plus a porter at Wyrley station called Edgar and 'Edalji the lawyer'. He boasted that he had been recruited by the gang because of his skill with animals. He expressed his desire to go to sea and offered to identify the gang members if the police would grant him immunity.[66] Because of the previous episode of poison-pen letters involving the Edalji family and police suspicions of George as the instigator, despite the unlikelihood of the perpetrator accusing himself, the authorities believed the allegations against him regarding the attacks on animals to be true. To prevent further atrocities, Captain Anson summoned special constables from far and near to patrol the district, with instructions to watch the vicarage closely.[67]

At this time, twenty-seven-year-old George Edalji, having completed his studies at Mason College with honours and won Law Society prizes, practised as a solicitor at a Birmingham law firm, and had previously published a well-regarded manual on railway law, *Railway Law for the 'Man on the Train'*. George was a slight, rather frail-looking, nervous young man with large, bulging eyes which gave him an odd appearance. He was shy, did not drink or smoke and liked to take long walks. He lived with his parents and led an ordinary family life.[68]

Then, early on 18 August 1903, a pony was discovered with its belly bleeding from a shallow cut, which the local veterinarian claimed had been made within the last six hours, even though twenty policemen had been patrolling the lanes and three of them had had the field under surveillance. Public pressure on the police to find the malefactor(s) was intense, so they arrested George Edalji as the most likely suspect.[69] Although other men had been mentioned in the three scurrilous letters in July, racial intolerance led them to focus on Edalji.[70] Andrew Lycett states in *The Man Who Created Sherlock Holmes* that Anson's belief in Edalji's guilt was based on his misinterpretation of Cesare Lombroso's 'scientific' categorisation of criminal types by physical facial features.[71]

Looking for blood stains and trace evidence to connect Edalji with the crime scene, Inspector Campbell, accompanied by several constables, searched the vicarage and impounded some of George's clothing. They also confiscated a set of four razors with dark stains, which might have served as the murder weapons. Campbell claimed that an old jacket George wore at home was damp (from the previous night's rain) and had horse hairs adhering to it, but both the vicar and Mrs Edalji denied the charges. Unfortunately, the clothing was packed up in the same bundle as a piece of the pony's hide, so when it was examined subsequently by the police surgeon, he found multiple horse hairs on it. Edalji was arrested at his office later the same day. Public anger was so intense that he was nearly lynched when he was transferred to the magistrate's court; the furious crowd tore the door off the cab. Local rumour opined that the attacks were ritual sacrifices to strange gods.[72]

Edalji's trial was horribly mismanaged. Instead of being tried by a Judge of the Assizes, he was tried on 23 October 1903 at the Staffordshire County Quarter Sessions by a local justice whose grasp of legal procedure was so weak that a barrister had to coach him.[73] The Prosecution's case was weak. Defying Sherlock Holmes' dictum not to theorise in advance of gathering the facts, the police tailored the evidence to support their belief in Edalji's guilt. Originally they accused Edalji of committing the offence between 8 and 9.30 p.m., but Edalji's bootmaker furnished him with an alibi for this period, and the police veterinarian insisted that the pony would not have survived until morning if the wound had been inflicted at that time.[74] So they devised a new theory claiming that Edalji stole out of the house unnoticed by both his father, with whom he shared a bedroom, and the police. The police were evasive about surveillance of the vicarage on the night in question. Later Anson admitted that no special precautions were in place at the rectory on the night of the pony slashing.[75]

Chemical analysis revealed that spots on the sleeve of George's coat were not blood stains but merely food residue, and the black mud on his trouser legs and boots did not match the yellow-red clay of the crime scene.[76] The stains on the razors proved to be rust. Thus the only physical evidence the police could advance to link Edalji to the crime scene was an inexpert comparison of one of his boots with a footprint made after the site had been contaminated with the prints of many officials and other visitors. Moreover, neither photographs nor casts were taken, and the said footprint had been measured unscientifically with bits of stick and a straw.[77] Furthermore, the graphologist Thomas Gurrin (whose expert opinion had helped to convict an innocent man in 1896) testified that Edalji's handwriting matched that in the letters accusing him of cattle maiming.[78]

Certainly, the Prosecution had not proved the means, motive, and opportunity for Edalji to commit the assault on the pony. They produced no instrument capable of causing the fatal wounds. There was no circumstantial evidence linking him to the crime site except the unreliable footprint. His father, a light sleeper, swore that George never left during the night, and no witnesses could place him at the crime scene. Their case depended chiefly on the testimony of the unreliable graphologist, Thomas Gurrin.[79] Except for impeccable character references from his former schoolmaster and his employer, Edalji's defence was weak because his legal advisors considered the Prosecution's charges so absurd that they did not prepare a strong case. The jury found him guilty under the Malicious Damage Act of 1861, and the layman-judge sentenced him to seven years' penal servitude.[80] As a result, George spent three years breaking stone in a quarry outside Portland in Dorset. Further attacks on animals in September and November while George was awaiting trial were dismissed as a diversionary tactic or smokescreen by 'Edalji's gang'.[81]

Outside the narrow confines of Wyrley there was a huge public outcry when Edalji was convicted. The Hon. Roger Dawson Yelverton, former Chancellor and Chief Justice of the Bahamas and current Chairman of the League of Criminal Appeal, who had been lobbying for the establishment of a criminal court of appeal since 1888, prepared a petition for reconsideration, in which he presented learned arguments illustrating the weakness of the case and impugning legal procedure. He collected 10,000 signatures, including those of several hundred lawyers, which he sent to the Home Secretary, but it was ignored by the Home Office.[82] In desperation, in May 1904, Edalji's father published his correspondence with the unresponsive Home Office.[83]

Whether these protests may have contributed to Edalji's release from prison on 19 October 1906 with a four-year ticket of leave, which meant that he was free but remained under police supervision, is unclear. The Home Office gave no explanation. He was not granted a pardon and he was given no reparation. Because he had been struck off the Solicitors Roll, he could not practise his profession and could only find work as a law clerk.[84] He had not been officially cleared of the charges against him so he existed in a state of legal limbo.

At this point Edalji aired his wrongs in a series of articles published in a Birmingham Sunday newspaper and then sent an account of his maltreatment to Conan Doyle, enclosing the press cuttings in December 1906.[85] Characteristically, Conan Doyle set about gathering the facts by sending for all available evidence, including official trial records, and writing to everyone who knew anything about the case. A review of legal depositions as well as press cuttings disclosed a complex affair.[86] Looking for practical strategies, he also studied the documentation gathered by the Crimes Club during their joint investigation with the *Daily Mail* into of the case of Adolph Beck, a Norwegian engineer who had been wrongly imprisoned for robbery (see Chapter 4). Spurred on by the relentless inquiries of the investigative journalist George R. Sims, the authorities had been forced to reopen the case. Beck had been declared innocent of his crime in 1901 and released, but was rearrested in 1904. He only escaped a second stretch of imprisonment when the guilty criminal was uncovered by Sims' indefatigable pursuit of the truth.[87] Like Sherlock Holmes, Conan Doyle studied the materials while smoking many ounces of tobacco and subsequently modelled his presentation on Sims' articles and letters.[88]

The next step was to interview the suppliant, so early in January 1907 he arranged an interview with Edalji in the foyer of the Grand Hotel, Charing Cross. Conan Doyle had no difficulty recognising the dark-skinned man in the hotel lobby. He noticed Edalji holding a newspaper 'at an angle close to his face'. As a trained eye surgeon, Conan Doyle recognised that Edalji's vision was severely impaired and greeted him as Joe Bell or Sherlock Holmes might have done: 'You're Mr Edalji. Don't you suffer from astigmatic myopia?'[89] Edalji confirmed Conan Doyle's quickly observed diagnosis and added that two ophthalmologists had been unable to fit him with eyeglasses because of his acute astigmatism. Conan Doyle realised that George would be half-blind in daylight and would be totally helpless in the dark, and thus he would have been unable to commit the crimes he was accused of. Nonetheless, as Joe Bell always advised, he verified his analysis by sending Edalji to a highly respected London eye specialist, Kenneth Scott, who reported eight dioptres of myopia, which meant he could not recognise anyone more than six yards away.[90]

Next, as Sherlock Holmes would have done, Conan Doyle travelled to Wyrley to inspect the crime scenes. He visited the vicarage and interviewed the Edalji family who reported their past history of persecution. None of this, which would have placed the accusations of cattle maimings into a pattern of continued persecution, came out at George's trial. Conan Doyle was appalled to learn that for nearly two decades the family had been the target of malicious pranks which the police had done little or nothing to clear up.[91]

When Conan Doyle traversed the route George was supposed to have taken from the vicarage to the scene of the last mutilation, he discovered that it would have been impossible for anyone with George's weak eyesight.

> The man was practically blind, save in a good light, while between his home and the place where the mutilation was committed lay the full breadth of the London and North-Western Railway, an expanse of rails, wires and other obstacles, with hedges to be forced on either side, so that I, a strong and active man, in broad daylight found it a hard matter to pass.[92]

Having completed his research and drawn his conclusions, Conan Doyle was unable to present his findings in a court of law or to the hostile police. So the press became his tribunal. He arranged for his findings to appear in two consecutive instalments on 11 and 12 January 1907 in the *Daily Telegraph* without copyright restrictions, which allowed for wide circulation in other newspapers. A week later, on 20 January, he published an 18,000-word pamphlet, 'The Story of Mr George Edalji'.[93] He reviewed in print the police case against Edalji, demolishing the evidence piece by piece and exposing the malicious persecution suffered by Edalji and his family. He rehearsed all the evidence in Edalji's favour: the fifteen-year campaign of persecution against his family in Wyrley, his blameless movements on the night of the pony's mutilation, the unreliable testimony of the handwriting expert who had been at fault in the Beck case, the unlikelihood of his accusing himself in the incriminating letters, and his disabling weak eyesight.[94] He also castigated the Home Office for releasing the victim without pardon, thus conferring on him an untenable status of being free but still guilty.

He even drew parallels with the infamous Alfred Dreyfus case in France, both in terms of prejudice and faulty handwriting analysis:

The parallel is extraordinarily close. You have a Parsee, instead of a Jew, with a young and promising career blighted, in each case the degradation from a profession and the campaign of redress and restoration, in each case questions of forgery and handwriting arise, with Esterhazy in the one, and the anonymous writer in the other. Finally … you have a clique of French officials going from excess to excess in order to cover an initial mistake, and that in the other you have the Staffordshire police acting in the way I have described.[95]

The report caused a sensation and the Edalji case became a cause célèbre overnight. Simultaneously, Conan Doyle launched a letter-writing campaign in the press.[96] Concurrently, Horace Voules, the editor of Henry Labouchere's *Truth*, which had been espousing Edalji's cause, published a series of articles demonstrating the impossibility of his guilt and urging a pardon. Other members of the press such as John Cuming Walters, editor of the *Manchester City News*, added their support. In March 1907 Churton Collins presented an outline of the case in the *National Review*.[97] The Rt Hon. Sir George Henry Lewis, one of most experienced solicitors of the age, exercised his influence behind the scenes with members of the legal profession.[98]

In the face of this concerted protest, the Home Office was forced to listen.[99] Finally, the Home Secretary, Herbert Gladstone (son of the late Prime Minister) appointed a committee to re-examine the case, which was composed of Sir Arthur Wilson, High Court Judge; the Rt Hon. John Lloyd Wharton, Conservative MP; and Sir Albert De Rutzen, Chief Magistrate of the Metropolitan Police Courts. The third member of this supposedly unbiased body was a second cousin of Staffordshire's Chief Constable Captain George Anson, who had been hostile to Edalji from the outset.[100]

While the committee were deliberating, Conan Doyle persevered in making local inquiries in Staffordshire. He realised that it would strengthen Edalji's position to identify the real culprits. In order to serve justice, there was still a case to prove. Between January and August of 1907, he strove to identify the real villain.[101] As early as 29 January he was following five lines of inquiry and was constructing a strong case.[102] Early on he became convinced that the culprit(s) were not only criminal but also mentally ill. Once he began defending Edalji and questioning the trial verdict, Conan Doyle himself began to receive threatening letters, which only confirmed to the police and Home Office that 'Edalji was the author of them all'.[103] Nor did they assist his inquiries.

One of the letters Conan Doyle received expressed

resentment against the headmaster of Walsall Grammar School. He had already deduced that references to Walsall Grammar School linked the first set of letters, between 1892 and 1895, to the second set in 1903.[104] By late January 1907 he had identified two brothers named Sharp as the letter writers.[105] After comparing the letters written between 1892 and 1895, rather as Holmes did in 'The Reigate Puzzle', he determined that they were written by two people: one an educated man and the other a foul-mouthed boy. He attributed the letters and the mutilations in 1903 to the boy. A long gap of seven years between spurts of letter writing might indicate that the writer was absent. An earlier letter had referred three times to life at sea, so the gap might indicate that he had gone to sea and then returned.[106]

The obvious next step was to inquire at Walsall Grammar School for a boy during the early nineties who had a grudge against the headmaster, who was innately vicious, and who later went to sea. Mr J. A. Aldis, the former headmaster, indicated that Royden Sharp fitted the profile. 'Royden ... had a taste for knives, for ripping up cushions in the train to school so that the horsehair spilled out. His father had had to pay compensation more than once for straps which he had cut off the carriage windows.'[107] While at Walsall, Sharp had had a feud with a fellow student, Fred Brookes, and his family became victims of hate mail between 1892 and 1895. After Sharp left school, he was 'apprenticed to a butcher where he learned to kill and cut up animals ... At the end of 1895 he was sent to sea as an apprentice,' returning in 1903 to live with his family 'during the year of the attacks on cattle and horses'.[108] For ten months Sharp had worked on 'a cattle boat in the Irish trade. He knew how to approach and handle animals.'[109] Conan Doyle completed his case by acquiring handwriting samples and the actual horse lancet used for the mutilations, as well as verbal testimony linking Sharp to the crimes.

A local woman, Mrs Greatorex, was of great assistance. One of the abusive letters in 1903 had been falsely signed with her son's name. She supplied samples of the handwriting of both Sharp brothers. The elder had qualified as an architect and emigrated to California, from whence Conan Doyle's hate mail came.[110] Mrs Greatorex also stated, while discussing the maimings from July 1903, that Royden had shown her a horse lancet and told her excitedly that it was used to kill cattle. Conan Doyle actually acquired this horse lancet, which Royden Sharp had obtained on the cattle boat, and, based on the nature of the wounds to the animals, he demonstrated, as Joe Bell might have done, that it was the only kind of instrument which could have caused them. In all of the attacks the incisions were shallow, cutting through skin and muscle but not penetrating the gut; the horse lancet is very sharp but could never cause more than superficial injuries.[111] Mr Robert Greatorex became Royden Sharp's trustee when his father died and admitted to Conan Doyle that he had had a great deal of trouble with the lad.[112]

When the Home Office committee reported on 16 May 1907, they concurred that George Edalji had been wrongly convicted. They admitted that the police investigation had focused merely on gathering evidence against Edalji, whom they already believed guilty, rather than on a thorough search for the culprit. However, the committee maintained that Edalji had written the letters and was, therefore, not entitled to any compensation.[113] Edalji was given free pardon as an act of clemency. So although Edalji was pardoned, he was denied any official reparation for his wrongful imprisonment.

Roger Dawson Yelverton was outraged. Prompted by Sir George Henry Lewis, the Law Society registered its contempt for the verdict by restoring Edalji to the Solicitors Roll on 25 November 1907, so he was able to practise law again.[114] After it became clear that Edalji would receive no compensation, a fundraising committee was set up in June under the auspices of *The Daily Telegraph*. Conan Doyle agreed to serve on it, along with Horace Voules and other influential advocates, such as George Henry Lewis of the Law Society, Jerome

K. Jerome, editor of *The Idler*, Professor John Churton Collins and J. Hall Richardson (Honorary Treasurer).[115] A subscription of £300 pounds was collected for Edalji, which he used to recompense an aunt who had paid his legal expenses.[116]

When Conan Doyle complained in person to the Home Office, he was told that the verdict was final and was referred to the committee report, which stated, 'These letters can have only a very remote bearing on whether Edalji was rightly convicted in 1903.'[117] However, he refused to abandon the struggle with only partial victory. He launched a campaign of letters to the press from June through August 1907. In addition, following the Home Office report, Conan Doyle wrote three articles about the handwriting, published in the *Daily Telegraph* on 23, 24 and 27 May. The first was titled 'Facsimile Documents'. It discussed both the handwriting and internal evidence, or content, of the anonymous letters. Conan Doyle supplied facsimiles of Edalji's script and that of the anonymous letter writer and compared them.[118] He cited the expert analysis of Dr Lindsay Johnson, the chirographer who had contributed to the Dreyfus defence. Conan Doyle had submitted the collection of letters for analysis much earlier. Johnson's method was to enlarge the writing on a screen so that the minutest of traits was visible, which facilitated comparison. It was also possible to superimpose words and phrases.

The handwriting analysis was followed by rational queries: 'Why should Edalji, an eminently sane young lawyer, with a promising career before him, write to the police accusing himself of a crime of which he was really innocent? And why would young Greatorex be involved?' In answer to his own queries, Conan Doyle replies that the enmity expressed toward both Edalji and Greatorex, who were unknown to each other, suggests a common foe trying to cause trouble for them both. This hypothesis is more sensible than the inherent improbability of the police theory. He contrasts the character and deportment of Edalji with that of the writer, who had neither grammar nor decency. He notes that references to people in Greatorex's neighbourhood would have been meaningless to Edalji. Finally, the enthusiastic allusions to the sea are totally alien to Edalji's experience. Conan Doyle's logical summary of his evidence asserts that a priori reasoning and internal evidence oppose the idea that Edalji wrote the letters.[119] His conclusion is as eloquent as it is logical, and entirely Sherlockian.

The second article, 'Who Wrote the Letters?', produces documents linking letters to earlier hate mail from 1892–96. Character analysis of the writers from internal evidence reveals three separate individuals – two adults and one boy – who live near enough to hand deliver letters to the vicarage. All use the same paper and envelopes, and at times a single letter combines messages from more than one person. From this proximity Conan Doyle infers that they are members of the same family united in a conspiracy of persecution. He also establishes a connection to Walsall Grammar School. Several families and the headmaster were sent scurrilous letters. Edalji attended Rugeley Grammar School, rather than Walsall, and was not acquainted with anyone there. The first writer frequently lapsed into the wild religious rant of a madman. The second writer was more controlled and tended to send postcards far afield with bogus orders of goods, urgent summonses, and advertisements over the rector's signature.[120]

In Conan Doyle's third piece for the *Daily Telegraph* – 'The Martin Molton Letters' – he connects the author of a current series of letters with the foul-mouthed boy of 1892. The handwriting is the same and the style is rude, coarse, and unformed. He compares parallels in script and phrasing in letters from 1892, 1903, and 1907 to prove the writer's identity. He concludes that the culprit is mentally deranged and that his ultimate destination should be an asylum rather than prison. The religious mania of the elder conspirator indicates a family weakness which is manifested by indiscriminate outbreaks of criminal madness in the younger boy.

Conan Doyle succinctly sums up the importance of clearing Edalji of writing the letters. Because he is held responsible for the letters, compensation for wrongful imprisonment is withheld. Writing poison-pen letters is a minor offence, so even if he had written them, Edalji is owed reparation. 'Redress for one unjust accusation has been refused by the simple process of making a second equally unjust.'[121] He is refused compensation for an offence for which he has been exonerated, but the denial is based on a charge of which he has been accused but not allowed to defend himself against in court. 'Therefore he is being severely punished for an offence of which he has never been proved to be guilty.' Conan Doyle complains further that the Home Office Committee report failed to consider the evidence he marshalled and submitted in Edalji's defence and accuses the Home Office officials of being hostile but polite when he presented documents and demonstrated crucial evidence therein. They preferred to support 'impeached officialdom'.

Although Conan Doyle believed he had proved, on the basis of internal evidence of the text and Johnson's analysis, that Royden Sharp was the principal author and his older brother the secondary writer of the threatening letters, he composed a separate report: 'Statement of the Case against Royden Sharp of Cannock, for the committing of those outrages upon Cattle from February to August 1903, for which George Edalji was Condemned to Seven Years penal servitude at Stafford Assizes, November, 1903', in which he presented the evidence he had compiled during his investigation and concluded with an admirable redaction of ten points (see above). He submitted it to the Home Office. They in turn sent it to Captain George Anson, the Chief Constable of Staffordshire who had been responsible for the mismanagement of the Edalji case from the beginning. Not surprisingly, Anson rejected Conan Doyle's findings and the Home Office took his advice.[122] Although the committee probably had received Conan Doyle's report about Royden Sharp before issuing their findings, they took no notice of it then.

Herbert Gladstone wrote that the lawyers for the Crown advised that there was not a prima facie case.[123] Conan Doyle also showed his report to the Edalji Committee, including John Churton Collins, Jerome K. Jerome and Sir George Lewis. Although the latter did not deny a prima facie case, he opined that there was insufficient evidence to secure a conviction.[124] So for once lawyers on both sides of the issue were in agreement. In answer to parliamentary questions, the Home Secretary announced that nothing new had come up.[125]

The Staffordshire police warned Conan Doyle that he would be open to accusations of libel if he published his report, even if he changed the names. So he never accused Royden Sharp in public print. Nor did his biographer, John Dickson Carr, who referred to Sharp by the pseudonym Hudson when discussing the Edalji case.[126] Conan Doyle's suspicions about Royden Sharp's criminal propensities were subsequently vindicated when Sharp was convicted for several crimes including arson, theft and damage.[127]

Conan Doyle was furious and expressed his disgust at the establishment's closing of ranks. He felt that the rejection of his report discredited his findings when he had only intended that they be used as a basis for an official inquiry.

> There was a strong prima facie case, but it needed the goodwill and co-operation of the authorities to ram it home. That co-operation was wanting, which was intelligible, in the case of the local police, since it traversed their previous convictions and conclusions, but was inexcusable in the Home Office. The law officers of the Crown upheld their view that there was not a prima facie case, but I fear that consciously or unconsciously the same trade union principle was at work.[128]

In his mind their stand reduced his role in the Edalji controversy from crucial investigator to mere publicist.[129] That Conan Doyle was both angry and disillusioned is indicated in his autobiography:

> The sad fact is that officialdom in England stands solid together, and that when you are forced to attack it you need not expect justice, but rather that you are up against an unavowed Trade Union ... which subordinates the public interest to a false idea of loyalty. What confronts you is a determination to admit nothing which inculpates another official.[130]

Two decades later Conan Doyle was still disturbed by the unsatisfactory outcome of this case when he wrote in his autobiography: 'After many years I can hardly think with patience on the handling of this case.'[131]

George Edalji was never compensated for false imprisonment. He moved to London and practised law until he died in 1953. The slashings went on long after he went to live in London. Conan Doyle tried unsuccessfully to reopen the case under two successive governments. When Edalji's sister Maud died, she left all the papers connected with George's case to the Law Society, but they have disappeared. Sir Compton Mackenzie claimed that they had been destroyed by an official of the Law Society to protect the reputations of some of the lawyers associated with the case.[132] In 1934 a local labourer from Darlaston, Enoch Knowles, was convicted of sending menacing and obscene letters and sentenced to three years' penal servitude. His offences stretched back over the early years of the century.[133] Upon his conviction, George Edalji wrote an article in the *Daily Express* but did not renew his claims for compensation.

Largely owing to the gross injustice in the Beck and Edalji cases, a Court of Criminal Appeal was established in 1907.

The Case of Oscar Slater

The Slater affair was another instance of police scapegoating. Conan Doyle played a less active role than in the Edalji case, functioning more as a consultant and publicist rather than conducting an investigation himself. Slater was a less sympathetic figure who had a debauched lifestyle and was involved in various sordid enterprises, such as operating gambling clubs in London, some of which were not strictly legal. A dark-haired German Jew from Silesia with a sallow complexion, whose real name was Joseph Leschziner, he was an obvious foreigner among the Glaswegian Scots. He was arrested and convicted for the capital crime of murder and nearly hanged. Conan Doyle considered Slater a blackguard, but believed that even a blackguard deserved justice, which made his crusade all the more admirable. Slater's was a much more serious case than Edalji's because a man's life was at stake.

For Conan Doyle the case began when lawyers representing an improperly imprisoned man appealed for his help. His motivation was the same as in the Edalji case: the moral certainty that injustice had occurred and the resolution to combat it. However, there were many qualitative differences between the cases. He was involved intermittently over sixteen years between 21 August 1912, when he published *The Case of Oscar Slater*, and 19 July 1928, when Slater was cleared of all charges by the Scottish Court of Criminal Appeal.

The murder of the elderly Miss Marion Gilchrist, battered to death with a blunt instrument in the dining room of her flat, was what Dupin would have judged a 'simple' crime and, therefore, difficult to solve. And so it proved. The police behaved just like the dunderheaded gendarmes in Poe's stories, failing to search the house and seek among her family for a motive. And they did indeed arrest an innocent suspect. There the analogy breaks down, for Poe did not allow for deliberate misinterpretation of facts by the police and perversion of justice in a court of law.

At seven o'clock on 21 December 1908, Miss Gilchrist sent her maidservant Helen Lambie to fetch an evening newspaper, and during her absence of ten minutes, Miss Gilchrist was bludgeoned to death. Because she was fearful of burglars, her downstairs neighbour Mr Adams had agreed to check on her if she knocked three times on the ceiling. So when he and his sisters heard knocking and a loud thud above their heads that evening, he answered the signal only to discover the street door open but the flat door firmly secured by two locks. He rang the bell but got no response. While he waited, Helen Lambie returned and heard about the loud noises; she assumed that a clothes-drying apparatus in the kitchen had collapsed. As she moved down the corridor toward the kitchen, a man emerged from the spare bedroom and walked toward the front door, passing Adams, and hurried down the stairs to the street. Lambie and the man did not greet each other. Adams then asked Lambie where Miss Gilchrist was, and only then was her body discovered in the dining room. Adams rushed to get a doctor and a policeman, while Lambie ran to tell the shocking news to a family relation who lived nearby.[134]

A police search of the flat revealed that a wooden box had been broken open and Miss Gilchrist's private papers scattered on the floor of the spare bedroom, but that none of her expensive jewellery had been taken except for a diamond crescent brooch. Within a few days the police learned that a man known as Oscar Slater had tried to sell a pawn ticket for a diamond brooch at a local club. However, the brooch had been pawned months earlier and did not belong to Miss Gilchrist. They also interviewed witnesses who might have seen the unknown man in the flat. Adams and Lambie supplied descriptions, as well as Mary Barrowman, a fourteen-year-old girl who had seen a man rush away from the house as she was passing. Her very detailed description did not match those of Adams and Lambie, but Lambie later came to agree with Barrowman about his clothes. Upon finding that Slater had embarked on the *Lusitania* for New York, the police decided to interpret his departure as flight and to pursue him across the Atlantic with their witnesses. They were shown photographs of him, and when he was escorted down the corridor to the courtroom, they were able to observe him before being asked to identify him during the court proceedings.[135]

In vain Slater pleaded that he did not know Miss Gilchrist or anything about her jewellery. He had only recently arrived in Glasgow and had arranged his trip to New York weeks earlier. Against the advice of his American lawyer, who urged that the mistake about the brooches undermined the charges against him, Slater waived extradition proceedings and, with touching but mistaken faith in the Scottish judicial system, returned willingly to Scotland with the police.[136]

Slater was tried on 3 May 1909 in the High Court of Justiciary in Edinburgh. The Prosecution produced a small tin-tack hammer found in Slater's luggage as the murder weapon, but both medical practitioners had misgivings about it. Slater's alibi was discounted because it was offered by his mistress and servant. Lambie and Barrowman both identified him but Adams would not swear positively that Slater was the man he encountered in the flat. The counsel for the Crown did not address important questions such as how Slater got in and out of the flat and how he knew Miss Gilchrist had valuable jewellery. Despite his piteous pleas that he knew nothing of Miss Gilchrist or her murder and that he had willingly returned to Scotland to help the police with their enquiries, the jury brought in a majority verdict: Guilty – 9, Not Proven – 5, Not Guilty – 1. He was sentenced to hang on 27 May 1909 at Glasgow prison. There was a public outcry, and 20,000 people signed a petition against his execution. As a result, two days before his scheduled execution, his sentence was commuted to life imprisonment with hard labour and Slater was sent to Peterhead prison for life.[137]

Having accepted the baton passed to him by Slater's lawyers, Conan Doyle wrote *The Case for Oscar Slater*, based on William Roughead's account in *Notable Scottish Trials*. Conan Doyle's manifesto was plain: 'It is impossible to read and weigh the facts ... without feeling deeply dissatisfied with the proceedings, and morally certain that justice was not done.'[138] He attacked the evidentiary arguments in sequence, omitting none and raising relevant questions. Conan Doyle noted the inconsistencies in the case, the witnesses' contradictions, the trivial explanations proffered by the Prosecution. He challenged theft as an insufficient motive, and suggested that documents rather than jewels were the focus of the burglary.[139]

Why had Helen Lambie not expressed surprise when a man coming from the spare bedroom passed her en route to the front door? Was he not a stranger? On the same tack, why had Miss Gilchrist admitted her killer to the flat? Was she expecting him? He seemed to be familiar with the flat. After assaulting her, he went unerringly to the right room and rifled her papers, ignoring the valuable jewellery in plain sight. Was he interrupted or was he only interested in the documents?[140]

Conan Doyle concluded that the identification was tainted, that Slater had been pointed out to the witnesses in the corridor before the hearing in New York and that Lambie and Barrowman had been coached. The Prosecution had not proved means, motive and opportunity for Slater to commit the crime. The police case against him relied heavily on testimony of witnesses who swore they had seen him near the Gilchrist flat on the night of the murder. Conan Doyle pointed out the early date on which Slater pawned the brooch to raise funds for his transatlantic journey, the impossibility of inflicting such severe wounds with Slater's tack hammer and the absence of blood on his clothes. The Prosecution case also emphasised his unsavoury activities as pimp, gambler and jewel dealer rather than proof of the murder. Oscar Slater's defence was badly handled. He was not allowed to testify in his own behalf. His alibi was disallowed. The judge misdirected the jury which, consequently, submitted a guilty verdict.[141] He concluded with a demand for a retrial.

Unfortunately, Conan Doyle's polemic did not stimulate an indignant backlash. However, he did receive a letter from a juryman who expressed dissatisfaction with the trial because it was not shown how the killer got into the flat. Moreover, if the crime had been committed as described, there should have been blood on Slater's clothes.[142] He also urged the readers of the *Daily Mail* to lobby to reopen the case. He was joined by Sir Herbert Stephen, who wrote a letter to *The Times*, but it, too, failed to incite the public.[143]

Although *The Case for Oscar Slater* did not encourage the general public to mount the barricades, it did raise questions in Parliament and led to demands for a retrial. Then, in March 1914, Detective Lieutenant John Trench, a police officer with a troubled conscience who had been worried about the Slater case for five years, confessed to a solicitor David Cook that some evidence had been suppressed which might have exonerated Slater. Conan Doyle joined forces with Cook and Trench in campaigning for an inquiry. It was duly convened in April by the Secretary for Scotland and presided over by James G. Millar, KC, who called the Procurator Fiscal for Lanarkshire and the Chief Constable. But it met under conditions which foredoomed it to failure. It was not allowed to address the conduct of the trial or question the actions of the police; moreover, testimony was not taken under oath and Slater was not present. However, new evidence was introduced when Slater's alibi was verified by a respectable grocer. As one of the first responders in the Gilchrist murder investigation, Trench had interviewed Helen Lambie and Miss Gilchrist's cousin Miss Birrell and recorded their remarks in his notebook. He stated that when Lambie had called on Birrell to inform her of Gilchrist's death, she had identified the man in the hall, but Birrell cautioned her not to tell the police. Birrell and Lambie both denied Trench's allegations, especially about the identity of the man in the hall on the evening of the murder.[144] The Scottish Secretary announced that no case had been made to justify retrial. So Oscar Slater remained in prison.

Conan Doyle expressed his disgust in the Letters to the Editor column of the *Spectator*: 'The whole case will, in my opinion, remain immortal in the classics of crime as the supreme example of official incompetence and obstinacy.'[145] Despite his dissatisfaction, he continued to plead Slater's case as each new Secretary of State for Scotland took office.[146]

As usual with whistle-blowers there was a backlash against Cook and Trench for breaking ranks. The establishment sought revenge. Cook and Trench were arrested on a false charge of receiving stolen property but were acquitted in 1915. Nonetheless, their lives were ruined. Trench was dismissed from the police force and lost his pension.[147]

Ten years later, in 1925, Slater appealed to Conan Doyle to take up his case again on humanitarian grounds, so once more he wrote letters to the Secretary of State for Scotland plus others to influential friends and the press. He made speeches and gave press interviews reviewing the details of Slater's case and explaining why he believed a miscarriage of justice had happened. He was joined by Sir Herbert Stephen and other prominent men. The campaign gathered momentum, but never enough.[148]

Then, in July 1927, a Glaswegian journalist, William Park, who had found new evidence, entered the scene. He had uncovered a witness who had seen a man running away from Miss Gilchrist's house on 21 December and insisted that it was not Slater. Park also maintained that the brooch which had played such a major part in Slater's arrest was not stolen.[149] Encouraged by Conan Doyle, Park wrote a book entitled *The Truth about Oscar Slater*, which was published in 1927 by Conan Doyle's firm, The Psychic Press. Park denounced the police management of the case, censured the judge and accused Miss Gilchrist's nephew of murder.[150]

Of course this was sensational news. Conan Doyle wrote a new introduction to his *The Case of Oscar Slater* and sent a copy to every Member of Parliament. *The Daily News* published a series of articles analysing the Slater case. In October 1927, the *Empire News* carried a statement from Helen Lambie, now living in America, who admitted that she had 'blundered' and withdrew her official evidence. She disclosed that she had told the police the name of the man she had seen in the flat at the time of the murder, who was a regular visitor. She also insisted that the police had pressured her to identify Slater. A month later, the *Daily News* printed Mary Barrowman's retraction, in which she claimed that the police had not only dictated her statement but also that the procurator fiscal rehearsed her courtroom testimony.[151] It was revealed that she had been given £100 as a bribe and Lambie had received £40.[152] Consequently, in mid-November the Secretary for Scotland arranged Slater's release on the specious pretext of a 'reward for good behaviour' while he was incarcerated.[153]

The case was sent to the Scottish Court of Appeals in June 1928 and heard in July. Conan Doyle attended and was able for the first time to see Oscar Slater in person instead of in a photograph. Craigie Aitchison presented the case, and it was admitted that aspects of the trial had been unfair. On 20 July the conviction was overturned. Slater was pardoned on the grounds that the judge had misdirected the jury and was awarded £6,000 compensation. (He retired and lived quietly in Ayr till his death in 1949.) Conan Doyle had the last word in the *Sunday Times* a few days later, still complaining that new evidence had not been heeded and that Mrs Hamilton, who had seen the killer and was prepared to swear that he did not resemble Oscar Slater, had not been called to testify at the original trial.[154]

Conan Doyle and members of the Jewish community had underwritten Slater's legal costs, which he refused to pay. As a wronged man, he felt he was entitled to keep all of the money awarded him. His gratitude to Conan Doyle and others for his release did not extend to paying his debts. Conan Doyle was furious, but was later persuaded that his long confinement had caused Slater to behave dishonourably.[155] Others might feel that Slater was behaving in character.

The results were also unsatisfactory on more serious moral and legal levels. Conan Doyle did not strive to bring a case against the actual murderer, as he did in the Edalji case. As in the Edalji case, Conan Doyle wanted to discover and prosecute the true culprit, who had been named, but no official action was taken. He and his coadjutors were convinced that the man in Miss Gilchrist's hall was her nephew Francis James Charteris, but he was not prosecuted.[156] Dr Charteris had been accused in Trench's notes and in Park's book, and Conan Doyle had little doubt about his guilt. His papers devoted to the Slater investigation spanning 1914 to 1929 are housed in the Mitchell Library in Glasgow.[157]

As with the Edalji affair, the Slater case was only a qualified success, although in both matters Conan Doyle's investigation and deductive analysis were truly Sherlockian. The most important issues were won, but full justice was not achieved. There was still a case to answer. Conan Doyle felt that even though the battle had achieved only a partial victory, it had been worth the struggle. He had fought for his principles and righted grievous wrongs. His unstinting dedication to both causes reveals him as 'tirelessly ready to support the rights of the individual, thus defending an ideal which transcended all categories of mankind and beliefs'.[158]

Conclusion

This chapter demonstrates that the affinity between Conan Doyle and his detective hero is undisputable and that he has the strongest claim to be considered the *real* Sherlock Holmes. He admired Dupin's inductive reasoning enough to attempt to write detective fiction, but he embellished

Poe's approach by adapting Bell's diagnostic methodology to detection. So Sherlock Holmes became the first scientific sleuth. Like Bell, Conan Doyle also investigated crime in the real world. However, an important difference exists between their criminal investigations. Bell functioned as a forensic pathologist when he was summoned by Littlejohn, Edinburgh's official police surgeon. Bell acted as an expert medical witness for the Crown. At times he took the lead in uncovering circumstantial evidence, as in the Chantrelle case, but generally his role was as a forensic examiner. Conan Doyle, on the other hand, often instigated his own inquiries – sometimes at the request of a distressed stranger – but frequently on his own initiative after noticing an intriguing problem in the press. (Sound familiar?) The chief distinction between them is that Bell functioned upon official request, whereas Conan Doyle acted independently and was not limited only to scientific analyses. As in the Edalji and Slater cases, he was motivated by moral rectitude and righteous indignation. Like Holmes, he fought injustice and championed the vulnerable. His altruism even extended to paying expenses himself, as in the Slater case. His life-long fascination with crime qualified him for his vocation. Applying Holmes' values and working habits in the real world was indeed second nature. Despite the influence of Poe and Bell, surely Conan Doyle is the *real* Sherlock Holmes!

Let final judgment of Conan Doyle's investigative abilities be left to an expert witness, a professional in the field, Sir Basil Thomson, assistant commissioner at Scotland Yard. 'Sir Arthur Conan Doyle would have made an outstanding detective had he devoted himself to crime detection rather than authorship. There was much of Holmes in Doyle.'[159]

PART II

THE REAL WORLD OF CRIMINAL INVESTIGATION

4

SHERLOCK HOLMES AND THE METROPOLITAN POLICE

How accurately did Arthur Conan Doyle represent the Metropolitan Police Department in the Sherlock Holmes stories? Because Holmes is a private detective whose assistance is often sought by clients wishing to avoid contact with the police owing to the delicacy or difficulty of their problems, the police do not appear in at least a third of his cases, make only token appearances in many others, and when they are actively engaged in trying to solve crimes, they are represented as incompetent bunglers. This emphasis on the exploits of a heroic single individual to counteract crime at the expense of the legally appointed officers of the law presents a myopic perspective. It does not reflect accurately how law breaking was dealt with in the real world. Although private enquiry agents did exist in the Victorian period, most criminal investigations were conducted by police officers, with varying degrees of success, as they are today.

When police officers do figure in Holmes' cases, they represent civil authority and impose due process of law, officially securing warrants, conducting searches, guarding premises, arresting suspects and committing villains for trial, but nonetheless they play subordinate roles in solving the crimes. Often they are only called in at the very end of a case to make an arrest, as in 'The Red-Headed League' or 'The Solitary Cyclist', and/or Holmes simply turns his evidence over to the police and leaves them to apprehend the villain, as in 'The Cardboard Box'. But there is very little actual police detection. When they do investigate, they usually fail to identify the malefactor or form incorrect theories and arrest innocent people because they misinterpret the evidence they collect.

When the police realise they are baffled in particularly difficult cases, they reluctantly consult Holmes. As he explains to Watson in 'A Study in Scarlet', 'I am a consulting detective ... Here in London we have lots of government detectives and lots of private ones. When these fellows are at fault, they come to me, and I manage to put them on the right scent. They lay all the evidence before me, and I am generally able, by the help of my knowledge of the history of crime, to set them straight.'[1] Ignorance of previous crimes is not their only shortcoming; they also lack imaginative intuition to interpret evidence correctly. Holmes clarifies his position in 'The Sign of Four': 'I have chosen my own particular profession, or rather created it, for I am the only one in the world ... The only consulting detective ... I am the last and highest court of appeal in detection. When Gregson, or Lestrade, or Athelney Jones are out of their depths ... the matter is laid before me. I examine the data, as an expert, and pronounce a specialist's opinion. I claim no credit in such cases.'[2]

On the whole Holmes maintains a good working relationship with law enforcement agents, as when he is co-opted by Inspector Hopkins in 'Black Peter' and 'The Abbey Grange' or collaborates with Inspector Martin in 'The Dancing Men' and with Inspector Morton in 'The Dying Detective'. Although his help is sought by Scotland Yard, Inspectors Lestrade and Gregson resent their own limitations and Holmes' infallibility. Having called Holmes in, they nonetheless continue to pursue their own lines of inquiry and compete with him to reach a solution. Lestrade frequently disparages and rejects Holmes' ideas, as happens in 'The Norwood Builder', 'The Boscombe Valley Mystery' and 'The Six Napoleons'. Athelney Jones scoffs at Holmes' theories and deprecates his suggestions in 'The Sign of Four'. Lestrade complains that Holmes has an unfair advantage: 'We can't do these things in the force ... No wonder you get results that are beyond us.'[3]

A spirit of competitive rivalry also stirs the superficially calm waters in the suburbs. In an offensively patronising and officious manner the nameless inspector in 'The Three Gables' rejects Holmes' help and teaches his grandmother to suck eggs: 'Well, Mr Holmes, no chance for you in this case ... Just a common ordinary burglary, and well within the capacity of the poor old police. No experts need apply ... I never pass anything, however trifling ... That is my advice to you, Mr Holmes.'[4] Inspector Baynes also prefers to play a lone hand in 'Wisteria Lodge' in order to seize the chance to advance his professional reputation, but these competitive feelings are assuaged when Holmes applauds Baynes' astuteness and relegates all honours of the case to him. Holmes also commends Gregory's competence in 'Silver Blaze' but regrets that his lack of imagination will prevent him from reaching the top of his profession, and predicts that Hopkins will share the same fate for the same reason. Inspector Mackinnon in 'The Retired Colourman' attributes Holmes' success to his unorthodox methods, forbidden to the police, which give him the advantage and enable him to receive all the credit. He is mollified when Holmes promises to retreat without claiming any kudos.[5]

Holmes is quick to acknowledge that the police are good at methodical tasks and does not waste his own time doing routine jobs better left to them. Moreover, Holmes gives credit where it is due in 'The Three Garridebs'; he acknowledges that 'they lead the world for thoroughness and method'.[6] Sometimes he relies on police assistance when manpower is required for apprehending physically strong culprits, such as Jefferson Hope in 'A Study in Scarlet', Patrick Cairns in

'Black Peter' and Colonel Moran in 'The Empty House'. Of course they are indispensable for large sting operations such as the coordinated apprehension of Moriarty's gang in 'The Final Problem'.

Although, according to Vincent Starrett, 'it is always eighteen ninety-five' in the world of Sherlock Holmes,[7] actually the dates in the stories range between 1880 and 1914, with forty-seven cases occurring prior to 1900 and only thirteen afterward.[8] So the fictional representation of the police force during that period must be compared with its actual state in the real world to judge how accurately Conan Doyle portrayed police officers and their work in the Sherlock Holmes adventures. The organisation and operation of the Metropolitan Police between 1888 and 1913 had evolved over the timespan of the stories.

For example, 'The Sign of Four', published in 1891 but set in 1888, concludes with a thrilling chase on the Thames in a police steam launch. The River Police, known at first as the Marine Police Institution, was established in 1798 by Patrick Colquhoun, who acted as Superintending Magistrate, and Master Mariner John Harriott, who functioned as Resident Magistrate. It was funded by private shipowners and merchants who were suffering enormous annual losses from cargo theft. Its autonomous magistrates and police court, or public office, was located at Wapping. It was staffed by 200 carefully selected men, mostly ex-sailors, and their officers. 'Certainly they were the most efficient body of police then existing.'[9] During the first year the River Police reported 2,200 misdemeanours, which were duly prosecuted by magistrates.[10] Two years later in 1800 it was transformed from a private to a public police agency by the Marine Police Bill. Because the River Police were employed full-time and earned commensurate wages, they were not allowed to accept gratuities.

In these early days of the Thames police their headquarters at Wapping was manned by a detachment of forty-one officers, surveyors, constables and watermen whose strength could be increased to a total of 221 if needed. Their 'fleet' consisted of two rowing boats or galleys, each with a surveyor overseeing a pair of constables. Ever vigilant, they patrolled between London Bridge and Blackwall. By 1829, in addition to the Wapping office, the Marine Force occupied two additional stations at Waterloo and Blackwall. In August of 1839 when the Thames police was integrated into the Metropolitan Force, it became known officially as the Thames Division. The Wapping Police Office became a court and was transferred to Arbour Square in Stepney; the old office remained as a police station.[11]

At first the new division was responsible for patrolling only as far up the river as London Bridge. Their beat was later extended to Fulham and farther still, under Commissioner Sir Edward Henry (1903–18), until their purview covered a thirty-five-mile stretch of the Thames from the Dartford Reach to Teddington, with five stations located at Wapping, Waterloo Pier, Barnes, Blackwall and Erith.[12] By 1913, the penultimate year in the Holmesian calendar, they were staffed by 240 officers and maintained fourteen launches, motor boats and row boats. Regular eight-hour patrols, each with two men plus a sergeant, went out in all weathers. Their duties included resuscitation of suicide cases, thwarting smuggling attempts, maintaining traffic regulations and many other tasks.[13]

Initially patrols were conducted in rowing boats, but as a result of the collision in 1878 between the steam collier *Bywell Castle* and the pleasure steamer *Princess Alice*, when 600 lives were lost, a parliamentary inquiry recommended that the police should have steam launches because the rowing galleys had proved inadequate to cope with the disaster. Two steam launches were introduced in 1885, and by 1898 a further eight had been requisitioned. However, 'it took a long time for the utility of these craft to become apparent to the official mind, and even at that they were so small ... as to be "only fit for fine weather and smooth water"'.[14] So Holmes' river chase in a police steam launch in

117

1888 could have occurred in real time, but they probably would not have caught up with the villain steaming ahead in Mordecai Smith's *Aurora*, 'as trim a little thing as any on the river'.[15]

Most historians date the foundation of the Metropolitan Police from 1829 when the Home Secretary Sir Robert Peel spearheaded through Parliament 'An Act for Improving the Police in and near the Metropolis'.[16] However, a rudimentary system of law enforcement was already in place, so for the first ten years the new Metropolitan Police coexisted with already established patrols of watchmen paid by the parishes as well as constables employed by the civil magistrates.[17]

According to Scotland Yard historian George Dilnot, 'every parish was supposed to appoint and pay its own watchmen with head-boroughs or constables in charge'.[18] In most parishes the arrangements were inefficient. Even the City of London and Westminster, the most conscientious among the boroughs, failed to fulfil their responsibilities. Kensington had three head-boroughs and only three watchmen. A dozen or more London parishes eschewed their responsibilities entirely and made no effort to keep a police force. Even when watchmen were hired, the chief concerns of parish officials were fiscal. They were paid as little as two pence per hour. Dilnot points out that 'the types of men employed were decrepit, lazy, dishonest, and cowardly'.[19]

The system of street patrols and plain-clothes officers known as 'runners' who executed magistrates' orders was originally instituted and managed by Sir Henry Fielding, Principal Acting Magistrate for Middlesex at the Bow Street public office, who was followed on his death in 1754 by his brother John.[20] A cadre of only eight constables was available to investigate crimes referred to them by watchmen and volunteer parish constables. Paid by the magistrates from government funds, they did not patrol but served writs and arrested offenders. Under John Fielding's supervision the Bow Street men became better organised and hence more effective, so conditions in the capital improved during the second half of the eighteenth century, but many problems persisted.[21]

The Middlesex Justices Act of 1792 instituted the principle of paid magistrates. It also mandated seven public offices in addition to Bow Street. Appointed by the Home Secretary, each court had three justices with a stipend each of £300 per year. Constables with the power to arrest were appointed to each office on a salary of twelve shillings per week. Passed by Parliament over strong objections that it was unconstitutional for magistrates to dispense punishments without juries and fears that constables with the power to arrest would oppress the poor, this Act was nevertheless renewed five years later and became the basis for other subsequent legislation. More courts were added. Each district remained independent of the others, and the parish watch remained outside the authority of the magistrates.[22]

Mounted patrols were added in 1805 by Richard Ford, John Fielding's successor. The 'old police' horse patrols comprised fifty-four men with six inspectors. Designed to combat highway robbery on the roads leading to London, horse patrols uniformed with blue coats and red waistcoats were composed largely of ex-military men armed with pistols, cutlasses and truncheons. Foot patrols operated on the main roads in the suburbs. Both the mounted and the dismounted patrols were on duty only at night, whereas the streets of inner London were patrolled both night and day. Dilnot notes that 'although they had many defects, they were at least under constant supervision, and did, to a point, succeed in holding crime in check'.[23]

At the beginning of the nineteenth century, when the first census estimated London's population at 1 million, there were only 189 full-time paid police officers in the metropolis. Most of them were untrustworthy, and the various contingents were riven by rivalry. For example, a Kensington officer would not assist one from an adjoining district. 'Watchmen did not concern themselves to assist the patrols. Graft and blackmail flourished amazingly, and, as might have been expected, crime was rampant.'[24]

Many of the runners attached to the magistrates' courts gained great repute for their investigative abilities and were regarded as experts in the techniques of detection. The Bow Street men were allowed to undertake cases on a freelance basis for private individuals who were willing to pay for their skills. Normally they received a guinea per week as a retainer, but for their private enquiries they earned a guinea a day. Despite their modest wages, several of these runners managed to acquire fortunes. For example, John Townsend left an estate of £20,000, and his colleague John Sayer amassed £30,000.[25] Their accrual of assets was managed by employing devious means when recovering stolen property. Releasing the thieves in exchange for the missing goods and then accepting a gratuity from the owners or splitting the reward money with the robbers was common practice. The inadequacies, weaknesses and flaws of this system became more and more evident in the early decades of the nineteenth century.[26]

The Metropolitan Police Force was created in response to widespread civil disorder, ubiquitous property theft and frequent personal assault. Parliamentary committee reports estimated that 115,000 people were involved in illegal, immoral, or criminal activities; 65,000 were openly engaged in criminal pursuits. It was acknowledged that the night watch and police patrols were unable to prevent or detect crimes because the individuals employed were unfit, their numbers insufficient, the scope of their authority curtailed, and their connection and cooperation with each other too limited.[27] In 1828 a House of Commons committee discovered some shocking facts. It was common knowledge that the runners took bribes, but beyond that a practice spread which was encouraged by the bankers and facilitated by the Bow Street men of 'compounding' robberies at a fixed percentage rate.[28] Strong measures were called for. The inability of disparate multiple agencies to maintain order and protect property led to a growing realisation of the need for the state to assume responsibility for the public welfare.[29]

With strong support of the Duke of Wellington, then Prime Minister, in 1829 the Home Secretary Sir Robert Peel took action and introduced into the House of Commons his 'Act for Improving the Police in and near the Metropolis'.[30] Impressed by the success of the Thames River Police in reducing the theft of cargo through surveillance, Peel endorsed a philosophy of crime prevention, which was to be achieved largely through police presence in the streets: 'The primary object of an efficient police is the prevention of crime; the next that of detection and punishment of offenders if crime is committed.'[31] Like the eighteenth-century Italian criminologist Cesare Beccaria, Peel believed that detection is a greater deterrent in the prevention of crime than vindictive punishment.[32] Peel encouraged people to regard a police officer as a paid civilian professional who was answerable to the public rather than a paramilitary deputy of government.

The 'New Police' did not subsume the former system of policing established in the eighteenth century, which was both confusing and inefficient. For the first ten years the Metropolitan Police coexisted with forces established from 1792 under stipendiary magistrates, who worked from police offices with separate squads of constables. The dual system resulted in rivalry and counterproductive jealousies.[33] John Moylan, receiver, asserted in his 1929 centenary history of the Metropolitan Police that 'the Bow Street Runners were more of a private detective agency than a public service ... The contrast between the Bow Street system and that of the new police was illustrated by the division of labour during the ten years (1829–1839) that the runners and the new police co-existed: the runners took all the jewel robberies and left the murders to the Metropolitan Police. All the murderers were discovered, but very few of the jewel thieves were brought to justice.'[34]

From the outset the intention was to create a coherent,

disciplined police force for the whole of London under the control of two justices (later called commissioners). Lieutenant Colonel Charles Rowan and Richard Mayne were appointed to head a force of eight superintendents, twenty inspectors, eighty-eight sergeants and 895 constables, whose duty it was to maintain order in a seven-mile radius around Charing Cross. Fourteen years older than Mayne, Rowan had had a successful career in the Army. He was 'dynamic, a brilliant organizer and a master of discipline'. In contrast, Mayne was an obscure barrister with a thorough knowledge of the criminal law and seven years' experience on the northern legal circuit. He had no special qualifications for being a commissioner of police, but he was intellectually gifted and had imagination and vision. Mayne foresaw future problems and planned remedies in advance. He realised 'very soon after taking up his post as Commissioner, that detection was a specialised occupation and that it could not be properly done – as was the practice at first – by any policeman who happened to be first at the scene of a crime'.[35]

Not only did Mayne invent the route paper system, an early method of communicating information between divisional offices to men out on patrol, but he also created the predecessor of the contemporary Criminal Records Office so that recognition of habitual criminals would not depend on eyewitness memory. He compiled statistics of crime rates in various districts, which permitted concentration of forces in the worst areas. In order to develop a more efficient force, Mayne reviewed types of crimes and their prevalence, and classified crimes into those which were capable of being solved and those which were not. He even monitored financial costs.[36]

Rowan devised the initial plan for demarcating London into six divisions in order to police an area from Islington in the north to the Elephant and Castle in the south, and from Whitechapel in the east to Shepherds Bush in the west.[37] Each division was divided into eight sections and each section into eight beats. Based on the model of an Army regiment divided into companies and platoons, this scheme was directly copied from Sir John Moore's Shorncliffe system. The hierarchical management structure was designed to provide unified central control as well as to promote independent initiative in an emergency and give cooperative support among the districts.[38] The only military rank Rowan assigned to the police was that of sergeant. The adaptable beat system of intersecting routes, by which constables could cross each other's tracks, enabled them to exchange information while on duty and come to each other's aid. Rowan was an excellent administrator, and having once established the organisational model of the police force, he focused on maintaining its smooth-running efficiency. However, he was also a charismatic leader of men, good at coping in emergencies and pragmatic.

He was concerned about the personal conduct of the men in the force and imposed strict standards of behaviour that demanded respect for the human rights of all citizens and unflagging courtesy to the public.[39]

Within a year Rowan had increased London's divisions from six to seventeen. These covered a twelve-mile radius from Charing Cross, including Kent and parts of Middlesex. They were identified by the letters A–H and K–V. Each division had a station or office with 144 constables under the command of a superintendent. Inspectors usually supervised four sergeants, who regulated squads of nine men. Three more divisions, designated W, X, Y, were added in 1865, and finally in 1886 J was included. I and J had been excluded earlier to avoid confusion because they were interchangeable in the Latin alphabet.[40]

Constables worked a six-day week with twelve-hour shifts for a weekly wage of nineteen shillings, sergeants earned twenty-two shillings and sixpence, while inspectors and superintendents received salaries of £100 and £200 each. Their plain, dark-blue uniforms with single-breasted swallowtail coats and tall black stovepipe hats distinguished them from red-jacketed soldiers. They were unarmed but carried rattles to call for help. Recruited from various walks of life, by 1832 their ranks were composed of former butchers, bakers, shoemakers, tailors, labourers, servants, carpenters, bricklayers, blacksmiths, clerks, shop assistants, mechanics, plumbers, painters, weavers and stonemasons, as well as soldiers and sailors.[41] Except for the latter, few had previous experience of the kind of self-discipline and teamwork required by the police force, much less of maintaining public order or crime fighting. Of the 3,247 men recruited in the first six months, over half (1,644) were dismissed – mostly for drunkenness.[42]

Ten years after the Metropolitan Police Department was created, the Metropolitan Police Act of 1839 attempted to achieve a more streamlined structure through consolidation by differentiating duties and eliminating duplication. It separated the judicial from the executive functions of the police office magistracy in London, abolished their constabulary forces, and conferred sole authority for policing in London on the Metropolitan commissioners, except within the City of London, which has always maintained an independent force. Though some officers previously employed by the magistrates joined the Metropolitan Force, no discrete detective body was formed.[43] This Act also assimilated the River Police. The next reorganisation, three years later, when the Detective Branch was created, further refined functions and led ultimately to separation of the investigative officers from the rank and file constables in 1842. Two cases especially influenced these changes.[44]

In 1840 the murder of Lord William Russell, brother of the Duke of Bedford, in Mayfair caused a huge sensation. The combined efforts of Inspector Beresford of local C Division and Inspector Nicholas Pearce, the former Bow Street Runner co-opted from Whitehall's A Division, solved the case. Lord Russell's Swiss valet, Francois Courvoisier, became the most likely suspect when Beresford found a chisel in his bag whose shape matched marks on some of the drawers that had been forced open. However the valet had not left the premises since the murder and none of the stolen property, which therefore had to be somewhere in the house, was found among his possessions. After much fruitless searching, Pearce finally discovered some freshly disturbed plaster by a skirting board in the valet's pantry and behind it a cache of coins and a medal from the Battle of Waterloo. On the basis of this circumstantial evidence Courvoisier was arrested and tried, but there was no direct link between him and the stolen goods. It materialised during the trial when the English wife of a French hotelier, for whom Courvoisier had worked as a waiter, produced some of Lord Russell's engraved silver spoons which Courvoisier had lodged with her for safekeeping.[45] He was convicted and finally confessed. Despite the successful conclusion of the case, the press complained of police inefficiency because it took several searches to find the stolen goods.[46]

The second case occurred two years later in 1842 when a young woman called Jane Sparks was killed by a coachman, Daniel Good, who wished to be free of her in order to pursue another woman. He came to the notice of the police when a pawnbroker accused him of stealing a pair of trousers and a constable sent to search his quarters discovered part of a female torso in the stable. Although temporarily delayed by being locked in the barn when Good fled, Constable Gardner still managed to notify stations within a sixty-mile radius by four o'clock the next morning, via the route-paper system, to be on the watch for Good. Devised by Commissioner Mayne, this system mandated that when a crime was committed in an inspector's district, he must record the details and send them with a reserve officer to the next division, which would do the same until every division had been informed. Copies were also sent to sergeants of beat patrols. The time of receipt was written on the back and initialled before passing it on. All were centrally checked so the system could be monitored.

Not all division officers acted immediately so Inspector Tedman, in charge of Division D where Sparks lived, missed an opportunity to apprehend Good when the latter removed property from Sparks' lodgings at 5.15 a.m. and took a cab to the home of his first 'wife' in Spitalfields. The sergeant who traced him that far was so inept that Good again eluded capture. Good was finally apprehended quite by chance when Thomas Rose, formerly a police officer but then working on the railway, recognised Good and arrested him. Good was tried, convicted and executed within seven weeks of the murder.[47] This comedy of errors generated much derision in the press.

Stephen Wade pointed out that 'these two cases clearly pointed to the shortcomings of the current preventive system and the lack of specialists'.[48] The latter case elicited a diatribe in *The Times* about the misplaced emphasis on patrolling the streets to control drunkards rather than engaging in inquiries to identify dangerous villains like Courvoisier and Good. It lamented the loss of the former Bow Street detective police and compared adversely the new military style of the present force with the older detective agents. It urged the formation of an elite branch of detectives composed of old Runners and current officers which could gather information and keep potential lawbreakers under observation. 'Something else was needed – something relying on the kind of expertise that comes with intimate knowledge of location and demography.' When lords were being murdered in their beds, even plain-clothes police were not so terrifying a thought. As Stephen Wade put it, 'The police were on trial as well as Courvoisier that week at the Old Bailey.'[49]

Although establishment of the uniformed Metropolitan Police had occurred in 1829 in the face of opposition, the employment of plain-clothes detectives had been even more vigorously resisted because it was associated in the public mind with spying and the notorious French secret police. Commissioners Rowan and Mayne disapproved of the use of plain clothes because when a police officer carried out his duties without his uniform, he was engaging in a kind of fraud. Impersonation is fraud. Furthermore, it gave the appearance of spying on the public by those paid to protect them.

However, surveillance was an important part of preventing and solving crimes. In order to be effective it had to be unobtrusive, so wearing plain clothes was indispensable. It began as early as the 1830s as a means of catching pickpockets at work.[50] Four officers in each division wore plain clothes in order to catch beggars. When testifying before a Commons select committee in 1833 in the wake of the Popay scandal, Mayne admitted that both Peel and Melbourne, when acting as Home Secretary, had condoned the practice because crime could not be prevented solely by using uniformed police.

PC Popay, on his own initiative, had posed as a member and attended meetings of the dissident organisation of the National Union of the Working Classes. When he learned that a forbidden meeting was to occur, Popay informed the commissioners who sent officers to disperse the group. Their forceful tactics caused a riot, during which a police officer received a fatal stab wound. At the subsequent trial, the jury was so outraged at Popay's 'spying' that they returned a verdict of Not Guilty. Because Popay acted independently, he was dismissed from the force and the commissioners were exonerated. Nonetheless, this episode hardened the public hostility against police use of plain clothes. Police spying was considered to be against the Constitution.[51]

Rowan and Mayne feared a similar recurrence and throughout the 1850s issued directives against officers wearing plain clothes except in very special circumstances. Hence the thirteen-year delay before even a small detective unit could be contemplated.[52] But finally, in the aftermath of the brutal murders in 1842, the advantages of plain-clothes detectives were publicly acknowledged, and Commissioner Mayne decided that some men should be employed to observe 'known or suspected criminals' and to detect crime.[53] A failed attempt to assassinate the queen in 1842 also added to the discontent with the inefficiency of police protection.[54]

The result was the creation of the Detective Department at Scotland Yard. In June 1842 Commissioner Mayne convinced the Home Secretary, Sir James Graham, to employ for a trial period two inspectors and six sergeants as detectives. The inspectors were paid an annual salary of £200, and the sergeants earned £73 per year. Nicholas Pearce, who had performed well in the Russell case, headed the group with John Haynes as his deputy. The other six men were Stephen Thornton, William Gerrett, Frederick Shaw, Charles Goff, Jonathan Whicher and Sergeant Braddick.[55] They were the first 'Serious Crimes' unit and investigated cases operating without jurisdictional limits, sometimes travelling to other parts of the country and even abroad.[56]

The negative attitude toward the police was somewhat ameliorated by positive press in the 1850s. Charles Dickens' article 'A Detective Police Party' in *Household Words* praised the wisdom and competence of the Detective Department, especially of inspectors Charles Field and Jonathan Whicher. He compared them with the former Bow Street detectives to the latter's disadvantage. Inspector Field was also lauded in *The Times* in 1853. In 1856 *The Quarterly Review* praised the Detective Department in a long article, 'The Police and the Thieves', claiming that it produced officers equal to those of Bow Street.[57]

In the 1860s (Frederick) Adolphus Williamson became head of a detective branch with approximately thirty men. 'Williamson saw the Branch through a period of tremendous growth of crime in London.'[58] Under Superintendent Williamson, the detective branch undertook government enquiries, naturalisation matters, extradition cases and the more serious criminal investigations. A crime wave in the mid-1860s produced a panic because of an increase in violent crimes, especially garrotting. To combat this widespread menace, an increased number of plain-clothes officers were assigned to night duty. In the 'Empty House', Holmes identifies one of the men watching for his return to 221b Baker Street as 'a garrotter by trade'.[59]

1. Edgar Allan Poe, late May to early June 1849. (Courtesy of the J. Paul Getty Museum, Los Angeles)

2. Sherlock Holmes smokes while pondering a problem in 'The Man with the Twisted Lip', by Sidney Paget, *The Strand Magazine*. (Courtesy of Roger Johnson)

Above: 3. Holmes and Watson discuss the case in 'The Copper Beeches', by Sidney Paget, *The Strand Magazine.* (Courtesy of Roger Johnson)

Left: 4. Dr Joseph Bell, a brilliant medical diagnostician at Edinburgh, whose appearance, personality and methods inspired Conan Doyle to create Sherlock Holmes. (Courtesy of Wellcome Library, London)

5. Dr Robert Christison, one of Conan Doyle's professors at Edinburgh, who published results of experiments with *cuca* or *coca*. (Courtesy of Wellcome Library, London)

6. Dr James Syme, the Napoleon of surgery at the Royal Infirmary in Edinburgh and mentor of Joseph Bell. (Courtesy of Wellcome Library, London)

7. Dr Henry Littlejohn, Professor of Medical Jurisprudence and Chief Surgeon to the City Police in Edinburgh, who co-opted Bell to assist on forensic investigations. (Courtesy of Wellcome Library, London)

8. Dr Patrick Heron Watson, surgeon and forensic scientist who served as expert witness in the Monson/Hambrough case with Joseph Bell and Henry Littlejohn. (Courtesy of Wellcome Library, London)

Right: 9. Arthur Conan Doyle. (Courtesy of the Wellcome Library, London)

Below: 10. Arthur Conan Doyle at his writing desk. (Courtesy of Wellcome Library, London)

Above: 11. Holmes examining a crime scene in 'The Boscombe Valley Mystery', by Sidney Paget, *The Strand Magazine*. (Courtesy of Roger Johnson)

Left middle: 12. Oscar Slater, extradited from USA and convicted of murdering a Scottish woman he had never met, but released after Conan Doyle publicised his case. (Courtesy of TopFoto)

Left bottom: 13. George Edalji, who was falsely imprisoned for cattle maiming but released after Conan Doyle gathered evidence proving his innocence. (Courtesy of TopFoto)

Above: 14. Police detectives in contemporary dress, *c.* 1911. (Courtesy of Metropolitan Police Heritage Centre)

Below: 15. Police detectives in plain clothes for drug operation, *c.* 1911. (Courtesy of Metropolitan Police Heritage Centre)

16. Detective Inspector
Walter Dew arrests
Hawley Harvey Crippen.
(Courtesy of TopFoto)

17. Crippen and Le Neve
at their trial in 1910.
(Courtesy of Wellcome
Library, London)

18. A police photograph of Mary Kelly's body where it was found on her bed. This is thought to be the first crime-scene photograph taken in Great Britain. (Courtesy of the Evans/Skinner Archive)

19. Alfred Swaine Taylor, forensic pathologist. (Courtesy of Wellcome Library, London)

Above: 20. Dr Bernard Spilsbury, the forensic pathologist who identified Belle Crippen's remains. (Courtesy of TopFoto)

Left: 21. Francis Galton (1892) published the first book on fingerprint analysis. (Courtesy of Special Collections, University College Library)

Opposite and overleaf: 22 & 23. Galton's charts of fingerprints. (Courtesy of Wellcome Library)

This form is not to be pinned.

MALE

C.R.O. No.

Name

Aliases

Prison

Prison Reg. No.

Classification No. $\dfrac{13 \cdot U \cdot 10}{18 \cdot U \cdot 10}$ 14

RIGHT HAND

1.—Right Thumb.	2.—R. Fore Finger.	3.—R. Middle Finger.	4.—R. Ring Finger.	5.—R. Little Finger.

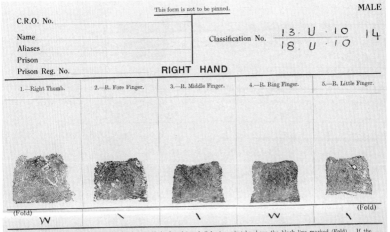

(Fold) ＼＼

＼

＼

＼／＼／

＼

(Fold)

Impressions to be so taken that the flexure of the last joint shall be immediately above the black line marked (Fold). If the impression of any digit be defective a second print may be taken in the vacant space above it.

When a finger is missing or so injured that the impression cannot be obtained, or is deformed and yields a bad print, the fact should be noted under *Remarks*.

The "rolled" and "plain" impressions are to be obtained first, then the prisoner should sign his name, and lastly an imprint of the right forefinger is to be impressed on the back of the form.

LEFT HAND

6.—L. Thumb.	7.—L. Fore Finger.	8.—L. Middle Finger.	9.—L. Ring Finger.	10.—L. Little Finger.

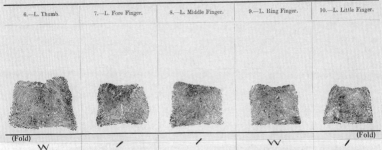

(Fold) ＼／

／

／

＼／＼／

／

(Fold)

LEFT HAND
Plain impressions of the four fingers *taken simultaneously.*

RIGHT HAND
Plain impressions of the four fingers *taken simultaneously.*

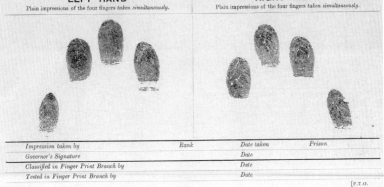

Impression taken by	*Rank*	*Date taken*	*Prison*
Governor's Signature		*Date*	
Classified in Finger Print Branch by		*Date*	
Tested in Finger Print Branch by		*Date*	

21057

PLATE 2

[P.T.O.

[*To face page 118.*

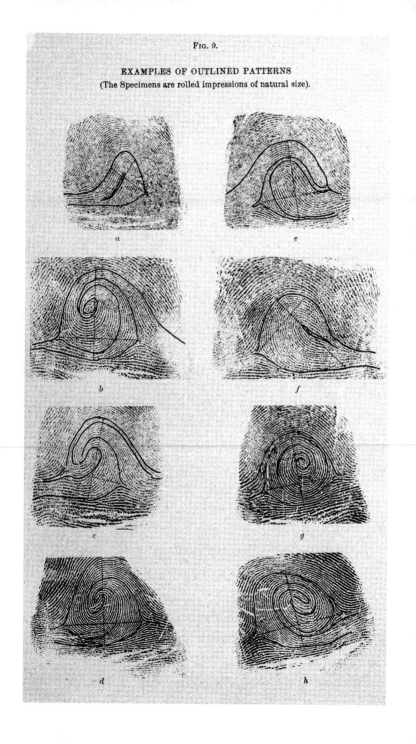

FIG. 9.

EXAMPLES OF OUTLINED PATTERNS
(The Specimens are rolled impressions of natural size).

a

e

b

f

c

g

d

h

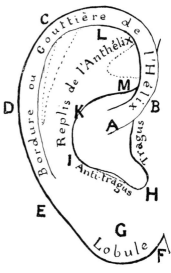

Above left: 24. Dr Edmond Locard formulated the theory that all physical contact leaves traces. (Courtesy of TopFoto)

Above right: 25. Alphonse Bertillon invented a system of physical measurements to classify criminals. (Courtesy of TopFoto)

Right: 26. Bertillonage measuring methods. (Courtesy of Wellcome Library, London)

Fig. 27. — Oreille schématique.

Bordure A B C D E décomposée en partie **O**riginelle A B, **S**upérieure B C, **P**ostérieure C D et inférieure D E.

Lobule E F G H considéré sous le rapport du **c**ontour E F, de l'**a**dhérence à la joue F H, du **m**odelé G et de sa **D**imension.

Antitragus H I examiné au point de vue de son **i**nclinaison, de son **p**rofil, de son degré de **r**enversement et de sa **D**imension.

Plis internes séparés en branches **i**nférieure I K, **s**upérieure K L, et médiane K M.

Left: 27. Holmes soothes Helen Stoner in 'The Speckled Band', by Sidney Paget, *The Strand Magazine*. (Courtesy of Roger Johnson)

Below: 28. Holmes inspires Miss Cushing's trust and confidence in 'The Cardboard Box', by Sidney Paget, *The Strand Magazine*. (Courtesy of Roger Johnson)

Above: 29. Holmes respects Violet Hunter's womanly instinct in 'The Copper Beeches', by Sidney Paget, *The Strand Magazine.* (Courtesy of Roger Johnson)

Right: 30. Holmes expresses compassion at the abuse suffered by Beryl Stapleton in 'The Hound of the Baskervilles', by Sidney Paget, *The Strand Magazine.* (Courtesy of Roger Johnson)

31. Holmes tries to prevent Anna's suicide in 'The Golden Pince-Nez', by Sidney Paget, *The Strand Magazine*. (Courtesy of Roger Johnson)

32. Holmes accuses Susan of eavesdropping in 'The Three Gables', by Sidney Paget, *The Strand Magazine*. (Courtesy of Roger Johnson)

The police used less fancy-dress disguise than has been suggested in popular fiction. For example, false moustaches and beards and wigs were considered too obvious; however, a detective would 'assume a character' and maintain a false identity to gather information, facilitate surveillance and/or make an arrest. A detective might attire himself as a sailor, a professional man, a scavenger, a peddler, or a chimney sweep to fit into his surroundings.[60] All of the police detectives in Holmes' cases wear plain clothes, but none ever don a costume. Holmes, on the other hand, excels at the art of impersonation. He masquerades as a stable hand and an elderly clergyman in 'Scandal in Bohemia' (p. 170), a rakish young workman in 'Charles Milverton' (p. 576), as an old lady in 'The Mazarin Stone' (p. 1016), as a sea captain in 'Black Peter' (p. 571) and as a poor old bibliophile in 'Empty House' (p. 485). In the latter role the deception is so complete that he nearly gives Watson a heart attack when he discards his disguise. Holmes assumes these personae to gather information, to recover stolen property and effect an arrest, and for self-protection.

As a sign of the times, London had its first railway murder. When Thomas Briggs, a senior bank clerk in the City, was brutally battered in a first-class carriage of the North London Railway while travelling from Fenchurch Street to Hackney on 9 July 1864, the attack aroused enormous outrage prompted by feelings of incipient danger. Twenty minutes after two bank clerks had discovered the blood-spattered upholstery in Briggs' empty carriage at Hackney Wick, the driver of a train travelling in the opposite direction saw the severely injured man lying at the side of the tracks between the lines near the Duckworth Canal and sent a guard to investigate. They raised the alarm and Briggs was carried to a nearby pub. As medical aid was summoned, the local beat police officer took charge. Briggs died that evening of his injuries.

This shocking crime was given top priority by Commissioner Mayne, who assigned Scotland Yard's best detective, Richard Tanner, to investigate. Although Briggs' stick and bag were found in the railway carriage, his watch, chain and hat were missing. Tanner distributed descriptions of Briggs' missing property throughout London. Almost at once a jeweller named John Death notified the police that a young foreigner had traded a similar watch and chain. Then a cab driver named Jonathan Matthews identified a young German tailor called Franz Müller, who had given his daughter an empty jewellery box with Death's logo, and also recognised a hat found in the carriage as Müller's. In addition, Matthews supplied Müller's address and photograph. The jeweller recognised the picture of Müller as well as the box. Tanner went to Müller's address only to learn that Müller had sailed to New York. Then Tanner made a bold and unprecedented decision that earned him an international reputation. Taking another officer as well as Death and Matthews, he embarked on a faster ship and arrived in New York three weeks before Müller. After his witnesses identified Müller, Tanner arrested him and discovered Briggs' watch and hat in his luggage. Extradition followed and then prosecution in London. The weight of the evidence was so convincing that the jury returned a guilty verdict within fifteen minutes. The transatlantic chase had excited public interest in both countries. His execution attracted a crowd of 50,000 and created such public disorder that public hanging was abolished.[61]

Increasingly during the 1860s the detective branch had to extend its agenda to deal with political crimes.[62] A crisis occurred in 1867 after a failed attempt to mount an armed uprising by the proponents of Irish self-rule, called Fenians. In September Colonel Thomas Kelly, the leader of the Irish Republican Brotherhood (IRB), was arrested in Manchester. He had been involved in organising a gang to assassinate informants and the police officers that were trying to combat the IRB. While Kelly was being transported to gaol, the police van was attacked by armed men and a police sergeant was killed when he refused to turn over his keys. A comrade cut through the roof so Kelly did escape, but five men were arrested. A nationwide manhunt for Kelly ensued. Inspector

James Thomson, based in London, received information that Captain O'Sullivan Burke and his associate Casey, who had organised the audacious Manchester escape, were staying in the capital. After they were identified in the street by an informer, Thomson challenged and arrested them at gunpoint. They were charged with treason felony and sent to the Clerkenwell House of Detention. Rumours of an attempted prison break were rife, so two or three officers were assigned to observe an outer wall. Commissioner Mayne also warned Captain Codd, the prison governor, and advised separating the prisoners and moving them to different quarters. Although Codd scoffed at the warning, he did shift the prisoners. In spite of these precautions, on 13 December a huge explosion destroyed fifty-five metres of the prison wall enclosing the exercise yard, killing six people and injuring 126. Although immense damage resulted, the prisoners were not freed. This tragedy caused a serious loss of public and parliamentary confidence.[63]

As a result of the debacle the number of detectives was increased. Although the staff of detectives had reached fifteen earlier in 1867, Mayne requested an increase in their number. Following the Clerkenwell calamity, in January 1868 he requested thirteen additional men and recommended that a group of full-time plain-clothes detectives be added to the divisions. Consequently, in February 1868 Home Secretary Gathorne Hardy appointed a departmental committee to review the administration of the Metropolitan Police. The committee report in May recommended that detectives form a separate division under the control of a special superintendent who would report directly to the head of the police. Unfortunately Mayne died before this initiative could be implemented, but Edmund Henderson, the new commissioner, increased the central force by twenty, bringing it to thirty-three, and allocated twenty sergeants and 160 constables, seconded from the unformed ranks, to the divisions.[64] The central Detective Department at Scotland Yard remained largely unchanged, but had no authority over the divisional detectives who continued to be responsible to their divisional superintendents. Informal specialisation developed, by which divisional detectives undertook inquiries unsuitable for beat patrolmen. This move merely ratified an already existing practice whereby some plain-clothes officers engaged in special inquiries.[65]

Divisional and central detectives had different kinds of duties. Divisional detectives were instructed to become well acquainted with all the criminals in their districts as well as their associates, habits and residences. They used three methods: 1) Twice weekly they visited different prisons in order to be able to recognise convicts recently arrested or about to be discharged to their districts. 2) After the Habitual Criminals Act was passed in 1869, they studied divisional registers of thieves. Criminal records were not centralised; there was not much collaboration or exchange of information within the Metropolitan Police. 3) Finally, when not otherwise occupied, divisional detectives frequented criminal dens and patrolled the streets. Unless directed by the commissioner, central detectives did not investigate ordinary criminal cases. They focused on more important, high-stakes cases, including swindles and fraud.[66]

Within a decade another crisis, prompted by perfidy within the elite plain-clothes corps, erupted. The Turf Club fraud scandal, which shocked the nation, brought disgrace on the whole department and resulted in its reorganisation. On 13 August 1877, Home Secretary Richard Assheton Cross appointed a confidential departmental commission to inquire into 'the state, discipline, and organization of the detective branch'.[67]

The tale is soon told. In 1873 Harry Benson and William Kurr were peddling fraudulent tips on horse races to gullible punters with great success. Because their system was so 'infallible', they claimed the bookmakers had refused to accept their bets. Promising to reimburse all winnings at 5 per cent interest, they persuaded people to place bets for them, using their own names and money. Of course anyone foolish enough to do so lost their money. When their victims complained to the police, the miscreants avoided prosecution by bribing Scotland Yard detectives to warn them when arrests were imminent. Four detective inspectors who regularly policed race meetings were involved in covering up the fraud: John Meiklejohn, Nathaniel Druscovitch, William Palmer and George Clarke. Impatient with the slow progress of the case, Superintendent Williamson took charge. While Druscovitch and others went to Holland to arrest Benson and other gang members detained there, Sergeant John George Littlechild travelled to Edinburgh to apprehend Kurr and his cronies. Once in custody, the conmen identified the officers who had protected them and testified against them in court. Meiklejohn, Druscovitch and Palmer were convicted and sentenced to penal servitude, but Clarke was acquitted.[68] This trial became a huge cause célèbre.

Detectives had long been regarded with suspicion and distrust because they worked covertly and independently, remote from supervision and control. Therefore the greatest care had to be exercised in selecting them and ensuring they conducted their duties honestly and assiduously. One of the most shocking aspects of the Turf Fraud scandal was that the detectives were able to proceed without arousing suspicion for so long. The case exacerbated latent fears that inadequately supervised and poorly paid detectives would become corrupted through close association with criminals. Nonetheless, the scandal did not lead to the dissolution of the detective branch but to a demand for a more efficient system of management.[69]

Three official inquiries were conducted between 1877 and 1879. The first dealt specifically with the detective system, and the second examined other functions of policing. The third, which remained incomplete, enquired into relations between the commissioner and the receiver, the Crown officer responsible for the finance and supply of the force who reported to the Home Secretary directly. All of these reports were private, as was that of 1868–69.[70] Both the

1868 and 1878 inquiries were chaired by the then Home Office parliamentary undersecretary.

All of the reports stressed the constant problem of the lack of proper qualifications, which contributed greatly to the department's inefficiency. Throughout the Victorian period there was such a dearth of educated officers with clerical skills that civilian clerks were employed in the offices of the commissioners and the receiver.[71] Haia Shpayer-Makov notes that 'most detectives in this period originated from working-class homes and were themselves ordinary workers before joining the police'.[72] Police administrators' reports were full of complaints concerning hiring and retaining staff. Recruitment figures for 1874 reveal that 31 per cent of new applicants came from land jobs, 12 per cent from military service, 5 per cent from other police jobs and the rest had done some sort of manual labour.[73] Some exceptions did occur. For example, Adolphus Williamson, son of the first superintendent of T Division, rose through the ranks to become the first chief constable of the Criminal Investigation Department.[74] Williamson gave evidence in both 1868 and 1878 inquiries, and insisted that it was essential for the Detective Department to recruit men with above-average skills and offer them a higher rate of pay. He acknowledged that the men were often experienced in the habits of thieves, but alleged they were mostly illiterate and ignorant, with very little knowledge of the world or mankind outside their own social circles. Many of them could not write a daily report of their activities.[75]

The system of rewards or gratuities, dating back to the days of the Bow Street Runners, was vigorously debated in the 1878 inquiry. Williamson endorsed retaining them as incentives. Opponents felt that they should be abolished on the principle that all cases should be handled alike to avoid preferential treatment based on anyone's ability to pay. The payment of rewards for results was also blamed for inciting negligence of duty. Edmund Coathupe, Chief Constable of Bristol, testified in 1878 that 'not one of the officers of

Scotland Yard would ever look at a case of picking up a thief in the streets; it was beneath them. "It does not pay" used to be their answer.'[76] They would wait for cases which offered rewards. Despite being warned that abolishing gratuities would simply lead officers to take them surreptitiously, the 1878 committee voted nonetheless to abolish them. As an alternative to compensate for the loss, they considered raising pay levels higher than those of the uniformed branch. Instead of the system of posting rewards and thus identifying their sources before they were distributed, they advocated paying gratuities into a general fund from which the commissioner could dispense sums to be awarded at the discretion of the head of the detective branch. Ultimately, gratuities were not abolished, and the system of declaration was retained.[77]

Another source of complaint was the lack of coordination between the divisions. Testimony from twenty-two witnesses revealed that divisional detectives were jealous of each other and therefore reluctant to cooperate, often refusing to share information. Constantly short-staffed and overworked, the divisional detectives complained that jurisdictional limitations interfered with following suspects outside the divisional boundaries. Both central and divisional detectives were concerned that confidentiality could not be preserved during an inquiry. Vital information could be 'leaked' throughout the system. Uniformed divisional officers could learn when and where a criminal was to be arrested, and clerks and messengers at headquarters were privy to similar information, which could be passed on for a fee.

The commission contended that a prerequisite of overcoming jealousy and achieving greater efficiency was 'the abolition of the divisional detective system' and the establishment of 'a united and distinct' detective force for 'all purposes of organisation and control'.[78] 'The commission's damning conclusion was that "the present division of detective power" had "utterly failed in leading to a proper detection of crime, or in supervising those who are known to live by it".'[79] Hence, the commission's report in January 1878 was 'a striking indictment of the effectiveness of detectives in dealing with criminals'. However, the committee's recommendation that the detective function be separated from the uniformed hierarchy was accepted. As a result of this report the Criminal Investigation Department (CID) replaced the Detective Branch. Howard Vincent, a barrister who had studied Parisian detectives, was appointed in March 1878 as its director, and reported directly to the Home Office.[80] Placing all detectives under one administrator was designed to eliminate jurisdictional conflicts and encourage centralised coordination.

Vincent introduced important reforms. His 'new Department was intended to consist of 280 officers, 254 of them to be based in the divisions under local inspectors', but within six years the CID roster grew from 250 to 800.[81] He increased both wages and allowances for them. He also published information about wanted criminals in the press. Other improvements included transforming the *Police Gazette* into a useful vehicle for circulating updated information among the divisions and establishing the Convict Supervision Office, which organised the collection of records and compiled photographs in a 'rogues gallery' of habitual offenders. In 1882 Vincent published the *Police Code and Manual of Criminal Law*, later known as the *Police Guide*, with a compilation of the laws and a code of conduct needed by police officers. It was regularly updated for the next eighty years.[82]

When Vincent resigned in 1884 detectives had still not completely proven their worth. Although from 1874 to 1884 arrests by detectives for criminal offences in London increased from 13,128 to 18,344, they dealt predominantly with petty crimes.[83] In 1885, when London's population was 5,255,069, the strength of the force numbered 13,319, but only 1,383 officers were available for daily beat duty.[84] Vincent had a low opinion of divisional detectives, claiming they were mostly illiterate and that many of them became plain-clothes officers to hide personal defects which prevented them from making a smart appearance in uniform. Even sixteen years later in 1901 when Edward Henry became commissioner, he took charge of a detective force that was of mediocre calibre at best. Like Vincent, Henry strove to improve qualifications, initiating a training course in 1902 plus lectures on criminal law and procedure in 1913.[85]

Revelation about corruption among detectives in the Turf Club fraud scandal (1877) and the inability of detectives to eradicate crime and find perpetrators in a number of celebrated murder cases, like those attributed to Jack the Ripper, perpetuated this negative image. 'It was only towards the end of the century that the reputation of the CID detectives began to change significantly for the better, but the change was gradual and the feeling among members of the police organisation was that a great deal still needed to be done to refute the prejudices harboured by the public.'[86] This was supported by fictional representations of police officers as unintelligent plodders by writers such as Edgar Allan Poe and Arthur Conan Doyle. From its very beginning in 1842 the Detective Department of the Metropolitan Police had been the object of criticism.

> The slow development of the detective force – from a unit of eight at Metropolitan Police headquarters in 1842 to a force of approximately 300 with a presence in all divisions by 1889 – was accompanied by censorious public discourse. However, during the course of the century, the public gradually came to accept the necessity of a police force in each locality, and then acceptance slowly extended to detectives as well, but because of the lingering suspicion of plain-clothes policing, the work of the police and their detective units was constantly subject to closer public scrutiny.[87]

The formal structure of the Metropolitan Police was well defined and the CID well entrenched at Scotland Yard between 1880 and 1914, the fictional time period during which Sherlock Holmes was exercising his professional skills.

The hierarchical structure of the organisation is revealed in the stories by the delegation of professional responsibilities assigned to the various ranks of divisional officers, and the importance of the CID at Scotland Yard made manifest. Detectives from the Yard are always sent to investigate murders, but there are no specific allusions to the Murder Squad formed in 1907 by the Home Secretary Herbert Gladstone to address problems occurring when detectives were summoned to remote crime sites. They often found that time delays had contaminated or destroyed evidence at the crime scene and/or that local officers resented their 'interference' and withheld crucial information. So Gladstone created a special group of experienced detectives who would be ready to leave immediately if a provincial chief constable decided the local force lacked the expertise to solve a crime. Superintendent Frank Froest led the first five-man team and also appointed chief inspectors Frederick Fox, Walter Dew, John Kane and Charles Arrow. They had all proved their worth in major investigations.[88]

How closely do Lestrade, Athelney Jones, Gregson and Hopkins resemble their opposite numbers in the real world? Lestrade – who travels to rural areas in 'The Boscombe Valley Mystery', 'The Norwood Builder' and 'The Problem of Thor Bridge' – always follows the obvious trail, which usually proves false. Jones, Gregson and Hopkins also overlook subtler clues that lead Holmes to the truth. The difficulties in finding well-qualified staff mentioned above, as well as low retention rates, could justify Holmes' perception of the Metropolitan Police on the whole, and even the CID, as second rate, especially prior to 1900 when the majority of the stories occur. Thirteen tales take place between 1900 and 1913, but only two happen after the creation of the fabled Murder Squad in 1907. During the first decade of the twentieth century, new, more reliable, scientific techniques such as fingerprinting and blood testing improved methods of criminal investigation significantly and yielded a higher rate of success.

Divisional methods of crime prevention included dividing criminals into two types: habitual or professional villains and occasional or opportunistic culprits.[89] Divisional officers would get to know the career criminals in their districts and learn their methods so as to aid in identifying perpetrators of fresh offences. A great deal depended on eyewitness identification, which was enhanced when the Habitual Criminals Register was introduced in 1869 and space for photographs added in 1870. Howard Vincent's introduction of a rogues gallery at the Convict's Supervision Office also contributed.[90] In 'The Six Napoleons', Lestrade is confident that the Italian victim and villain will be identified quickly by Inspector Hill, who is familiar with the Italian community around Saffron Hill, and he is right. Hill identifies the corpse immediately as a Neapolitan cutthroat with Mafia connections. Detectives also relied heavily on networks of informers. Holmes himself gives an example of this kind of networking in 'The Illustrious Client' when he employs Shinwell Johnson, a former criminal, to discover information about Baron Gruner.

There were several sensational murder cases in the years between 1880 and 1914, but most of them were not solved by police detectives' brilliant insights and logical deduction à la Sherlock Holmes, but rather through routine procedure and 'information received'. A brief review of their investigative work in some of these high-profile cases will indicate whether contemporary detectives were reliably depicted as deserving Holmes' contempt.

A most egregious example of police ineptitude occurred in the case of Adolph Beck, who was arrested and imprisoned twice on false charges of fraud and theft on the basis of mistaken identification. It began in December 1895 when Madame Ottilie Meissonier sought help from a constable, accusing Beck of stealing her jewellery. At the police station it transpired that during the past two years twenty-two women had lodged similar complaints against a grey-haired man resembling Beck. Not surprisingly, they all identified

Beck in a police line-up of randomly selected men, because he was the only one with grey hair and a moustache. Beck was charged with ten misdemeanours and four felonies because a police officer thought he recognised Beck as John Smith, whom he had arrested and who was convicted for similar offences in 1877.

At the trial a handwriting expert named Thomas Gurrin, who had compared samples of Smith's and Beck's writing, testified that current samples of Beck's script had been written in a disguised hand, implying that they were by the same author. But what convicted Beck was his mistaken identification by witness after witness as the swindler. In March 1896 Beck was convicted of fraud, sentenced to seven years of penal servitude and sent to Portland Prison, where he was assigned Smith's former ID number with the letter W added to indicate that he was a repeat offender. Between 1896 and 1901 Beck's solicitor presented ten petitions to the Home Secretary for the case to be re-examined, but all were denied.

The first break came in 1898 when a Home Office official reviewed Smith's dossier and noticed that he was Jewish and had been circumcised, whereas Beck had not been. The Home Secretary then conceded that Beck was not Smith, and authorised the removal of the letter W from his records, but insisted that Beck was still guilty of the fraud charges. Then a crusading *Daily Mail* journalist, G. R. Sims, wrote an article protesting that Beck had been tried and sentenced on the assumption that he was Smith, but that the judge had disallowed any evidence about Smith to be presented, which rendered the verdict invalid. Gradually he convinced others, including Conan Doyle, and Beck was paroled in July 1901. Three years later, on the basis of a similar complaint of fraud and theft lodged by a female servant, the inspector handling the matter – who was familiar with Beck's case – had him rearrested. When the woman did not recognise Beck, the inspector arranged to have her threaten Beck with arrest, at which point he panicked and fled.

When apprehended and tried again, five additional women identified him so the jury again found him guilty. Despite assurances by the police and the Home Office of his guilt and/or identity, the judge delayed sentencing. Ten days later a man was accused of trying to swindle a couple of actresses and was found in a pawnshop with their stolen property. Inspector John Kane of the CID, realising that Beck was already on remand, went to the prisoner's cell and found a heavier Beck lookalike with a scar on his neck, who was actually John Smith alias William Thomas alias Wilhelm Meyer. After notifying Scotland Yard, the inspector arranged for several women who had previously identified Beck to confront Smith. They all recognised him as their swindler and admitted their previous error. Smith's former landlord also identified him. In the face of this evidence, Smith confessed, so Beck was released.[91]

Beck was given a free pardon in July 1904 and eventually compensated for false imprisonment. In the aftermath the Metropolitan Police were exonerated, but the judges involved, as well as the Home Office, were censured, not only for malfeasance, but also for preferring to countenance injustice rather than risk loss of credibility. The committee, chaired by the Master of the Rolls, cited the prison authorities' failure to describe Smith's physical characteristics as the primary cause of the miscarriage of justice.[92] As a result of the horrific travesty of justice experienced by Beck, a Court of Criminal Appeal was established, and warnings were issued about the unreliability of eyewitness identification. In a Gilbert and Sullivan operetta this Cox and Box comedy might generate amusement, but it was no laughing matter for Adolph Beck and revealed the great ineptitude of the law enforcement system. Similar injustice happened in the George Edalji and Oscar Slater cases mentioned above, wherein prejudiced investigations produced unsound verdicts.

The most notorious cases of the period, the obscenely violent serial murders of eleven East London prostitutes between April 1888 and February 1891 which were attributed to Jack the Ripper, remain unsolved to this day, despite tenaciously sustained efforts by the police.[93] Another killer who preyed upon prostitutes, Dr Thomas Neill Cream, managed to poison four women with strychnine in South London before he was arrested in 1892 when an intended victim sought help from the police. Frederick Henry Seddon, a district superintendent with the London and Manchester Industrial Assurance Company, was convicted in 1912 of poisoning his lodger Eliza M. Barrow with arsenic after he converted her property to an annuity of £3 per week. He was exposed when one of her relations complained to the police. Success in these cases depended upon 'information received' by the police.[94]

George Joseph Smith, a serial bigamist, drowned a series of three 'wives' in the bath between 1910 and 1914 before the similarity of their deaths as reported in the press was called to the attention of Scotland Yard.[95] Unlike the Ripper and Dr Cream, who clearly shared a pathological hatred of prostitutes, sheer greed motivated Seddon and Smith. The closest parallels to the latter two villains among Sherlock Holmes' cases were Dr Grimsby Roylott in 'The Speckled Band', who murdered his stepdaughter in order to continue to enjoy her income, and Dr Schlesinger, who robbed and drugged Lady Frances Carfax and attempted to bury her alive.

Apart from the unsolved Ripper cases, Dr Crippen's murder of his wife in 1910 was the most infamous case of the pre-First World War era because, like Inspector Richard Tanner's race across the Atlantic in 1864 to capture the culprit in the first railway murder, it involved a dramatic transatlantic police chase. Although Inspector Walter Dew gained great acclaim for the pursuit and extradition of Dr Hawley Harvey Crippen and his secretary-cum-lover Ethel Le Neve, he did not at first suspect them of foul play. It was only after they fled and he had searched the house four times that he finally discovered the remains of Crippen's wife buried in the cellar. This is not brilliant investigative work. Moreover, the captain of a transatlantic liner alerted him by telegraph that the fugitives were embarked for Canada. Thereafter, like the police detectives in Holmes' adventures, he tenaciously followed the trail, scrupulously observing bureaucratic regulations until he had Crippen and Le Neve behind bars. He also performed well in court. The case attracted further attention because of the brilliant forensic analysis of human scar tissue performed by Dr Bernard Spilsbury that identified the remains as those of Mrs Crippen.[96]

Perhaps the final word on this comparison should come from Scotland Yard. According to George Dilnot, writing in 1913, 'There is no other great city in the world which can boast of no murder mystery in which for two years the perpetrator remained undiscovered.'[97] In each of the twenty-four murders in 1912 the guilty person was identified. Of the twenty-five cases in 1913, there were eleven arrests: one of a man who killed two people, and nine cases in which the killer committed suicide. Three cases, which involved illegal operations, were not immediately reported, and one foreigner fled abroad. These results are possible because of the superior training of the detectives. 'There are 650 men attached to the Criminal Investigation Department, and they have all learned their trade by tedious degrees. They all started, even the superintendents at their head, as constables on street duty.'[98]

This confidence is echoed in the statement of Assistant Commissioner Basil Thomson:

> Real life is quite unlike detective fiction; in fact, in detective work fiction is stranger than truth. Mr. Sherlock Holmes … worked by induction, but not, so far as I am able to judge, by the only method which gets home, namely, organization and hard work … Scotland Yard has the enormous advantage over Mr Sherlock Holmes in that it has an organisation which can scour every pawnshop, every laundry, every public-house, and every lodging-house in the huge area of London within a couple of hours.[99]

As Chief Constable Frederick Porter Wensley insisted in a deliberate disparagement of the inferences Sherlock Holmes drew from Watson's watch in 'The Sign of Four', 'There have been all kinds of successful [police] detectives, but they haven't got anywhere near the top by making flashing deductions from the scratches on a watch and enmeshing a criminal by the exercise of pure reason.'[100]

Police professionals generally concur that their success depends on hard work, including long hours spent observing or tracking suspects even over great distances, as opposed to the middle-class private detective of fiction, who often solves puzzling crimes while sitting in his armchair and using scientific deduction.[101]

On the other hand, James Berrett in *When I Was at Scotland Yard* gives a definition of a detective which also fits Sherlock Holmes perfectly: 'If a man is a real detective, long hours mean nothing to him. He is naturally industrious and naturally observant. He possesses a wide knowledge and applies it with intelligence.'[102]

5

ADVANCES IN DETECTION: TECHNOLOGY AND FORENSIC SCIENCE

The reputation of the Metropolitan Detective Police improved in the late nineteenth and early twentieth centuries as their methods of detection were enhanced, largely through applied technology and science.

Wikipedia defines technology as the joining of 'art, skill, cunning of hand' with 'the collection of tools, including machinery, modifications, arrangements and procedures used by humans'. Engineering is the discipline that seeks to study and design new technologies.

Many people regard the term 'forensic science' to mean the application of science for practical purposes and, in the case of criminal investigations, the application of science to solve crimes. However, professionals in the field define it as 'the scientific method of gathering and examining information about the past'. '[F]orensics are also carried out in other fields, such as astronomy, archaeology, biology and geology to investigate ancient times.'[1]

Thus Sherlock Holmes' investigations fulfil the formal

definition of forensic analysis in 'Study in Scarlet', 'The Sign of Four', 'Boscombe Valley Mystery', 'Silver Blaze', 'Priory School' and 'Black Peter' when he observes a crime scene and interprets its features in order to explain what happened there.[2] He is reconstructing the immediate past. It is worth mentioning that Hans Gross's seminal study *Handbuch für Untersuchungsrichter* (*Manual for Examining Magistrates*, 1891), the first textbook on criminal investigation, appeared after the first two Holmes stories had been published.

At a recent international conference, Dr Ian Burney of the Centre for the History of Science, Technology and Medicine at Birmingham University defined the standard methodology of Crime Scene Investigation (CSI) as comprising three principles: 1) protecting a crime scene from contamination, 2) preserving and recording the relationships between all objects in the scene, no matter how trivial, and 3) submitting trace evidence to scientific scrutiny. This creed epitomises Sherlockian practice. Burney also gives credit to Holmes for anticipating CSI procedure; the goal is to 'make the invisible, visible and the inconsequential, consequential'.[7] It was not until the 1920s that CID (Criminal Investigation Department) investigations included dedicated CSIs to lead scientific operations accompanied by police photographers.

Edmond Locard, head of the police research laboratory at Lyons and author of a seven-volume treatise, *Traité de criminalistique*, frequently urged his students of forensic science and colleagues to read Sherlock Holmes' investigations to learn a proper scientific approach and obtain insight into the future directions that scientific inquiry might take. In 1906 one of Locard's colleagues even wrote a thesis on the medico-legal aspects of Conan Doyle's work and presented it to the Lyons medical faculty. Locard's *Policier de Roman et de Laboratoire* (1924) contains two essays directly inspired by Conan Doyle's visit to his institute in March 1921. One discussed Edgar Allan Poe as a detective, and the other, the methods of Sherlock Holmes; both were published previously in French journals. Locard, the most celebrated forensic scientist of the time, even named one of the rooms at the laboratory after Conan Doyle.[3]

After subjecting several of Holmes' adventures to careful analysis, Locard distilled the essence of Holmes' detective methods and discoursed on how modern they were. He also performed the appropriate research indicated by Holmes' disquisition *Upon the Distinction between the Ashes of Various Tobaccos, an Enumeration of 140 Forms of Cigar, Cigarette and Pipe Tobacco*, and published a learned paper on ashes left at crime scenes.[4] In addition, he imitated Holmes' practice and maintained a collection of mineral, fibre, animal hair, dust and soil samples to assist in identifying objects with trace elements from crime scenes.[5] He was flattered to be called the Sherlock Holmes of France.[6]

The criminologist Harry Ashton-Wolfe, former assistant to Alphonse Bertillon, also paid homage:

> Many of the methods invented by Conan Doyle are today in use in the scientific laboratories. Sherlock Holmes made the study of tobacco-ashes his hobby. It was a new idea, but the police at once realized the importance of such specialised knowledge, and now every laboratory has a complete set of tables giving the appearance and composition of the various ashes, which every detective must be able to recognise. Mud and soil from various districts are also classified much after the manner that Holmes described ... Conan Doyle made Holmes a complex personality: not only a tracker, but a logician and an analyst, and thus evolved and disseminated successfully the constructive method in use to-day in all Criminal Investigation Departments.[7]

Photography: Mugshots, Crime Scenes, Bodies

One of the earliest technological aids adapted to police work was photography. Prior to its use, most officers had to rely on memory to identify criminals. They paid regular visits to prisons in order to be able to recognise convicts recently arrested or about to be discharged to their districts. A great deal depended on personal knowledge. They also visited places believed to be frequented by villains and studied divisional registers of thieves. When the Habitual Criminals Act was passed in 1869, it included provision of a Habitual Criminals Register. Records were not centralised, and there was limited exchange of information between divisions. A criminal could easily escape detection simply by moving his activities to another district.

Howard Vincent, who was appointed Director of the Criminal Investigation Department (CID) in March 1878, instituted reforms which included the establishment of the Convict Supervision Office, which organised the central collection of records and compiled offenders' photographs into a rogues gallery.[8] Vincent had studied Parisian police methods, including the techniques of Alphonse Bertillon, who had invented and standardised the use of the 'mugshot' by 1888. Bertillon insisted that two images be recorded: one full face and one profile. All photographs were to be taken from the same angle with the same lighting. Bertillon also advocated the *portrait parlé*, or word picture, listing eye and hair colour, complexion, shape of the head, general physique, identifying marks and even tone of voice. This was the forerunner of the verbal description found today on 'Wanted' posters.[9] Vincent realised the utility of this method in identifying criminals and introduced it in England. As an aid in identifying suspects, a photograph is worth a thousand hazy memories.

Photography became indispensable in compiling reliable records of crime scenes and the condition of human remains, or in fact any evidence subject to deterioration or degradation. Pictures of objects, entrances and exits, premises *et alia* contributed to evidence of each case file.

Fingerprints

The greatest asset in positive identification of suspects was the discovery and adoption of fingerprinting. 'A fingerprint in its narrow sense is an impression left by the friction ridges of a human finger ... Fingerprints are easily deposited on smooth surfaces by the natural secretions from the eccrine glands that are located in the epidermal ridges.'[10] As early as 1823 Professor Jan Evangelista Purkinje, a Czech pathologist and physiologist at the University at Breslau, identified nine general types of fingerprints and developed a system for classifying them but did not recommend using them for identification. It was not until seventy years later that Henry Faulds, a Scottish medical missionary in Japan, first suggested that fingerprint identification might be used in criminal investigations and cited two cases in a letter to the journal *Nature* in 1880. 'When bloody finger-marks or impressions on clay, glass, &c. exist, they may lead to the scientific identification of criminals.'[11] In response to Faulds' article a month later, William Richard Herschel, a British civil servant in India, notified *Nature* that he had been using fingerprints for identification since 1860.[12] When Faulds returned to the UK in 1886, he presented his research to the Metropolitan Police, but they failed to see its value.

Disappointed but undaunted, Faulds sent a description of his work to Charles Darwin, who in turn passed it on to his cousin Francis Galton. The anthropologist read the reports in *Nature* and began studying fingerprinting. He corresponded with Herschel and came to believe that fingerprinting was the most accurate and facile means of establishing human identity. In 1892 Galton published a detailed statistical model of fingerprint analysis and identification, advocating its use in forensic science to identify criminals. His book *Finger Prints* presents his system for classifying the patterns of whorls, loops and triangles found in finger marks.[13]

Faulds and Galton developed similar systems of fingerprint classification working independently.

Having studied Galton's book, Juan Vucetich, an Argentinian police officer in charge of the Statistical Bureau, set up the first fingerprint bureau (1892). He had immediate success in solving a particularly brutal murder of two children when one of his colleagues found a bloody thumb mark on a door. It matched that of the chief suspect, who confessed when presented with the evidence. This is the first murder case on record to be solved using fingerprint evidence.[14]

Five years later, in 1897, a fingerprint bureau was established in Calcutta by means of a directive of the Governor General's Council for the purpose of classifying criminal records. Two Indian fingerprint experts, Azizul Haque and Hem Chandra Bose, of the Anthropometric Bureau, devised the initial fingerprint classification system, which was eventually named after their supervisor, Sir Edward Richard Henry, the Chief of Police of Bengal. Inspired by Galton's work, Henry had been developing a practical fingerprint classification system, which he published in 1900. Consequently, he was asked to report at a committee meeting in London on the 'Identification of Criminals by Measurement and Fingerprints'. As an expert witness he testified that fingerprinting was superior to 'bertillonage' or anthropometry, a system measuring parts of the body to ascertain identity. He demonstrated the retrieval facility from within a pool of seven thousand items.

The Henry Classification System is a method for classifying fingerprints and excluding potential candidates. It allows for logical categorisation of ten-print fingerprint records into primary groupings based on fingerprint pattern types. This system reduces the effort necessary for searching large numbers of fingerprint records by classifying fingerprint records according to gross physiological characteristics. Subsequent searches (manual or automated) utilising granular characteristics are greatly simplified.

As a result of his demonstration, the Henry Classification System was adopted in England and Wales in 1901 when

Scotland Yard created the United Kingdom Fingerprint Bureau at Metropolitan Police Headquarters. Henry was appointed its head and became commissioner a year later when Robert Anderson retired.

> The Henry Classification System assigns each finger a number according to the order in which it is located in the hand, beginning with the right thumb as number 1 and ending with the left pinky as number 10. The system also assigns a numerical value to fingers that contain a whorl pattern; fingers 1 and 2 each have a value of 16, fingers 3 and 4 have a value of 8, and so on, with the final two fingers having a value of 1. Fingers with a non-whorl pattern, such as an arch or loop pattern, have a value of zero. The sum of the even finger value is then calculated and placed in the numerator of a fraction. The sum of the odd finger values is placed in the denominator. The value of 1 is added to each sum of the whorls with the maximum obtainable on either side of the fraction being 32. Thus, the primary classification is a fraction between 1/1 to 32/32, where 1/1 would indicate no whorl patterns and 32/32 would mean that all fingers had whorl patterns.[15]

This method of classification is still in use in much of the English-speaking world. The Galton-Henry system divides fingerprints into three basic patterns: loop, whorl and arch. They constitute, respectively, 60–65 per cent, 30–35 per cent and 5 per cent of all known prints. Henry subsequently made several improvements to dactyloscopy. By 1910 this system had been adopted throughout Europe and established the reputation of Scotland Yard worldwide.[16]

The new fingerprint system produced gratifying results immediately. By the end of the first half-year, ninety-three identifications had been authenticated and by the end of 1902 the totals exceeded those of the previous six years.[17] In 1905 fingerprints were used for the first time to identify the perpetrators of a particularly heartless and savage double murder. During a robbery in Deptford, an elderly shopkeeper and his wife were battered to death. The crime was discovered when an employee could not gain entry to the shop and sought help. When entry was gained through the rear premises, the couple's bloodied bodies were found. Actually, the wife was still alive but died within a few days. A witness came forward who had seen the injured husband at the door at 7.30 a.m. but, having watched him close the door and having been unable to find a policeman, left the area. Other witnesses testified to seeing two men slam the door and leave the shop at about 7.15 a.m. Another witness claimed to have seen Albert and Alfred Stratton nearby at the relevant time and gave a description of their clothes, which matched that of the unknown men seen leaving the shop. Albert Stratton's landlady testified that she had given him some old black stockings and had later seen the masks he made from them between his mattresses. But the crucial clue was a thumbprint on an inner tray of the cash box, which matched that of Alfred Stratton. The brothers were arrested and tried at the Old Bailey. Although the fingerprint evidence was contested, the jury were convinced after the fingerprints of one of its members were taken to demonstrate the reliability of the technique. Nonetheless, such was the general ignorance of the new technology that the judge advised the jurors to consider it as collaborative rather than primary evidence. After two hours they returned a guilty verdict and the brothers were hanged a fortnight later.[18]

Across the channel Dr Locard, although a former student of Bertillon, nonetheless became an enthusiastic supporter of fingerprinting. Qualified in both medicine and law, he was appointed the director of a small police laboratory in 1910. Locard soon built it into a highly efficient state-of-the-art forensic facility. Basing his work on Galton and Henry's system, he created the first standards for the minimum number of ridges that must exist to establish a fingerprint match. Twelve clear points were essential. These points are sometimes referred to as 'Galton's Details'. In 1913 he discovered that it was possible to create false fingerprints by using an Indian-rubber base for an artificial finger. Horrified that it was so easy to counterfeit fingerprints, he was driven to develop a supplementary technique which he named 'poroscopy'. It focused on the patterns formed by thousands of pores between the ridges of fingerprints. Because so many more pores exist than ridges, pore patterns would be infinitely more difficult to imitate.[19]

Locard also used iodine fumes to develop latent prints, which were then carefully photographed before they could fade. He was very particular about using powders with contrasting colours to the background on which the latent print was exposed. Because only the photographs could be shown in court, every step of the process was recorded to obviate any charges of counterfeiting prints.[20] Here technology and science were joined to produce convincing evidence.

Although Conan Doyle kept abreast of the latest developments in forensic science, he only mentions fingerprinting in seven stories, and then it is 'more honoured in the breach than in the observance'. More often than not, Holmes notes the presence of a finger mark but does not study it or attempt to retrieve and/or register it. For example, in 'Sign of Four' Holmes detects a thumb mark on the envelope sent by Thaddeus Sholto to Mary Morstan (95); in 'Man with the Twisted Lip' he suggests that the greasy thumbprint on the note from Neville St Clair was made by the Lascar (239); and in 'Cardboard Box' Holmes sees two 'distinctive' thumb marks on the box sent to Susan Cushing (891). But he does not attempt to derive leads from any of them. In 'Three Gables' the local inspector demonstrates how efficient he is by flourishing a diary page which may have latent fingerprint evidence on it. Holmes is unmoved (1030). In 'Three Students' (599) and 'Red Circle' (903) Holmes remarks on the absence of fingerprints, that is, negative evidence, like the dog which did not bark. Only in 'Norwood Builder' does he express any interest in a finger mark, and again it is a red herring. He realises that it is a fake because it had not been there the previous day when he examined the wall. The appearance of a bloody thumbprint after the owner of the thumb had been arrested enables Holmes to save a young man from the gallows. Conan Doyle introduced the concept of the fabricated fingerprint in 1903 prior to Locard's concern to develop a technique to counter such frauds.

Footprints

Through the end of the nineteenth century, there was no established legal or scientific protocol for the collection and analysis of footprints. Although footwear was made to order rather than mass produced as it is today, the value of footprints as evidence in identifying criminals was not generally recognised. One of the first forensic scientists to realise their potential was Charles Meymott Tidy, who devoted a lengthy section of his *Legal Medicine* (1882) to 'Marks of the Hands and Feet'. Having conducted several experiments, he discerned that footprints may be larger or smaller than the boot or foot that produced them. For example, with footmarks made in soft sand or soil, particles at the edge of the print may sift into the impression as the foot is withdrawn. An impression in wet clay may be enlarged if the foot is extracted in the opposite direction to that in which it was inserted. Tidy concluded, therefore, that the medium in which a print is created influences its size and shape.

Tidy devised techniques for making plaster casts of footprints as well as for identifying bloodstains or other foreign elements in them. He advocated removing floorboards with bloody footprints in order to preserve them as evidence. Opinion differed on the relationship of the foot to its image. Some specialists in medical jurisprudence disagreed about whether a foot was larger or smaller than its print.[21] At the end of the nineteenth century, Hans Gross recommended that evaluating footprints should not be restricted to medical doctors but suggested that shoemakers also be consulted. However, final responsibility for weighing evidence should reside with the criminal investigator. Despite Gross's belief in the importance of footprint comparisons, this aspect of forensic science was neglected.[22]

'There is no branch of detective science which is so important and so much neglected as the art of tracing footsteps,' claims Sherlock Holmes in 'A Study in Scarlet' (84). He was so convinced of the importance of boot marks that he published his views: 'Here is my monograph upon the tracing of footsteps, with some remarks upon the uses of plaster of Paris as a preserver of impresses' ('Sign of Four', 91). Holmes' interest is seconded by Bertillon, who created many forensic techniques, including the use of galvanoplastic compounds to preserve footprints.[23] Holmes expresses his admiration for Bertillon's anthropometric system of measurement in 'The Naval Treaty' (460) but is irritated when Dr Mortimer ranks Bertillon above him as the best crime expert in Europe (672).

Analysis of footprints or boot marks focuses not only on tracking or trailing someone, but also on identifying an individual by the unique features of his foot or boot. As a glove moulds itself to the wearer's hand, so the boot or shoe exhibits the sui generis shape of the owner's foot and pattern of his walk. In 'The Boscombe Valley Mystery' Holmes says to Lestrade, 'That left foot of yours with its inward twist is all over the place.' He chides Lestrade for allowing the crime scene to become trampled. 'Oh, how simple it all would have been had I been here before they came like a herd of buffalo and wallowed all over it!' (p. 212). Despite its corrupted condition, Holmes identifies the footprints of the murder victim and his son, plus those of his assailant. From the trace evidence left on the site and scrutiny of the footprints of the three men in the soft ground, Holmes reconstructs their movements to form a coherent sequence of action, and he deduces a physical description of the culprit. He 'is a tall man, left-handed, limps with the right leg, wears [square-toed] thick-soled shooting boots and a grey cloak, smokes Indian cigars, uses a cigar-holder, and carries a blunt pen-knife in his pocket.' (p. 213). *En passent* during his forensic analysis, he retrieves the murder weapon. Like any good CSI he has made 'the invisible, visible and the inconsequential, consequential'.

Holmes solves a robbery in 'The Beryl Coronet' by interpreting footprints in the snow. Apart from the evidence of a housemaid's rendezvous with her wooden-legged lover near the back door, he discovers deep boot prints in the snow outside a downstairs window where someone had waited. In the stable lane he detects the impressions in the snow of two men coming and going. The first had walked but the second man had run, as indicated by the deeper impression of his weight on the front of his foot and shallower impression of the heel. The barefooted prints of the second man were sometimes superimposed on those of the first, showing that he had followed the first. The snow at the end of the lane revealed signs of a struggle before the man wearing boots had run away. A few drops of blood showed he had been hurt. His trail ran out at the paved highroad. Holmes infers that the thief had stood outside the window until the coronet was delivered to him and then left via the stable lane. He was pursued by the barefooted man, who struggled with him and wrested the coronet from him, breaking it in the process and injuring his opponent. Holmes also observed the wet footprint of the second man on the windowsill as he climbed back into the house. It then only remained to trace the thief and the missing fragment of the coronet. Holmes deduces his identity from a very limited field of suspects and, having secured a cast-off pair of his shoes, is able to match them to the prints in the snow (pp. 315–16) QED.

Footprints are also important in 'The Hound of the Baskervilles' because Holmes realises that Sir Charles is running away from the house instead of toward its safety when he has a fatal heart attack. Of course, there are also the tracks of a gigantic hound. In 'The Priory School' Holmes faces the challenge of interpreting tracks made by bicycles and livestock as he tries to follow the trail of a missing boy and his schoolmaster. His tracking skills enable him to determine the direction the bicycles take and to differentiate their routes. By close examination of the pattern made by the hooves of the cattle he is able to distinguish the inappropriate gait of the animals and penetrate the subterfuge perpetrated by the villain, who has laid a false trail.

Forensic Pathology

The science of forensic pathology was pioneered in Europe in the eighteenth century, when the focus of dissection broadened from mere anatomical exploration to investigation of causes of physical changes – particularly those resulting from unnatural deaths, that is, criminal acts. An autopsy is performed with the explicit purpose of determining the cause of death: 'the pathologic process, injury, or disease that directly results in or initiates a series of events that lead to a person's death'. The pathologist also tries to ascertain, if possible, the time of death. In addition, forensic pathologists investigate the particular locale and circumstances of death. During the autopsy a pathologist considers the manner of death and collects trace evidence to aid in identifying the deceased. Steps in the post-mortem examination include: examining and documenting wounds and injuries, collection and microscopic analysis of tissue specimens to identify signs of natural disease or foreign bodies in the organs or wounds, collection and analysis of toxicological samples from body tissues and fluids. In cases of sudden or unexpected deaths forensic pathologists are expected to liaise with area medico-legal authorities and, when required, to testify as expert witnesses in civil or criminal trials.[24]

Two Parisian doctors, Paul Brouardel and Ambrose Tardieu,

studied the signs of suffocation and hanging on cadavers. The marks made on the neck by hanging and the damage to the hyoid bone caused by manual strangulation were recorded by Brouardel in *La Pendaison, la strangulation, la suffication, la submersion* (1897). Tardieu, in a paper with a similar title, 'La Pendaison, la strangulation, et la suffocation', described small blood spots in the heart (petechiae) and under the pleura caused by quick suffocation.[25] Dr Alexandre Lacassagne, chairman of the Médecine Légale de la Faculté de Lyon, studied changes occurring at death, especially the phenomena of rigor mortis, livor mortis and algor mortis. He realised that all three states could be measured to determine the time of death, which is important in cases of unnatural death. Lacassagne also assessed conditions which could distort the normal pattern of these developments, such as the temperature of the environment, the circumstances and the age and physical condition of the deceased. Concurrently, in the British Isles, a mixture of religious practices, superstition and affectionate feelings for the deceased produced resistance to the post-mortem study and autopsy of human remains. In addition, the tradition of displaying eviscerated corpses of criminals in public engendered an attitude of shame toward dissection. Hence, a shortage of cadavers existed which impeded forensic pathology.[26]

However, in the mid-nineteenth century Alfred Swaine Taylor, who had trained in Paris, was appointed to teach forensic medicine in London. His *Manual of Medical Jurisprudence* (1873) contained a carefully couched argument with cogent examples justifying examination of violent death. This work on pathology and toxicology exerted a profound influence.

> A medical man, when he sees a dead body, should notice everything. He should observe everything which could throw a light on the production of wounds or other injuries found upon it. It should not be left to a policeman to say whether there were any marks of blood on the dress or on the hands

of the deceased, or on the furniture of the room. The dress of the deceased as well as the body should always be closely examined on the spot by the medical man.[27]

Taylor was followed shortly by Charles Meymott Tidy, who was appointed professor of chemistry and medical jurisprudence at London Hospital in 1876. He also became public analyst and deputy medical officer of health for the City of London as well as analyst to the Home Office, and produced a seminal work in two volumes, *Legal Medicine* (1882).[28]

Perhaps the most famous of Home Office pathologists in the early twentieth century was Bernard Henry Spilsbury, who testified for the Crown in some of the most sensational cases of the period. After qualifying with degrees in natural science and chemistry at Magdalen College, Oxford, he did further study at St Mary's Hospital in Paddington, London, specialising in forensic pathology, and was appointed resident assistant pathologist at St Mary's in 1905. Though of longer duration, his relationship with the senior pathologist at St Mary's, Augustus Pepper, resembled somewhat that of Conan Doyle and Joe Bell. Spilsbury succeeded Pepper when he retired in 1909.[29]

Spilsbury was catapulted into the public eye when he gave evidence at the trial of Hawley Harvey Crippen for murdering his wife, Cora Turner, who performed as Belle Elmore in music halls but was born Kunigunde Mackamotski. Crippen was an American dentist who had been selling patent medicines in London. Belle was demanding and domineering, so Crippen had sought solace in the arms of his office typist, Ethel Le Neve. Then Crippen announced to Belle's circle of friends that she had left him and gone to America. Shortly thereafter, he announced that she had died in California. Since Belle had not spoken of leaving, her friends became suspicious, especially when Crippen was seen at a ball with Ethel wearing Belle's jewellery. Inquiries in California about the missing Belle produced no results, so they went to the police.[30]

When Inspector Walter Dew interviewed Crippen, he was completely taken in by his story that he announced Belle's death to avoid the humiliation of admitting she had left him for another man. He made no objection when Dew searched the house. Returning a few days later to clarify a few details, Dew discovered that Crippen and Le Neve had fled. Then he had the house searched more thoroughly. Under some loose bricks in the cellar floor they discovered the decaying remains of most of a torso without bones, limbs, head or neck, but most of the internal organs were present and in good condition. Other items included some dark bleached hair, a hair curler and some portions of clothing. The remains had been wrapped in a man's pyjama jacket. Pepper and Spilsbury were called in to do the post-mortem examination.

Using standard police procedures, Dew raised a hue and cry for the runaways. Captain Kendall of the SS *Montrose* en route to Montreal from Antwerp had purchased a copy of a newspaper featuring the story of Crippen's flight on the day his ship sailed. Thanks to the newspaper photographs and modern wireless technology, the captain not only recognised the fugitives but was able to telegraph Dew notifying him that they were bound for Canada disguised as a father and son named Robinson. He observed that they were more affectionate toward each other than most fathers and sons. The latter had an unusually high-pitched voice and his clothes fitted poorly. As in the Oscar Slater case, a thrilling transatlantic race ensued when Inspector Dew, disguised as a harbour pilot, boarded the ship off Quebec before it docked and made the arrest.

Various kinds of evidence were produced at the trial. The Prosecution was able to prove that the pyjama jacket in which the human remains were wrapped was purchased by Crippen himself. Belle's hair and hair curler were identified. Chemical analysis of the stomach contents produced a concentration of the alkaloid poison hyoscine, and they found proof that Crippen had purchased five grains of hyoscine from a well-known chemist. Spilsbury's analysis of scar tissue on a portion of abdominal skin identified the remains as those of Belle, who was known to have had a long scar on her lower stomach. With Pepper at his side, Spilsbury conducted a microscopic examination of the tissue. He stated, when testifying, that

> sebaceous glands, tiny features of the skin, did not exist in scar tissue. He examined cross sections of the abdominal tissue. The outer skin, the epidermis, had mostly gone. The inner skin, the dermis, consisted of a close network of fibrous tissue resting on subcutaneous fat. The remains of sebaceous glands were visible, embedded in the dermis on the right margin of the specimen and also in a piece of skin from a fold near the left upper part of the specimen. Signs of sebaceous glands were apparent even in the middle of the fold. In a specimen taken from the suspected scar, however, sebaceous glands were found at each end (but not in the middle) for a distance of an inch and a half, a length of tissue where the dermis was noticeably denser and thinner than elsewhere.[31]

He concluded that 'the area of altered skin indicated an old, and probably stretched, scar'.[32] The forensic evidence, which included collection and microscopic analysis of tissue specimens to identify signs of natural disease or foreign bodies in the organs or wounds as well as collection and analysis of toxicological samples from body tissues and fluids, established the identity of the remains and also the cause of death to be poison. It was both dramatic and convincing. Without it, Crippen might not have been convicted.

Spilsbury also conducted autopsies on the victims of George Joseph Smith, who murdered several wives by drowning them in the bathtub. Using geometry, he demonstrated that the bathtubs were too small for the victims to have simply slid under the water and drowned. Instead, they could only have died if an assailant had placed his left arm under their knees and lifted while simultaneously pressing his right hand on the top of their heads and forcibly submerged them. It was a simple matter of the laws of physics. Spilsbury had the bathtubs brought into court and gave a demonstration of the technique. The Brides-in-the-Bath murder case was another high-profile trial, which attracted a great deal of attention and helped advance Spilsbury's career.[33]

Blood Testing

When Holmes first meets Watson at St Bartholomew's Hospital in 'A Study in Scarlet' (1887), he is jubilant at having discovered a reagent which is precipitated by haemoglobin and shocked that Watson does not realise its significance. 'It is the most practical medico-legal discovery for years. Don't you see that it gives us an infallible test for bloodstains?'[34]

It is very difficult to distinguish blood from mud, rust and fruit stains, especially after time has elapsed. So the focus on developing a test which is specific for human blood was very important. Haemoglobin was the focus of these experiments because it is the principal component in red blood cells. ('The function of hemoglobin is the transportation of oxygen and the exchange of carbon dioxide between tissues.')[35]

Holmes feels that his test is superior to an unsatisfactory test employing the resin from the West Indian guaiacum tree, which would change colour if mixed with blood and hydrogen peroxide, but other substances could produce the same sapphire-blue hue. Since its reaction was not exclusive to blood, it was not an infallible test. According to Christine Huber,

> There is a modern version of this test called the Hemoccult Test, used to detect blood in fecal specimens. In the Hemoccult Test, filter paper is guaiac-impregnated. The fecal specimen

is applied to the paper, and then a few drops of hydrogen peroxide are applied. If blood is present in the specimen, a blue color develops on the filter paper. A newer version of this test called the HemoQuant Assay has been widely touted recently as *the* Sherlock Holmes Test! However, neither the Hemoccult nor the HemoQuant Assay is the Sherlock Holmes Test!'[36]

Holmes fails to mention a third test based on spectrum analysis which was used as early as 1864 in the famous trial of Franz Müller, the railway killer. Having employed a spectroscope, constructed of a lens, a prism and a small telescope, Dr Henry Letheby analysed stains in the railway carriage. He was able to verify the presence of Fraunhofer lines (dark bands which occur when blood interrupts the flow of light) in the railway car specimens and thus identify them as bloodstains. This discovery was an enormous advance for crime-scene investigation. On the basis of blood spatter patterns, he then reconstructed the crime. Spectroscopic analysis had the advantage of being able to detect blood in stains that were several years old, but was a complex procedure – perhaps too complex for Conan Doyle's average reader.[37]

Conan Doyle indicates his awareness of a very important issue in forensic science by focusing Holmes' experiment on a blood test in the very first story.

Throughout the nineteenth century, European scientists had been conducting an intensive search for a reliable test to identify human blood in various states. No fewer than eleven tests, with varying degrees of efficacy, had been devised and published between 1800 and 1881. Raymond McGowan reviews and evaluates all of them in 'Sherlock Holmes and Forensic Chemistry'.[38] McGowan asserts that Sherlock Holmes' knowledge of forensic chemistry excelled that of nine of the eleven scientists searching for a valid blood test. His test was based on the chemical composition of the blood. Holmes was cognisant of the oxidation-reduction reaction which he used to precipitate the iron in haemoglobin.

McGowan states that only two of the eleven tests are still in use today: the Teichmann and Sonnenschein Tests.[39] Both of these tests employ the oxidation-reduction reaction which precipitates the haem in haemoglobin containing iron pigment. He states that the Sonnenschein test precipitate is identical to that in the Sherlock Holmes test. To further verify results, McGowan performed additional tests on plasma and haemoglobin using the Sonnenschein method. The results were negative and positive respectively. However, McGowan notes that Sherlock Holmes did not use the same reagents as Sonnenschein, whose test was also based on an oxidation-reduction reaction. The application of the reagents in the Sonnenschein test differs from that of the Holmes test. 'In the former, the reducing agent (sodium tungstate) and the catalyst (acetic acid) are combined to acidify the sodium tungstate prior to adding the reagents to the test solution.'[40] Holmes used a reducing agent (white crystals) and an acid (clear liquid), which would be the catalyst. McGowan conducted further experiments to determine whether, if these reagents were added separately to the test solution, the results would be the same. The results proved negative. Therefore, Holmes did not use the same reagents that were used in the Sonnenschein test.

Christine Huber, writing later the same year, goes beyond McGowan in her article 'The Sherlock Holmes Blood Test: The Solution to a Century-Old Mystery'.[41] Huber quotes Holmes' jubilant cry at the outset of 'Study in Scarlet': 'I have found a reagent which is precipitated by haemoglobin, and by nothing else! ... Don't you see that it gives us an infallible test for blood stains?' (p. 17). She infers that Holmes has overcome the limitation of the guaiacum test; his test reacts exclusively to haemoglobin. Nor does it matter how old the test sample is. The test itself is simple. Holmes adds a drop or two of blood to a jar of water, pointing out that the concentration would be in proportion about one in a million. He then adds a few white crystals followed by a few drops of a transparent fluid. The water turns a dull mahogany colour and a brownish dust is precipitated to the bottom of the jar.

As McGowan indicated, scientists searched for most of the nineteenth century for a reliable blood test. Huber reveals that for most of the twentieth century Holmesians – when they have not assumed it to be fictional – have been trying to discover the constituents of Holmes' formula. She maintains that

> the principles of Holmes' Test *are* used today as the *first steps* in preparing blood to quantify the types and concentrations of hemoglobin by electrophoresis. When blood is added to water, the red cells rupture, releasing their contents. If the solution is then made alkaline with a base chemical, the hemoglobin molecule is denatured. With the addition of another chemical, most human hemoglobins are precipitated. Normal adult hemoglobin consists of a majority of hemoglobin A, some hemoglobin A_2, and a very small amount of hemoglobin F (fetal hemoglobin).
>
> The Holmes Test was based on Sherlock Holmes' knowledge of theories of his time, his knowledge of chemistry, and methods employing trial and error ... Holmes' Test ... consists of a procedure in which blood is added to an amount of water, and white crystals are introduced into this, followed by a transparent liquid. In fact, chemicals introduced by such a procedure and in just such an order are used in preparing hemoglobin for electrophoresis.[42]

Huber reveals the mysterious elements of Holmes' formula to be sodium hydroxide (available today as white pellets but usually dispensed as white powder or in crystalline form in Holmes' time), and a saturated solution of ammonium sulfate, a clear liquid. She then lists exact amounts of materials to be used and the precise order of steps to be followed. 'The Holmes Test ... employs blood dissolved in water, the addition of white crystals, and finally the addition of a transparent liquid. All of these substances must be added in a precise order to obtain the dull mahogany colour of the liquid and then the brownish dust precipitate.'[43] She gives the results when this test is administered with human whole blood, human plasma, human serum and dog whole blood. The reaction Holmes achieved only occurred with human whole blood.

Like McGowan, Huber disqualifies the Sonnenschein test because the sodium tungstate must first be acidified by being mixed with the acetic acid *prior to* being added to the haemoglobin solution. Unlike McGowan, she goes on to identify exactly the reagents Holmes used and to validate Holmes' claim to have discovered a test to precipitate haemoglobin.

This challenging problem was finally solved outside fiction in 1901 at the Institute of Hygiene in Greifswald, Germany, when Paul Uhlenhuth developed the means of distinguishing human blood from that of animals. He noticed that when injected with human blood, rabbits' blood would produce a defensive serum called precipitin. The serum reacted strongly to further contact with human blood and also to bloodstains. However, it reacted only to the blood of species whose blood had been previously injected, so it became possible to distinguish which species was the source of stains. This discovery contributed enormously to the improved success rate of the CID.[44]

Trace Evidence

As early as 1890, in 'The Sign of Four', Holmes gives Watson a 'curious little work upon the influence of a trade upon the form of the hand' with illustrations of the hands of various tradesmen (p. 91). And three decades later in 'The Creeping Man' (1923) he advises Watson, 'Always look at the hands first

... Then cuffs, trouser-knees, and boots.' During the interim, forensic scientists introduced trace evidence into criminal investigations (p. 1080). In 1893 Hans Gross emphasised the importance of occupational dust, echoing Holmes' precept: 'There are a surprising number of callings which leave their traces on the clothing and under the fingernails of those who practice them.'[45] In 1904 this concept was applied in solving the murder of a young seamstress in Germany who had been strangled with her own bright red and blue scarf. Dr Georg Popp, a chemist in Frankfurt, Germany, who had specialised in analysing tobacco and ashes in arson cases, was asked to analyse a stained handkerchief left at a murder scene. Microscopic examination revealed red and blue fibres identical to her scarf adhering to the handkerchief, plus sand, coal, snuff and crystals of the mineral hornblende. The police were able to link his findings to a suspect who worked at a gasworks and also at a gravel pit which would have exposed him to the materials on the handkerchief. Moreover, he habitually took snuff.[46]

In the same period, Dr Edmond Locard followed similar paths and, like Sherlock Holmes, created a collection of soil, mineral, fibre and animal hair samples in order to facilitate the identification of trace evidence found at crime scenes. According to Locard, 'The microscopic debris that covers our clothing and bodies are the mute witnesses, sure and faithful, of all our movements and all our encounters.'[47] In 1912 Dr Locard's analysis of fingernail scrapings led to the conviction of Marie Latelle's killer in Lyons, France. He formulated what is known as Locard's Exchange Principle, which asserts that every physical contact leaves traces. Holmes echoes this principle in 'The Adventure of Black Peter' (1904). 'As long as the criminal remains upon two legs so long must there be some indentation, some abrasion, some trifling displacement which can be detected by the scientific searcher' (p. 562).

'The Adventure of Shoscombe Old Place' (1927) opens with Holmes bending over a microscope and triumphantly listing the items of trace evidence on his slide, including tweed threads, dust, skin cells and glue blobs, found on the cap left at a murder scene by a suspect who makes picture frames using glue. He also tells Watson that since he identified a counterfeit coiner by the copper and zinc filings found in his cuffs, the police have begun to realise the importance of the microscope (p. 1102).

Handwriting

The importance of scientific evaluation of written documents was not generally acknowledged in the nineteenth century, but some precedents were set. Although forgery was a constant threat, it was difficult to deal with. A few methods of analysis were established, largely based on comparative examination by a skilled professional such as an engraver or scrivener, someone who copied documents as a trade. Such individuals acquired a 'trained eye' over time and through experience, much as a naturalist is able to identify species in the wild. A common technique to test the validity of a handwritten passage was to compare it with known samples written by the same person. This included signatures on deeds, wills and other legal papers. As E. J. Wagner suggested, 'Forgery has an old and dishonourable history, and the evaluation of questioned documents is one of the most complex disciplines in the forensic sciences.'[48]

Because of the mischief caused by poison-pen letters, called 'hate mail' today, forensic document examiners have devised methods of identifying handwritten examples when suspects are identified. Having examined over 300 pernicious effusions by such a troublemaker, Edmond Locard spent several hours dictating to a suspect and whisking away what was written sheet after sheet. Attempts to disguise the normal script broke down over time and permanent characteristics were manifested. Confronted with the mass of evidence, the woman confessed.

What today is officially termed Forensic Document Examination was known as chirography in the nineteenth century. Chirography deals with all aspects of penmanship and handwriting. Another approach to handwriting analysis is known as graphology, and differs from chirography in attempting to infer psychological characteristics of the writer from his script. Experts in these fields, called chirographers and graphologists, often testified as expert witnesses at criminal trials.

One of the first trials concerned with a disputed document at which expert testimony was recorded occurred in Boston, Massachusetts. Both a man who was employed to sign multiple documents for a busy executive accused of writing an incriminating letter, and an engraver, also familiar with the executive's signature, swore that the disputed signature was genuine. He was convicted and later confessed.[49] In this case a disputed sample was compared with authenticated examples.

The primary purpose of forensic document examination is to provide evidence about a suspicious or questionable document using a variety of scientific processes and methods. Criteria to be evaluated might include possible alterations, provenance, damage, forgery, source and/or authenticity. A forensic examiner may be asked whether a document originated from the same source as another one. He may be asked to trace its history, determine when it was created, or decipher information which has been obscured, obliterated, or erased. Common criminal charges involved in document examination include false claims of identity, forgery, counterfeiting, fraud or passing forged documents such as cheques.[50] Sometimes the outcome of extremely consequential trials have depended on handwriting analysis, as in the cases of Captain Alfred Dreyfus, Adolph Beck and George Edalji.

Perhaps the most unjust case involving faulty handwriting

analysis at the end of the nineteenth century was the deliberately false attribution of incriminating documents to Captain Alfred Dreyfus. His victimisation became an international cause célèbre. In 1894, when a memorandum detailing French military secrets was recovered at the German embassy in Paris, a group of French military officers accused Dreyfus of having written it although there was strong evidence that a man called Esterhazy was guilty. Handwriting experts (chirographers) disagreed with each other. Alphonse Bertillon testified that Dreyfus had tried to disguise his script but was undoubtedly the author of the memorandum. He supported his opinion with complex mathematical computations based on the laws of probability. Because he was so highly respected his opinion convicted Dreyfus, who was sentenced to imprisonment on Devil's Island. However, the verdict was contested by influential people and Dreyfus was tried again, only to be convicted a second time. The public was outraged and proof emerged that French Intelligence officers had manufactured the evidence against him. He was ultimately awarded a phony pardon (rather like that of Oscar Slater) and released in 1906. This whole farce was based on forged documents which were accepted as valid, thus causing forensic document examination to be in low repute at the turn of the century.[51]

In England at the trial of Adolph Beck in 1896 a handwriting expert named Thomas Gurrin, who had compared samples of John Smith's and Beck's writing, testified that current samples of Beck's script had been written in a disguised hand, implying that they were by the same author. His testimony contributed to Beck's false conviction. The same 'expert' testified at the trial of George Edalji that he had written anonymous letters of a scurrilous nature which were linked with charges of mutilating livestock and again contributed to a false verdict. In contesting Edalji's case, Conan Doyle consulted the chirographer Dr Lindsay Johnson, who was involved in the repeal of the conviction of Alfred Dreyfus. Johnson's method was to enlarge the writing on screen so that the minutest characteristics were visible in order to facilitate comparison. It was also possible to superimpose words and phrases to determine likeness (see Chapter 3).

Holmes' interest in handwriting analysis is mentioned in several stories, beginning with 'Study in Scarlet', wherein he notes the peculiar features of the message on the wall left by the murderer. He points out the inconsistencies in spelling as a clumsy attempt to suggest the writer is German. Like the engraver and the scrivener at the American trial, Holmes' judgment is based on his personal knowledge because chirography is a special hobby. He utilises these same skills in observing the idiosyncratic characteristics of Mr Windibank's typewriter in 'Case of Identity', pointing out that some slight slurring occurs over the 'e' and a defect in the tail of the 'r' and mentioning fourteen additional indicators (p. 199). So even machines acquire individual identity.

In 'The Adventure of the Reigate Squires' (1893) the entire solution to the murder depends on Holmes' analysis of the writing in a fragment of an incriminating letter sent to entrap the victim. Holmes discerns two different hands in the note and extrapolates a series of stunning conclusions from his observations. Prompted by an overall irregular appearance of the text, he contrasts the strength of the letter 't' in support of double authorship. He also infers an age difference between the two from the contrast in their scripts. The leader wrote out the message leaving gaps for the other to fill, but some were so small that they forced the other to squeeze his words in. The motive was to involve both equally in some dangerous enterprise. Holmes infers kinship between them because both use the uncommon Greek 'e'. Other discrepancies in the account of the crime, such as lack of powder burns on the victim supposedly shot at close range, lack of footprints in the soft earth along the escape route taken by the putative villain, and inability to see events from windows as described, confirm Holmes' suspicions that Alec Cunningham killed the coachman. In his imagination Holmes constructs the scenario of what must have happened at the time of the murder and realises that the killer would not have had time to dispose of the larger portion of the note found in the dead man's hand. He must have quickly shoved it in his dressing-gown pocket to hide it. So solving the case depends on retrieving the incriminating paper, whose whereabouts he correctly surmises. Several of Holmes' deductions follow his usual pattern of inference based on observation and would seem to encompass the handwriting analysis. However, his remarks about deriving age, kinship, and character from the script fall within the province of graphology. 'Even a highly trained forensic document examiner cannot reliably tell handedness, gender, or age from handwriting'. Graphologists' claims that psychological traits can be deciphered from handwriting have no basis in empirical evidence.[52]

In conclusion, between 1880 and 1914, the period during which the Sherlock Holmes stories took place, several achievements occurred in technology and science which greatly enhanced criminal investigation, but surprisingly Holmes takes advantage of very few of them. Some important discoveries had been made earlier in the nineteenth century. For example, as early as 1836 James Marsh reported a reliable chemical test for arsenic in *The Edinburgh Philosophical Journal*. Technological improvements had been made in taking casts to preserve impressions of footprints and/or boot marks. In 1882 Charles Meymott Tidy published observations on foot marks and suggested methods of taking plaster casts. For most of the century chemists had been experimenting to find a means of distinguishing bloodstains from lookalike substances such as mud, rust and fruit with varied success. The most reliable blood test required a complex instrument called a spectroscope, attached to a microscope, which was able to detect haemoglobin when light was passed through a solution of blood. It functioned well enough to help convict Franz Müller when Dr Henry Letheby provided evidence in the 1864 railway murder case. Less satisfactory but easier to administer, the guaiacum test introduced by Izaak Van Deen in 1861 produced results not exclusive to blood. No wonder Holmes was so elated when he discovered a simple chemical formula to precipitate haemoglobin in 1887.

More interest and activity was centred on the Continent than in the British Isles, but in 1873 Alfred Swaine Taylor published his *Manual of Medical Jurisprudence*, the first text in English on forensic medicine. Taylor joined the medical faculty at Guy's Hospital in 1831 and was appointed lecturer in chemistry, toxicology and medical jurisprudence a year later. His seminal study was followed within ten years by Charles Meymott Tidy's *Legal Medicine* (1882) and within a further decade by Hans Gross's *Handbook for Coroners, Police Officials, and Military Policemen* (1893). A new age of forensic medicine had dawned.

These publications were succeeded by the founding of forensic science institutes and laboratories. Almost simultaneously, Alexandre Lacassagne founded the Médecine Legale de la Faculté de Lyons and Archibald Reiss established the Institut de Police scientifique in Lausanne. The next year, staffed by two assistants in two attic rooms in Lyons, Edmond Locard organised the first police laboratory, and Hans Gross created the Institute of Criminalistics at the University of Graz Law School (1912).

Advances in technology and science also appeared in the UK. In 1888 Alphonse Bertillon's card system for identifying criminals was adapted with space for front and profile views of each offender, which was of great assistance in identifying villains. Edward Henry's fingerprint classification system was implemented in 1901 and yielded almost immediate results. It was enhanced by Edmond Locard, who established the twelve-point standard for print verification. In 1913 his discovery of pores in fingertips (poroscopy) made it almost impossible to fabricate finger marks.

In the 1890s in Germany Hans Gross improved methods of comparing foot marks and in France Bertillon developed galvanoplastic compounds for better preserving footprints.

In 1900 Karl Landsteiner at the Institute of Pathology and Anatomy in Vienna discovered blood types. His theory was applied in 1901 to establish the guilt of a serial killer. Finally, in 1901, all that searching for a chemical test to identify blood was perfected by Paul Uhlenhuth at the Institute of Hygiene in Greifswald, Germany. He created the precipitin test by injecting rabbits with human blood, which produced a specific reaction to it if they were subsequently injected a second time. By 1904 the precipitin test was standard procedure in most forensics laboratories.

Clearly, the twenty years spanning the last decade of the nineteenth and the first decade of the twentieth century was an exciting time in the field of forensic science. All of these forensic techniques had the potential to improve criminal investigations – and did – but progress was slow, especially in the provinces. How did these events affect Sherlock Holmes and his investigations? What technology did he utilise? Photographs feature in three stories. Irene Adler's picture becomes his treasured souvenir in 'Scandal in Bohemia'. In 'Six Napoleons' he shows a photograph to a workshop owner to identify a villain. In 'Charles Augustus Milverton', Holmes and Watson identify the mysterious wronged woman who shot Milverton among photographs of socialites in a fashionable shop window. But Holmes did not take any of these pictures. He does not use a camera to take any photographs to assist in solving his cases. Usually he relies on his excellent memory to recall faces and record facts.

Holmes receives and sends telegrams in several stories but never waits on tenterhooks for one to arrive with the vital clue to resolving an enigma. He subscribes to numerous newspapers and relies on them for information and also corresponds through them, even inserting a notice which lures Colonel Walter into a trap in 'Bruce Partington Plans'. He knows enough about typewriters to expose Mr Windigate in 'Case of Identity', but does not own one himself. He has had a telephone installed at Baker Street which both he and

Watson use in 'Three Garridebs'. So Holmes is *au courant* with technology but does not always use it to the full extent that he might.

Holmes prides himself on being a scientific detective – but how much science does he really employ? He insists on the importance of footprints and indeed has even written a monograph on the subject. He searches for them and interprets them to useful effect in several cases, and he follows patterns of boot marks in order to reconstruct action at a particular place, but the reader never sees him actually preserve an impression with plaster of Paris. Fingerprints, the most important technique in the period for identifying criminals, are mentioned in only seven tales out of sixty and assume only negative importance in one story. The bloody thumbprint in 'Norwood Builder' is a red herring. Holmes rejoices when he discovers an effective chemical blood test but never employs his test to solve a case. And what of the ostentatious display of chemical apparatus? Again, he never solves a case, or at least none that Watson relates, by conducting a chemical experiment. The microscope is much in evidence in 'Naval Treaty' and in 'Shoscombe Old Place', but the narratives of the cases these experiments refer to remain in Watson's tin box. On the whole not much detection is achieved with chemistry.

How does Holmes solve his cases? What methods does he apply? Does he ever use scientific techniques? He excels at acute crime-scene observation and accurate interpretation of even the most trifling physical trace evidence present. He is able to link details in his imagination to form a coherent scenario of the action that occurred there, that is, to reconstruct the past. He has no difficulty construing the events that took place in Black Peter's cabin or in predicting the behaviour of Beppo on a rampage to smash busts of Napoleon. The most extraordinary example of this exercise occurs in 'Veiled Lodger' when Holmes imagines, when given the facts, how the lion would have acted in the circumstances. His ability to imagine the behaviour of individuals involved in a crime sets him apart from Lestrade who, like Dupin's prefect, is inextricably enmeshed in the here and now. Indeed, Holmes complains to Watson of the lack of imagination at Scotland Yard. Intuitive insight into human character is indispensable to his process of detection. Once the facts are established through observation of crime scenes and human behaviour, Holmes assesses inconsistencies in statements by witnesses, suspects and clients and considers motives. Finally, he applies his superior powers of logical analysis to prove means, opportunity and motive. Like any successful CSI, he makes 'the invisible, visible and the inconsequential, consequential'.

6

SHERLOCK HOLMES AND THE FAIR SEX

Sherlock Holmes has gained the reputation of being a misogynist because he was a confirmed bachelor. According to Watson, 'His aversion to women, and his disinclination to form new friendships, were both typical of his unemotional character.'[1] In 'The Five Orange Pips' he confides, 'I do not encourage visitors.'[2] Holmes defended his choice to eschew relationships with women because he needed to preserve his rational judgment in order to function as a detective. As he remarks to Watson in 'The Sign of Four', 'love is an emotional thing, and whatever is emotional is opposed to that true cold reason which I place above all things. I should never marry myself, lest it bias my judgment.'[3]

In a letter to Joseph Bell in June of 1892, Conan Doyle confessed, 'Holmes is as inhuman as a Babbage's Calculating Machine, and just about as likely to fall in love.'[4] When Holmes remains impervious to Mary Morstan's charms, Watson echoes Conan Doyle as he accuses him of being 'an automaton – a calculating machine'. Holmes replies, 'It is of the first importance ... not to allow your judgment to be biased by personal qualities ... The emotional qualities are antagonistic to clear reasoning.' He adds, 'I assure you that the most winning woman I ever knew was hanged for poisoning three little children for their insurance-money.'[5]

Twenty years later in 1912, Conan Doyle admitted in a letter to Ronald Knox, 'Of course ... Holmes changed entirely as the stories went on. In the first one ... he was a mere calculating machine, but I had to make him more of an educated human being as I went on with him. He never shows heart.'[6] Evidence of the softening of Holmes' attitude is revealed in 'The Lion's Mane'. Contrary to his claim that 'the client was merely a unit, a factor in the problem',[7] and that he was impervious to female charms, Holmes responds to Maud Bellamy's beauty: 'Women have seldom been an attraction to me, for my brain has always governed my heart, but I could not look upon her perfect clear-cut face ... without realizing that no young man would cross her path unscathed.'[8] Of course, he 'shows heart' on multiple occasions.

Over time Arthur Conan Doyle softened Holmes' austerity and developed the softer side of his nature, not only toward women, but also toward Watson. Conan Doyle's assertion that Holmes never showed heart can, therefore, be contested. In the early stories Holmes takes no heed of Watson's feelings, as he complains more than once that Watson ruined the account of an investigation by sensationalising what should have been presented as a purely rational exercise. For example, in 'The Sign of Four' he alleges, 'Detection is, or ought to be, an exact science and should be treated in the same cold manner. You have attempted to tinge it with romanticism, which produces much the same effect as if you worked a love-story or an elopement into the fifth proposition of Euclid.'[9] He changes his mind later and compliments Watson on his good judgement and moderation, but what he gives with one hand he takes back with the other. In 'The Copper Beeches' he exonerates Watson from choosing the most sensational cases they have investigated but instead reporting 'those incidents which may have been trivial in themselves, but which have given room for those faculties of deduction and of logical synthesis which I have made my special province'.[10] In the face of Holmes' gracious remark, Watson admits that he cannot quite absolve himself from the charge of sensationalism. Holmes agrees: '[Y]ou have erred, perhaps, in attempting to put colour and life into each of your statements, instead of confining yourself to the task of placing upon record that severe reasoning from cause to effect which is really the only notable feature about the thing ... Crime is common. Logic is rare. Therefore it is upon the logic rather than upon the crime that you should dwell ... At the same time ... you can hardly be open to a charge of sensationalism, for out of these cases which you have been so kind as to interest yourself in, a fair proportion do not treat of crime, in the legal sense, at all ... But in avoiding the sensational, I fear that you may have bordered on the trivial.'[11]

On the few occasions when Holmes sends Watson to do reconnaissance, he uses harsh language to criticise his efforts. In 'The Solitary Cyclist', Holmes tells Watson that he has 'done remarkably badly'.[12] Holmes cannot think of 'any possible blunder which [he] has omitted' in 'The Disappearance of Lady Frances Carfax': 'The total effect of your proceedings has been to give the alarm everywhere and yet to discover nothing.'[13]

Further, in 'The Hound of the Baskervilles', when Watson tracks Holmes to his hiding place in the stone hut, his feelings are wounded that Holmes has not confided his plans: 'You use me, and yet you do not trust me! ... I think I have deserved better at your hands, Holmes.' Holmes offers a handsome apology: 'My dear fellow, you have been invaluable to me in this and in many other cases, and I beg that you will forgive me if I have seemed to play a trick upon you.' Watson is insulted that young Cartwright has been acting as a second pair of eyes locally and angry that his reports have been superfluous. Holmes hastily reassures him: 'I must compliment you exceedingly upon the zeal and intelligence which you have shown over an extraordinarily difficult case.'[14] So Watson is mollified. Holmes' conciliatory attitude and placating words provide a sharp contrast to the harsh judgment and censorious tone cited above.

Throughout the canon, Watson accepts his secondary role and moulds his own behaviour to suit Holmes' moods. He demonstrates his loyalty and devotion to Holmes over and over again, asking for nothing more than the privilege of assisting his friend, but hoping for a word of praise and longing for a sign of affection. Watson treasures moments of intimacy, as in 'The Illustrious Client': 'Both Holmes and I had a weakness for the Turkish Bath. It was over a smoke in the pleasant lassitude of the drying room that I found him less reticent and more human than anywhere else. On the upper floor of the Northumberland Avenue establishment there is an isolated corner where two couches lie side by side, and it was on these we lay.'[15]

Despite Conan Doyle's insistence that Holmes 'never shows heart', Holmes does reveal his feelings for Watson. In 'The Devil's Foot' when Watson saves Holmes' life as they begin to be overcome by lethal fumes from burning fragments of the devil's foot root, Holmes gasps, 'Upon my word, Watson! ... I owe you both my thanks and an apology. It was an unjustifiable experiment even for oneself, and doubly so for a friend. I am really very sorry'. Watson, 'who had never seen so much of Holmes' heart before', answers, 'You know ... that it is my greatest joy and privilege to help you.'[16]

The most dramatic demonstration of Holmes' feelings for Watson occurs in 'The Three Garridebs' when 'Killer' Evans shoots Watson: 'You're not hurt, Watson? For God's sake, say that you are not hurt?' Watson thinks, 'It was worth the wound – it was worth many wounds – to know the depth of loyalty and love which lay behind that cold mask. The clear, hard eyes were dimmed for a moment, and the firm lips were shaking. For the one and only time I caught a glimpse of a great heart as well as of a great brain. All my years of humble but single-handed service culminated in that moment of revelation.' As further proof of his feelings, Holmes tells Evans, 'If you had killed Watson, you would not have got out of this room alive.'[17]

'His Last Bow' concludes with a sentimental moment. As evidence of the enduring bond in their last adventure Holmes detains Watson: 'Stand with me here upon the terrace for it may be the last quiet talk that we shall ever have.'[18]

As Holmes' feelings for Watson warmed, so too his position toward women gradually mellowed; nevertheless, Holmes does voice his general distrust of the female gender as a whole on several occasions. In 'The Sign of Four' he insists, 'Women are never to be entirely trusted – not the best of them.'[19] His professional principle to remain celibate is buttressed by his perception of the female sex as mysterious and unknowable. Sounding rather like G. B. Shaw's Professor Higgins wondering why a woman cannot be more like a man, he complains to Watson in 'The Illustrious Client': 'Woman's heart and mind are insoluble puzzles to the male. Murder might be condoned or explained, and yet some smaller offence might rankle'.[20] In the same vein he states in 'The Second Stain' that 'the motives of women are so inscrutable ... Their most trivial action may mean volumes, or their most extraordinary conduct may depend upon a hairpin or a curling-tong'.[21]

Despite his reservations, Holmes interacted with women of every social class – from genteel society matrons under threat and exploited single women of private means, to working women such as anxious young governesses, worried elderly landladies and resourceful adventuresses – and he exercised his talents to resolve their difficulties. Holmes' empathy enabled him to understand their dilemmas and settle their problems – often waiving his fee. In addition, he induced countless housekeepers, nursemaids, lady's maids, housemaids and cooks to provide vital information. He definitely 'had a way with women'. His easy relationships with them reveal his empathy, sympathy, concern and compassion. It would be a mistake to regard him as a misogynist. Despite his harsh remarks spoken to Watson, his actions speak louder than his words. His behavior reveals – despite statements to the contrary – that he *does* understand women's feelings and values and he attempts to befriend and protect them from harm whenever he can.

The best testimonial of Holmes' dedicated concern for vulnerable women is registered in 'The Disappearance of Lady Frances Carfax': 'One of the most dangerous classes in the world ... is the drifting and friendless woman. She is the most harmless, and often the most useful of mortals, but she is the inevitable inciter of crime in others. She is helpless. She is migratory. She has sufficient means to take her from country to country and from hotel to hotel. She is lost, as often as not, in a maze of obscure *pensions* and boarding-houses. She is a tray chicken in a world of foxes. When she is gobbled up she is hardly missed. I much fear that some evil has come to the Lady Frances Carfax.'[22]

Holmes' treatment of Mary Sutherland in 'A Case of Identity' exhibits sympathetic insight into her feelings which fosters a reluctance to destroy her dreams of romance. Moreover, he admits that he finds his client a more interesting study than her problem. She begs Holmes to find her fiancé who disappeared en route to their wedding. Her grief at the loss is all too evident as she breaks down sobbing. Holmes, who realises that she has been deceived, advises her, 'Let the weight of the matter rest upon me now, and do not dwell on it further ... Let the whole incident be a sealed book, and do not allow it to affect your life.' The simple faith in her response – 'I cannot do that. I shall be true to Hosmer' – inspires his respect.[23] Although Holmes decides not to reveal the truth to his client because he realises that she wants to cling to her phantom lover, in the cause of justice he subsequently threatens her stepfather with physical reprisals unless he desists in his fraudulent schemes to retain her income.

Holmes also shows great sensitivity in dealing with Helen Stoner, who is terrified of her abusive stepfather following her sister's death. His compassion finds tactile expression. Bending forward and patting her forearm, he comforts her: 'You must not fear ... We shall soon set matters right, I have no doubt.' He also generously reassures her about paying his fees: 'As to reward, my profession is its reward; but you are at liberty to defray whatever expenses I may be put to, at the time which suits you best.'[24] He also expresses distress over her physical abuse: 'Holmes pushed back the frill of black lace which fringed the hand that lay upon our visitor's knee. Five little livid spots, the marks of four fingers and a thumb, were printed upon the white wrist. "You have been cruelly used."'[25] A parallel moment occurs in 'The Abbey Grange' when he sees similar marks on Lady Brackenstall's arm and his sympathy is aroused.[26]

Having been convinced of Grace Dunbar's innocence by perceiving her strength of character when he visits her in gaol in 'The Problem of Thor Bridge', Holmes vows to assist her: 'Never mind, my dear lady ... With the help of the God of justice I will give you a case which will make England ring. You will get news by tomorrow, Miss Dunbar, and meanwhile take my assurance that the clouds are lifting and that I have every hope that the light of truth is breaking through.'[27]

In 'The Red Circle' he calms the hysterical landlady, Mrs Warren, with a touch of his hand: 'Holmes leaned forward and laid his long, thin fingers upon the woman's shoulder. He had an almost hypnotic power of soothing when he wished. The scared look faded from her eyes, and her agitated features smoothed into their usual commonplace. She sat down on the chair which he had indicated.'[28]

He also defends mistreated married women and on several occasions becomes a champion of the institution of marriage and family life, even acting as marriage counsellor. He chastises men for mistreating their wives, children and other dependents under their protection. For example, Holmes remonstrates with Neil Gibson for attempting to seduce Grace Dunbar. Gibson excuses himself by saying that he would have married her if he could. Holmes receives this evasion with scorn, sarcastically complimenting Gibson on his 'generosity' and accuses him of trying to ruin a defenseless girl under his own roof. He reveals his sincere concern for Dunbar when he accepts the case 'for her sake only'.

Holmes also admonishes the Duke of Holdernesse in 'The Priory School' for failing to exercise parental responsibility. 'To humour your guilty elder son you have exposed your innocent younger son to imminent and unnecessary danger. It was a most unjustifiable action.' He further urges a reconciliation with the estranged duchess. 'I suggest that you make such amends as you can to the duchess, and that you try to resume those relations which have been so unhappily interrupted.'[29]

In the 'Second Stain', Holmes is commissioned by the Prime Minister to find a state document purloined from the private dispatch-box of the Secretary for European Affairs, the Right Honourable Trelawney Hope. It had been taken by his wife, Lady Hilda, in order to prevent the blackmailer Eduardo Lucas from revealing to her husband an affectionate missive penned in her youth. 'It was a letter ... an indiscreet letter written before my marriage ... a letter of an impulsive, loving girl. I meant no harm, and yet he would have thought it criminal.'[30] Terrified that her husband would reject her if the truth emerged, Lady Hilda exchanged the state paper for her own letter, but later retrieved the document after Lucas was killed. After tracing her movements and offering to protect her, Holmes demands that she give him the missing paper: 'If you will work with me, I can arrange everything. If you work against me, I must expose you.'[31] She explains, '[Lucas] promised that he would return my letter if I would return him a certain document which he described in my husband's dispatch-box ... He assured me that no harm could come to my husband.' To her appeal – 'What was I to do?' – Holmes replies, 'Take your husband into your confidence,'[32] but she lacked the courage. Of course, she made matters much worse by stealing the state document, committing treason for which she could never expect forgiveness. Nonetheless, Holmes is moved by her pleas and assists in covering up her theft.

When Holmes' client Lady Eva Brackwell finds herself being blackmailed on similar grounds on the eve of her wedding, Holmes tries to bluff Charles Augustus Milverton by saying he will advise her to take her fiancé into her confidence, but Milverton merely laughs at him. When Holmes asks what harm lies in her letters, Milverton answers, 'They are sprightly – very sprightly ... The lady is a charming correspondent. But I can assure you that the Earl of Dovercourt would fail to appreciate them.' He adds inexorably, 'If the money is not paid on the 14th there certainly will be no marriage on the 18th.'[33] In the face of this ultimatum, Holmes decides to take the dangerous risk of burgling Milverton's safe. He regards his course of action as morally justifiable but technically criminal. He disdains the personal risk because a lady is in desperate need of his help. What could be more gallant? He considers Milverton's stance in the light of a challenge to his self-respect and his reputation. In the end he burns the letters to preserve Lady Eva's honour and ensure her wedding.

Milverton's threats of exposure are not idle, as is proven when a noblewoman's life is ruined after her titled husband dies upon receiving compromising correspondence written in the past to another man. Impelled by her grief at the wreck of her marriage and a desire for vengeance, she shoots Milverton dead on his own hearth rug. Despite recognising her photograph in a shop window full of society portraits, Holmes does not notify the police and refuses Lestrade's request for help on the grounds that 'there are certain crimes which the law cannot touch, and which, therefore ... justify private revenge'.[34]

In addition to treating women respectfully and kindly, Holmes' behavior belied his words about trusting them. He trusted several to follow his instructions at crucial moments in his investigations.

In 'The Speckled Band' Holmes instructs Helen Stoner to remove a lighted lamp in her bedroom window and open the shutters before retiring to safer quarters, so that he and Watson can enter:

> 'It is very essential, Miss Stoner ... that you should absolutely follow my advice in every respect.'
> 'I shall most certainly do so.'
> 'The Matter is too serious for any hesitation. Your life may depend upon your compliance.'
> 'I assure you that I am in your hands.'[35]

He and Watson then keep a vigil and discover the lethal snake whose bite caused her sister's death and could have caused hers.

Holmes also respects and trusts Miss Hunter in 'The Copper Beeches'. He says, 'You seem to have acted all through this matter like a brave and sensible girl ... Do you think that you could perform one more feat? I should not ask it of you if I did not think you a quite exceptional woman ... We shall be at the Copper Beeches by seven o'clock ... The Rucastles will be gone by that time, and Toller will ... be incapable. There only remains Mrs Toller, who might give the alarm. If you could send her into the cellar, on some errand, and then turn the key upon her, you would facilitate matters immensely.'[36] She agrees. Indeed, her cooperation allows Holmes and Watson free access to the attic room where Miss Alice Rucastle had been imprisoned by her greedy father. Ironically, their chivalrous mission was foiled because she had already been rescued with the aid of Mrs Toller.

In 'The Naval Treaty' Miss Ann Harrison agreed against her will to remain in Percy Phelps' bedsit room, formerly occupied by her brother, while the men toured the grounds looking for signs of an intruder. She was displeased at being left behind, but did as Holmes asked.[37] He had earlier discerned from her handwriting that she was a woman of rare character, when she penned Percy Phelps' request for Watson's help. Recognizing the depth of her devotion to

Phelps, he later urges that she stay in Phelps' sick room all day and evening. 'It is of vital importance ... When you go to bed lock the door of this room on the outside and keep the key. Promise to do this ... It is for his sake. You can serve him.'[38] Thus Holmes prevented any attempt by the culprit to re-enter the room until he was in place to observe. He reports later that 'she carried out every one of my injunctions to the letter' and insists that the recovery of the treaty depended on her.[39]

Holmes was usually courteous, kind and generous in his treatment of women. For a man who rejected the softer passions, he was extraordinarily chivalrous. As Watson declares in 'The Dying Detective', 'he had a remarkable gentleness and courtesy in his dealings with women'.[40] His chivalry might at times seem superficial or merely pro forma, however, his concern was usually genuine rather than indifferent or patronising.

In 'The Abbey Grange' Watson reports, 'Holmes answered in his gentlest voice, "I will not cause you any trouble, Lady Brackenstall, and my whole desire is to make things easy for you, for I am convinced that you are a much wronged woman."'[41]

In 'The Copper Beeches' he was capable of identifying with Violet Hunter, a vulnerable young governess, as if she were a personal relation. He tries to dissuade her from accepting a post with peculiar duties and a suspiciously generous salary: 'I confess that it is not a situation that I should like a sister of mine to apply for.' He fails to convince her, but agrees to answer any call for help. Although Violet Hunter is a competent young woman and in no obvious danger, Holmes continues to worry about her. Watson notes that '[Holmes] would always wind up by muttering that no sister of his should ever have accepted such a situation'.[42]

In 'The Illustrious Client', despite being frustrated by Violet de Merville's refusal to heed his warnings about Baron Gruner, Holmes absolves her because 'she is not in her senses. She is madly in love. She has been told all about him. She cares nothing.'[43] He is simultaneously infuriated by her impenetrable cold complaisance and appalled at the prospect of her violated innocence and subsequent degradation. Consequently, the prospect of her fate if she were to marry Baron Gruner stirs his chivalric nature and he struggles to save her in spite of herself. He is moved by strong personal feelings: 'I thought of her for the moment as I would have thought of a daughter of my own.'[44]

Yet it transpires that though habitually polite, Holmes is not always chivalrous. Watson boasts in 'The Golden Pence-Nez' that 'Holmes had ... a peculiarly ingratiating way with women, and ... he very readily established terms of confidence with them'.[45] This is evident when he interviews Miss Cushing and Mrs Maberley; however, he practices a kind of subterfuge, obtaining facts about family members without disclosing his purpose. While cordially chatting with Mrs Marker and Mrs Mordecai Smith, he manipulates the conversation so that they divulge information which they might not normally give if asked for it directly. For instance, he wants to discover whether Professor Coram might be concealing someone, so he discusses with Mrs Marker how Coram's excessive smoking affects his appetite to ascertain the amount of food consumed. In order to get a description of Mordecai Smith's steam launch, he pretends to want to hire it and promises his wife to deliver a message if he finds it. He tells Watson, 'The main thing with people of that sort ... is never to let them think that their information can be of the slightest interest to you.'[46] With the same technique he encourages Lady Brackenstall's devoted nurse, Theresa Wright, to give details of her journey from Australia to England, as well as her recent marriage to and mistreatment by Sir Eustace. He uses his reconnaissance to serve his own ends, but not always to his informant's advantage, as with Mrs Smith and Theresa Wright, who divulge information which leads to the apprehension of men they wish to protect.

Without compunction he cavalierly exploits Milverton's housemaid Agatha to learn the ground plan and routine of the household so that he can burgle Milverton's safe. When reproved by Watson, he shrugs and says pragmatically, 'You must play your cards as best you can when such a stake is on the table.' His following comment somewhat mitigates his offence: 'However, I rejoice to say that I have a hated rival who will certainly cut me out the instant my back is turned.'[47] Nonetheless, one feels that rival or no rival he would have deceived Agatha.

So while usually polite, Holmes was not always strictly ethical while investigating a case.

Watson also declares in 'The Dying Detective' that Holmes 'disliked and distrusted the sex, but he was always a chivalrous opponent'.[48] This comment deserves scrutiny. When in conflict with the fair sex, did Holmes always behave like a gentleman – even with blackmailers, thieves and murderers?

He treats Irene Adler and Isadora Klein similarly. During his encounter with the former, he employs an elaborate scam, tricking Adler into revealing the hiding place of the scandalous photographs, but is ultimately outwitted by her. Because he admires her feat, he does not begrudge her escape. In the case of the latter, he obtains evidence against Klein and her minions and is prepared to unmask her, but, aware of the devastating consequences his actions would have, he agrees not to sully her name in exchange for enough money to fund Mrs Maberley's world cruise.

In 'The Golden Pince-Nez' after exposing Anna's hiding place and hearing her tale, Holmes tries to prevent her suicide and agrees to deliver her papers to the Russian legation. He also chivalrously forbears to identify Milverton's murderer. He views her as a victim and because of the extenuating circumstances regards her crime as morally justified.

Moved by their plight, he generously offers assistance to Lady Hilda Trelawney Hope and Lady Brackenstall, even though they were complicit in the commission of crimes. He calmly and rationally presents evidence to Laura Lyons of Jack Stapleton's disloyalty and convinces her to give details involving him in Sir Charles Baskerville's death, and he is deeply compassionate upon finding the battered Beryl Stapleton and gently persuades her to help him find her husband.

However, he is not always so solicitous and gentle. Holmes ruthlessly uses Kitty Winter as a cat's paw in his efforts to defeat Baron Gruner's scheme to entrap Violet de Merville. He handles her roughly as he aborts her attack on the contemptuous young woman and forces her bodily from the premises. In addition, he exploits her knowledge of Gruner's house to obtain his incriminating diary.

He listens sympathetically to Eugenia Ronder's confession, but speaks in a brusque tone when he commands her not to commit suicide. He can also be sardonic and hectoring as he is with Mrs Maberley's servant Susan, alias Mrs Barney Stockdale, who is working undercover in her household. His tone with Annie Fraser is intimidating when he demands to see 'the man of the house' after Annie Fraser denies that Dr Schlessinger lives on the premises.

On the whole Watson's defense of Holmes' gallantry is justified, but he can also be opportunistic, intransigent, severe and ruthless if necessary.

The influence of women's love and sexual passion on human behavior – even in so far as it leading to crime – forms the basis for several of Watson's most powerful narratives. They include 'A Scandal in Bohemia' in *The Adventures*; 'The Musgrave Ritual' in *The Memoirs*; 'The Golden Pince-Nez', 'Charles Augustus Milverton' and 'The Second Stain' in *The Return;* as well as 'The Illustrious Client', 'The Three Gables' and 'The Problem of Thor Bridge' in *The Casebook*. In all of the eight stories in which women are the primary villains, violence occurs as the result of unfulfilled passion, jealousy, or threat to an established marital relationship.

In some other tales a woman also acts as an accomplice or instigator of crime. These stories focus on female sexual passion as a motive for disgraceful, illicit or criminal behavior. Mary Holder in 'The Beryl Coronet' and Eugenia Ronder in

'The Veiled Lodger' are sexually motivated women who act as accomplices in acts of theft and murder respectively, but are not the prime movers. Holder betrays her guardian for a dissolute roué, and Ronder conspires with a lover to assassinate her abusive husband. Although not guilty of shedding blood, Lady Brackenstall and her maid Theresa are complicit in a homicide when they shield her husband's killer in 'The Abbey Grange'. Until he betrays them, Beryl Stapleton and Laura Lyons both facilitate the nefarious activities of Jack Stapleton in 'The Hound of the Baskervilles' because they love him.

In 'The Three Gables' Isadora Klein commits a crime indirectly, propelled by desire to make a prestigious society marriage. She hires agents to obtain the manuscript of Douglas Maberley's fictional account of their illicit love affair, which would cause a scandal and prohibit her nuptials. They break into Maberley's mother's house, chloroform her and steal the book.

Sarah Cushing does not commit a crime in 'The Cardboard Box', but her jealousy leads to the break-up of her sister's marriage and her subsequent murder. As Iago poisoned Othello's mind in Shakespeare's eponymous play, Sarah alienates Mary's affections from her husband and sows discord between them, even encouraging her sister to keep company with another man. Sarah stokes the flames of Jim Browner's jealousy until he commits a double murder.

In most of these stories, crimes of passion are committed by temperamental 'foreign' women. The exceptions include the English aristocrat Madame X, who shoots Milverton after he destroys her marriage and drives her husband to a premature death of a broken heart; Kitty Winter, who, seduced and abandoned to a life of prostitution by Baron Gruner, flings acid in his face in a volatile fury of hatred, thereby preventing his further victimisation of women by destroying his good looks; and Rachel Howells, who suffers from brain fever when the butler Brunton prefers another woman and is impelled by her 'excitable Welsh temperament'

to bury him alive while assisting him in a robbery. All three of these 'wronged women' seeking revenge are British.

The American opera singer Irene Adler, enraged at being rejected when the King of Bohemia followed court protocol in choosing a wife of royal blood, threatens to cause a scandal by revealing intimate photographs of their illicit liaison. Her blackmail threat is prompted by jealousy – 'Hell hath no fury like that of a woman scorned.'[49] The threat is withdrawn when she herself marries, but she retains the compromising photographs to protect herself from future harassment.

Professor Coram's estranged Russian wife, Anna, stabs his secretary in a panicked attack when she is surprised while stealing papers concerning her past. Coram had betrayed his revolutionary political colleagues to save his own life, and from jealous motives had stolen Anna's diary and letters from 'the friend of [her] heart' in order to incriminate them. Having been released from prison in Siberia, she has come to retrieve the papers which can exonerate her wrongly convicted lover and bring about his release, thereby undoing the damage caused by jealousy. Her love and strong sense of injustice motivates her conduct, prevailing over prolonged years of incarceration.

Holmes' distrust of emotion and Anglo-Saxon prejudice against unrestrained temperamental behavior are confirmed in 'The Second Stain,' 'The Three Gables', 'The Problem of Thor Bridge', 'The Hound of the Baskervilles' and 'The Sussex Vampire'. They portray women from Latin backgrounds or tropical climes as dark-haired, dark-eyed beauties with tempestuous natures. Their torrid temperaments are attributed as much to climate as culture. Conan Doyle perpetuates the literary symbolism of the Snow White vs Rose Red stereotypic iconography throughout the canon: virtuous women are usually blonde and blue-eyed, while immoral women are dark-haired and dark-eyed.

In 'The Second Stain' the Parisian Madame Henri Fournaye stabs her husband, Eduardo Lucas, to death when she mistakenly assumes his late-night female visitor is his mistress. Creole by birth, she is characterised as having an extremely excitable nature and suffering from attacks of frenzied jealousy resulting from a dangerous and permanent mania.[50]

Promiscuous and predatory, Isadora Klein is one of these femmes fatale. 'She was, of course, the celebrated beauty ... She is pure Spanish, the real blood of the masterful Conquistadors, and her people have been leaders in Pernambuco for generations.'[51]

In 'The Hound of the Baskervilles' Beryl Stapleton, formerly Beryl Garcia of Costa Rica, is portrayed as a fascinating and beautiful woman with something tropical and exotic about her. Watson claims 'she was darker than any brunette whom I have seen in England – slim, elegant, and tall. She had a proud, finely cut face, so regular that it might have seemed impassive were it not for the sensitive mouth and the beautiful dark, eager eyes.'[52] The intensity of her hatred towards Stapleton for his physical and mental ill treatment and betrayal of her love is expressed in her eagerness to help in his pursuit. 'A woman of Spanish blood does not condone such injury so lightly.'[53] She reveals 'fierce merriment' as she realises he must have fled to his doom in Grimpen Mire: 'He may find his way in, but never out.'[54]

In 'The Problem of Thor Bridge' Conan Doyle again associates strong passion with a Latin temperament, and Mrs Gibson conforms to the stereotype. She is described as being 'rare and wonderful in her beauty. It was a deep rich nature, too, passionate, whole-hearted, tropical, ill-balanced.'[55] When the wealthy American Senator Neil Gibson became attracted to his children's governess, Grace Dunbar, and his affection for his wife cooled, Mrs Gibson, née Maria Pinto of Brazil, became intensely jealous of Grace Dunbar. Because she could not bear life without her husband's love, she devised a scheme to commit suicide which would incriminate Dunbar as her killer. She was portryed as being at the mercy of her heritage: 'A creature of the Tropics ... Tropical by birth and tropical by nature. A child of the sun and of passion. She had loved him as such women can love.'[56] Gibson explains that the romance lasted for years, but when it faded her love persisted: 'But you know the wonderful way of women! Do what I might nothing could turn her from me.' Reminiscent of Holmes' words in 'The Illustrious Client' and 'The Second Stain' about women's unknowable hearts and minds (cited above), Gibson comments further on the unfathomable depths of female nature: 'Women lead an inward life and may do things beyond the judgement of man.' He also shares his ruminations on the complexity and intensity of jealousy with Holmes: 'There is a soul-jealousy that can be as frantic as any body-jealousy ... she was aware that this English girl exerted an influence on my mind and my acts that she never had ... She was crazy with hatred, and the heat of the Amazon was always in her blood.'[57]

The power of love is manifested in unselfish but ill-judged guise in 'The Sussex Vampire' when another passionate Latin beauty from Peru, Mrs Robert Ferguson, loves her husband so devotedly that she cannot bear to hurt him by disclosing the murderous attacks upon their young child by his fifteen-year-old son of a previous marriage. Instead she beats off the older boy with a stick, giving no explanation except that she hates him; she risks alienating her husband in order to protect him from painful knowledge, so her ill will is attributed to jealousy. 'She is very jealous – jealous with all the strength of her fiery tropical love.'[58] This theory seems to be confirmed when she is found sucking blood from the child's neck to remove poison. Her overwhelming love dictated that she wait for someone else to disclose the facts to her husband. She commits no crime but makes a great error in judgment, because the teenage boy's jealousy of his stepmother and her baby is so ferocious.

These stories support Holmes' beliefs that frustrated sexual passion and perverted love have the power to distort judgment and ruin lives.

Fact Versus Fiction: Women in the Real World

Conan Doyle wrote for middle-class readers of *The Strand Magazine*, so most of the main characters of both genders are middle class, but the stories involve people from a cross section of society. Not surprisingly, no one among the fleets of servants ever consults Holmes as a client. Many provide essential information, but, apart from a few like Theresa Wright, they remain largely nondescript figures.

Holmes functioned in an intensely patriarchal society, interacting mostly with male clients, police officers, police informers, professional experts, witnesses and criminals. In almost a dozen cases no women appear at all, and in many others they might as well be wallpaper because they are merely mentioned or are seen but not heard – that is, they are characters in name only. Others are designated simply by their function, such as housekeeper, cook or maid. In several stories the actions of female characters who are central to the plot are merely reported or referred to rather than portrayed, thus their significance is subverted. As noted by Susan Rice in 'Doyle's Women', this failure to develop strong female characters was common practice in Conan Doyle's historical novels.[59] However, Holmes interacted with many women during the course of his investigations, especially while conducting interviews, and several sought his professional assistance as clients.

Holmes' client Lady Eva Brackwell, the *fons et origo* of the action in 'Charles Augustus Milverton', never appears. Mrs Hilton Cubitt, around whom the mystery swirls in 'The Dancing Men', enters the scene only at the climax and never speaks. Miss Dobney, whose inquiry about the missing Lady Frances Carfax initiated the search for her, is never seen – the lady herself is discovered comatose on the brink of death only at the end of the story bearing her name. In 'The Cardboard Box' Sarah Cushing – who has destroyed a marriage, caused two murders, and thereby delivered

195

her brother-in-law to the hands of the police to face trial for homicide – is not even glimpsed. Other key figures are represented only as corpses, as with Lady Beatrice Falder in 'Shoscombe Old Place' and Godfrey Staunton's dead wife in 'The Missing Three-Quarter'.

Given this anomalous situation, the question arises of how accurately Conan Doyle portrays women and their roles between 1880 and 1914. (All further references to the fictional time continuum will be taken from Brad Kefauver's electronic 'A Basic Timeline of Terra 221B', 2001).[60]

Women of all social classes are represented in the canon. Aristocrats like Lady Hilda Trelawney Hope, Lady Brackenstall, Lady Frances Carfax and Milverton's anonymous nemesis at the pinnacle. Upper-middle-class married women include Mrs Nevil St Clair, Mrs Cecil Forrester and Mrs Grant Munro. Independent gentlewomen like Miss Violet de Merville and Helen Stoner. Well-educated middle-class women who need to earn their living working as governesses, such as Mary Morstan, Violet Smith, Grace Dunbar and Violet Hunter, and the redoubtable Miss Stoper who manages an employment agency for governesses. Single middle-class women, some of whom work at secretarial jobs, including Mary Sutherland and Laura Lyons. Even the arts are represented by the opera singer Irene Adler, the danseuse Flora Millar and Madame Lésurier, who owns a couturier salon in Bond Street.

Owners of modest properties, like Mrs Mary Maberley and Miss S[usan] Cushing, also enjoy independent middle-class status, while landladies like Mrs Hudson, Mrs Merrilow, Mrs Warren and Madame Charpentier are forced to take in lodgers to make ends meet and maintain their middle-class respectability. Mrs Merrilow and Mrs Warren refer to themselves as 'poor' even though they own houses. In contrast to them, according to Watson in 'The Dying Detective', the princely sums Holmes paid Mrs Hudson for his rooms over the years would have been enough to purchase the whole house. Working-class women oversee and clean such premises, including the concierge Mrs Saunders in 'The Three Garridebs' and the commissionaire's wife, Mrs Tangey, in 'The Naval Treaty'. Most working-class women are in domestic service; several occupy positions of trust, such as Theresa Wright and Mrs Mason.

Within this gallimaufry of females, apart from widows, only a small group of unmarried middle-class young women have any autonomy – that is, initiate action to take control of their own lives. Five resist parental authority in seeking a husband (Mary Sutherland, Maud Bellamy, Helen Stoner, Mary Holder, Violet de Merville). Four are independent women who work as governesses (Morstan, Hunter, Smith, Dunbar). Two assume responsibility to assist men they care about (Alice Turner, Anne Harrison). One follows her fiancé to Baker Street and provides further information for Holmes' investigation (Edith Prestbury). Deserted by her husband, another sets up her own typing business (Laura Lyons). Fully autonomous, the final two – Irene Adler and Isadora Klein – are labeled 'adventuresses' and considered 'fallen women' because they have had sexual liaisons outside of marriage. Both are prepared to give up their independence to make respectable marriages.

Even the villainesses come from across the social spectrum and all have been victimised or betrayed by men. They range from Milverton's anonymous upper-class nemesis, to Lady Trelawney Hope and Mrs Neil Gibson, Madame Fournaye and Anna 'Coram', as well as the ventursome Irene Adler and Isadora Klein. The housemaid Rachel Howells completes the social cross section. Criminal accomplices are also recruited from across social classes, from Lady Brackenstall, to circus performer Eugenia Ronder, to the reluctant Mrs Elise Lysander Stark, to subservient wives like Mrs Toller and Mrs Hayes, and widowed domestic servants like Mrs Lexington. Actively enmeshed in crime as a way of life are Annie Fraser, co-conspirator of 'Holy' Peters, and the prostitute Kitty Winter.

Woman's Nature: The Weaker Sex's Role in Society

In the nineteenth century ideas defining the nature of woman and her role in society, as well as the institution of marriage, underwent seismic changes. 'Discoveries' about the female brain and nervous system led to new perceptions about women. In 1839 Alexander Walker posited the theory that a vast difference existed between the brains of men and women – that there existed a natural inferiority of female intellect which was balanced by a superiority of instinct. Hypothetically, instinct provided women with a quick, non-cognitive apprehension or insight. A man had a higher intellectual faculty, allegedly because he had a larger cranium. Walker claimed that man was a slave to reason and alleged that 'women were more physical, instinctual and emotional because they were dominated by their sexual functions'. Throughout the Victorian period this pernicious 'scientific'evidence of female intellectual inferiority supported resistance to women's education and employment in the professions.[61]

Walker maintained that the female nervous system was disposed to foster feelings of sympathy, delicacy and refinement. Female sensibility was thought to render women especially perceptive and susceptible to intangible impressions and to confer a special acuteness of feeling. According to Melanie Phillips 'this new ideology of femininity, associat[ed] sensibility with sympathy, compassion, benevolence, humanity and pity'. Emotions were considered indicative of fine feelings and of virtue. Unfortunately, women 'with the most refined nerves were most susceptible to nervous disorders, so they were both morally superior and weaker than men; indeed, their very weakness was the source of their superiority'. Thus woman's highest virtue was identified with her weakness.[62] Therefore, the phrase 'the weaker sex' was not a term of disparagement. Women's weakness became the *raison d'etre* of chivalry. Delicacy or refined genteel deportment was encouraged so as to protect women from nervous stress.

Because of the belief in the innate distinctions between the genders, women were taught to suppress willfulness and submit to traditional authority within the family. They were also told that to attract husbands they should be meek, submissive and resigned. Their role was defined as selfless devotion to others.[63] Domestic responsibilities, especially child-rearing, were considered better suited to the more compassionate and tender sex, so women were expected to stay at home. The figure of the mother in the home came to symbolise virtue and developed iconic significance. The home became a sanctuary, a temple of virtue. People believed that women should work for the happiness of others by guarding the comfort of the home. Men wanted to idealise women and hence the cult of the Angel in the House flourished.[64]

With their refined natures, women became the essential guardians of morality. They were expected to pursue 'the high and holy duty of cherishing and protecting the minor morals of life'. Female virtue was marshalled to combat social problems created by male vice. By the mid-nineteenth century women were generally accepted as more moral and virtuous than men; by gently correcting their husbands' errors, wives could create a ripple effect to improve society as a whole. According to Eliza Farnham, 'Nature meant women to be the chief agent for improving human behavior by moving man from savagery to civilisation.'[65] Charles Darwin's theory of natural selection in *The Origin of Species* (1859) was invoked by Robert Chambers (1844) and Herbert Spencer (1851) to support a belief that humanity was gradually evolving toward perfection.[66] In fact, Darwin actually believed that female intuition was characteristic of children and the lower races.[67]

On the whole, Conan Doyle's presentation of female characters endorses the prevailing mores. There are several references to women's instinct in the canon. In 'The Copper Beeches' Violet Hunter associates it with benevolence: 'From the moment that I understood that there was something about that suite of rooms which I was not to know, I was all on fire to go over them. It was not mere curiosity … It was more a feeling of duty – a feeling that something good might come from my penetrating to this place. They talk of woman's instinct; perhaps, it was woman's instinct which gave me that feeling.'[68] In 'The Beryl Coronet' Mary Holder is afraid that her step-brother will be blamed for her crime and protests, 'I am so sure that he is innocent. You know what women's instincts are.'[69] And in 'The Lion's Mane' Holmes welcomes Maud Bellamy's help: 'I value a woman's instinct in such matters.'[70] This idea of a female non-rational intuitive faculty survives into the twenty-first century.

No clearer example of the feminine ideal and Watson's approval of it exists than his account of Mary Morstan's behavior early in 'The Sign of Four': 'After the angelic fashion of women, she had borne trouble as long as there was someone weaker than herself to support, and I had found her bright and placid by the side of the frightened housekeeper. In the cab, however, she first turned faint and then burst into a passion of weeping.'[71] Morstan epitomises not only the unselfish ideal woman striving to serve others, but also the sensitive weaker vessel. Mrs Forrester represents the loving virtuous matron as she tenderly embraces Mary and greets her in a motherly voice. Watson is totally captivated by this sentimental image of domestic harmony as he drives away: 'The two graceful, clinging figures, the half-opened door, the hall-light shining through stained glass, the barometer, and the bright stair-rods. It was soothing to catch even that passing glimpse of a tranquil English home.'[72]

Opposed to this idealised view of women's nature and role in marriage were the practical realities of unjust sexual mores and their inequitable legal status.

Women's Virtue: Marriage and Sexual Mores

Because social status and wealth were passed on from generation to generation through marriage, the cult of virginity was enshrined to ensure that heirs were legitimate and the blood line unsullied, thus preventing alien claims on the family assets.[73] Titled and monied families intermarried and thereby often increased or consolidated their fortunes and social status. Young women were expected to make 'suitable' marriages – that is, to benefit their families by accepting a suitor of their parents' choice.

A bride was expected to accept the authority of her husband and to become a devoted and loyal wife, confining her interests and activities to the domestic sphere. Her tastes and opinions were shaped by those of her husband. In 1839 Sarah Stickney Ellis wrote that 'married women must accept the "the superiority of your [*sic*] husband simply as a man"'.[74] So strong was the cult of innocent virtue that no man wanted a woman with a past, but rather an ignorant virgin whose tastes he could mould to his own to please himself. It was the role of the husband to initiate his wife into sexual experience.

A woman's ignorance of sexuality was regarded as the greatest proof of her innocence or virtue. Sex was considered brutish or animalistic and associated with the lower classes.[75] As women were considered delicate, they needed to be protected from anything coarse. Consequently, a bride often entered marriage without basic knowledge of sexual matters. Emmeline Pethick-Lawrence, a prominent feminist, wrote that her mother 'when she married … was completely ignorant of what was expected of her as a wife'.[76] Because of women's innocence they were deemed to lack sexual appetite, and indeed it was regarded as indelicate and unseemly for a woman to manifest such interest.[77] A woman's honour and reputation depended on her sexual purity; like Caesar's wife, a married woman had to be above suspicion of infidelity.

Several of Holmes' cases reflect the importance of a woman's sexual purity in the period. The social transgressions of Lady Eva Brackwell, Lady Hilda Trelawney Hope and Madame X consisted merely of indiscreet correspondence with a member of the opposite sex in their youth. At the time, all were virgins with no carnal knowledge or physical experience, yet the mere existence of such letters was enough to ruin their reputations and render them social pariahs. In two of the cases the victims were married women whose loyalty and virtue had been tested by time, and yet they were threatened with losing their husbands' trust and respect if prior romantic attachments were revealed. Such fears also motivated the behavior of Mrs Hilton Cubitt in 'The Dancing Men' and Mrs Grant Munro in 'The Yellow Face', both of whom had been married previously and were frightened to acknowledge the legacy of their pasts lest they forfeit the affection of their current husbands.

Of course this social code of ethics applied only to the upper- and upper-middle classes who could afford to provide a sheltered life for their womenfolk. For lower-middle-class and working-class women life was much more pragmatic. Ideas of sensitivity and delicacy yielded to the practical necessity of earning a living, but unselfish, meek and submissive behavior was expected. Though the preferred role for a woman was that of a stay-at-home wife and mother, many working-class women entered domestic service or were forced to work menial low-paying jobs, such as that of seamstress, laundress or barmaid, or else they became prostitutes. The same code of sexual morality prevailed, which forbade sex outside of marriage, and giving birth to illegitimate children often resulted in social rejection.

Women as Property: The Legal Status of Women

Women had no legal rights and could not own property or vote. Because women had no legal status, they had no autonomy. They were under the control of their father or closest male relative until marriage, at which time they became the property of their husbands.

Conan Doyle reflects this reality in several stories. While investigating the death of Fitzroy McPherson in 'The Lion's Mane', Holmes asks to speak privately with Maud Bellamy, but her father forbids it: '"I tell you, Maud, not to mix yourself up in this matter," cried her father angrily.' While living under her father's roof, she was expected to obey him. 'She looked at me helplessly. "What can I do?"' Her father strongly disapproved of her attachment to the schoolmaster – 'I object to my girl picking up with men outside her own station.'[78] – and he had already complained to Holmes that McPherson's attentions to Maud were insulting because he had never suggested marriage. In 'The Hound of the Baskervilles' Mr Frankland disowned his daughter for marrying without his consent.

In 'The Dancing Men' Abe Slaney feels entitled to take Elsie Patrick Cubitt away on the grounds that he 'had a right to her. She was pledged to me years ago ... I tell you that I had the first right to her, and I was only claiming my own.'[79] Clearly, he argues that his claim precedes that of Cubitt because she was her father's property and her father had a right to give her to whomever he chose.

The legal status of married women was no better. A wife's identity was subsumed into that of her husband. Her property, earnings, liberty and conscience belonged to her husband. Writing in *The Subjection of Women* in 1869, John Stuart Mill complained, 'Wives had no legal personality. Husbands could force them to have sex, compel them to return if they left, and had sole rights over their children.'[80]

Legally married women had the same status as underage children, wards, lunatics, idiots and outlaws.[81]

According to the distinguished eighteenth-century jurist William Blackstone, husbands had the right to 'moderate correction' of their wives, as well as 'domestic chastisement', but they were to be meted out within 'reasonable' limits and violence was prohibited. However, though illegal, many jurists and most of the general population believed that it was permissible for a husband to beat his wife.[82]

This is illustrated by the brutal treatment of Peter Carey's wife and daughter in the story bearing his name: 'When he had the fit on him he was a perfect fiend. He has been known to drive his wife and his daughter out of doors in the middle of the night, and flog them through the park until the whole village outside the gates was aroused by their screams.'[83] Yet no one intervened to curb his violence and protect the women.

The most dramatic and horrific instance of spousal abuse in the Holmes stories is that of Beryl Stapleton, who is beaten, gagged and tied to a beam in order to prevent her warning Sir Henry Baskerville of the impending attack by the hound. Over her bonds 'two dark eyes – dark eyes full of grief and shame and a dreadful questioning – stared back at us'. When released, she faints and has to be revived with brandy. 'She shot her arms out from her sleeves, and we saw with horror that they were all mottled with bruises. "But this is nothing – nothing! It is my mind and soul that he has tortured and defiled."'[84] Mrs Stapleton introduces the issue of mental cruelty, which is a precedent.

Women had no rights at all over their children, except in cases of illegitimacy, when the mother alone was responsible for their support. The father of a child born in wedlock was entitled to exercise total control over the child, whom he had complete custody of, even if he were unfit or neglectful, and he could prevent the mother from all access.[85]

Many women were deterred from leaving their husbands for fear of losing custody of their children. To remedy this situation the Infants Custody Act 1839 was guided through parliament by Thomas Talfourd, MP for Reading, who was motivated by the plight of the Whig society hostess Caroline Norton, whose husband had denied her access to her three children all under the age of ten.[86] He also refused to return any of the money or property which were hers before the marriage. Cases such as this led Alexander Walker to conclude, 'Thus wives in England are in all respects as to property, person and progeny in the condition of slaves.'[87]

Property Rights

Since women had no legal status, they could not own property, nor could they make any claims on the dowry given to their husbands at the time of marriage. They were totally dependent on their spouses, unless they had retained some control through male trustees, which only a small percentage of upper-class women did. When equity for married women under the law was mooted, it was met with great disfavour because it threatened to interfere with the dynastic accumulation and secure possession of property through marriage. The possibility of the disestablishment of landed estates was extremely unsettling to the propertied classes.[88]

If a man behaved badly and their wife left them, she would have to find a source of income either by working to earn money or by securing the rights to their own property. The Married Women's Property Acts passed in 1870 and 1882 entitled married women to the same rights as unmarried women, so they could retain their own earnings and, a decade later, their own property – that is, possessions and capital.[89] These laws liberated many women from domestic tyranny and granted them autonomy.

However, not all women chose to accept it. The disadvantages are clear in Conan Doyle's 'The Yellow Face' when Mrs

Grant Munro, who was a widow when she married for a second time, voluntarily turned over her property to her new husband, and so had to ask him for funds when she wanted to arrange a visit with the secret child of her first marriage. A marital crisis occurred because, fearing his displeasure, she refused to tell him why she wanted the money.

Divorce: Divorce Acts 1857, 1878 and 1888

Men could divorce their wives merely if they committed adultery. However, women could obtain a divorce only if their husbands had committed incest or adultery with desertion, cruelty or unnatural offences.[90]

Central to the debate was the double standard. 'The double standard meant that sexual license was regarded as an understandable and even pardonable lapse by men, who were … at the mercy of their instincts, but an unpardonable and very serious offence by women, who were betraying theirs.'[91] Popular belief held that female adultery undermined the institution of marriage, whereas the same was not thought of unfaithful husbands. Of course, it was blatantly unjust to condone in men the same sexual misbehavior for which women were condemned and ostracised. As divorce became more frequent, the unfairness of the double standard attracted more negative attention. The prevalence of violence by upper- and middle-class men was also revealed and condemned.[92]

Inequality of the law governing marital rights led upper-middle-class women to campaign for reform of divorce law.[93] Divorce was perforce restricted to the very wealthy, as it required an expensive, complex annulment process or a costly private Bill in the House of Commons. The latter was regarded as detestable and disgraceful, because it often necessitated detailed discussion in public of a couple's intimate marital relationship.[94]

Opposition to divorce was based largely on Christian belief as articulated in the Bible and in the marriage ceremony: 'What God hath joined together, let no man put asunder.'[95] It was also feared that divorce would lead to serial polygamy because of the promiscuous sexual appetite of men. In addition, there were practical concerns that financially dependent wives would become destitute after a seperation.[96]

Mrs Barbara Leigh Smith Bodichon, who was the daughter of the radical peer from Norwich, Benjamin Smith, and Florence Nightingale's cousin, organized support in 1857 for the Married Women's Property Bill by gathering 24,000 signatures. Detractors claimed it would 'disrupt society, destroy the home and turn women into loathsome, self-assertive creatures'.[97] It was introduced by Sir Erskine Perry MP and passed a Second Reading, but was defeated on the final vote.[98]

The Matrimonial Causes Act of 1878 allowed women to obtain separation orders which included custody of children under ten on the basis of suffering from physical abuse, and the Act of 1888 extended this to desertion.[99] Not until 1923 did the Matrimonial Causes Act grant divorce on the same grounds for both genders.[100]

Conan Doyle vigorously campaigned to achieve equal divorce rights for women and served as chairman of the Divorce Law Reform Union for ten years. His support of this issue may have been inspired by his mother's predicament when his alcoholic father imperiled the family's welfare.[101] He clearly portrayed the difficulties of unhappily married women in some of Holmes' cases. In addition to Beryl Stapleton and Mrs Peter Carey, Holmes encountered several women who suffered mental and physical abuse from their husbands, including Laura Lyons and Lady Brackenstall.

The plight of a woman in an unhappy marriage is disclosed in 'The Hound of the Baskervilles' through the bitter words of Laura Lyons, whose husband deserted her. 'I made a rash marriage and have had reason to regret it ... My life has been one incessant persecution from a husband whom I abhor. The law is upon his side, and every day I am faced by the possibility that he may force me to live with him.'[102] The date on Dr. Mortimer's walking stick indicates that the story is set after 1884. By 1888 Mrs Lyons would have been able to obtain an order of separation on grounds of desertion, protecting her from any attempt to force her to cohabit with her husband. She seems confident that she can obtain a divorce if funds can be found, therefore it seems safe to conclude that the events occur after 1888.

Holmes' discovery of the bruises on Lady Brackenstall's arm in 'The Abbey Grange' unleashes her eloquent denunciation of unfair marital laws: 'Sir Eustace was a confirmed drunkard. Can you imagine what it means for a sensitive and high-spirited woman to be tied to him for a day and a night? It is a sacrilege, a crime, a villainy to hold that such a marriage is binding. I say that these monstrous laws of yours will bring a curse upon the land.'[103] Her words, uttered in 1897, seem at odds with reality, since the Married Women's Property Act of 1882 would have given her the right to claim assets owned prior to marriage and the Matrimonial Causes Act of 1888 would have enabled her to obtain her freedom on grounds of abusive treatment. Perhaps she shrinks from the inevitable public disclosure of details of her private life.

Education

Once a woman gained her liberty, her troubles were not over. She had to face the challenge of how to maintain herself. Very few had acquired any skills that were useful outside of the home. The generally accepted goal of education for women was to prepare them for their duties as wives and mothers. If the conventional role of woman was to be the helpmate of man, then her education should be fashioned to support her husband's goals and participate in and/or enhance her husband's pleasures and those of his family and friends.[104] General knowledge was not considered necessary.

For most of the nineteenth century there were three types of schools which girls attended: finishing schools, old-fashioned boarding schools and charity schools. At the finishing schools emphasis was placed on deportment, fashionable accomplishments and a smattering of the arts and sciences. They drew students from the upper- and upper-middle classes and produced both debutantes and governesses. Boarding schools were usually located in small towns and were attended by the daughters of local tradesmen and farmers. Illigitimate daughters as well as girls whose mothers were too busy with younger children and household duties to teach them were often placed in such schools. The third kind of institution was the charity school for orphans, semi-orphans or the daughters of professional-class parents in straitened circumstances. Admission was arranged by an influential patron.[105] However, in 1872 Maria Grey and her sister, Emily Shirreff, expanded these opportunities when they started the Girls' Public Day School Trust. In just under twenty years there were eighty endowed schools for girls.[106] Despite this progress, most of the graduates of these schools were taught only basic subjects. The majority of them would spend their lives as wives, but a few would become governesses.

To improve the qualifications of governesses, in 1848 a King's College professor, the Reverend Frederick Maurice, founded Queen's College in London to offer free evening classes in maths, geography, Latin, history, theology and moral philosophy. At the time most governesses simply relied on their own upbringing to prepare them for teaching. Few of these women had much formal schooling, so their level of education was generally low. Professor Maurice's academy fulfilled a genuine need.[107] As late as 1890 Charlotte Yonge advocates in *Womankind* that young women intending to become governesses should obtain a diploma from Queen's College in London or a similar establishment.

In 1850 one of Maurice's students, Frances Buss, opened the North London Collegiate School, and eight years later another, Dorothea Beale, established Cheltenham Ladies' College. Miss Browning's Blackheath School offered literature, art and music. Graduates were prepared to teach, but there were more jobs in people's homes than in schools. Most governesses offered instruction in simple arithmetic, English and French languages, music, drawing, needlework and deportment – sometimes supplemented by Latin, German and geography. There was a general consensus that this was enough to prepare a gentlewoman for her role as wife and mother.[108]

Higher education for girls began in the 1860s. As the result of the efforts of the energetic feminist Emily Davies to improve education for middle-class women, in 1865 girls were admitted to Cambridge University local examinations – a practice also followed by Oxford University.[109] 'By 1869, her schoolmistresses' associations were entering hundreds of girls for junior and senior exams.' That same year she founded what later became Girton College at Cambridge University, where the female students sat the same exams as the male students, although they were not granted degrees.[110] From 1881 the first women were allowed to take courses and sit examinations with recorded results, and from 1921 they were awarded diplomas of Bachelor of Arts, but not actual degrees until 1948. In 1878 London University admitted women to matriculate for degrees.[111] Despite their superior credentials, the limited opportunities for employment meant that most women took posts as teachers.

The vogue of governesses came to an end in the Edwardian era, when fashion changed and people preferred sending their daughters to school rather than educating them at home. Toward the end of the nineteenth century the number of girls' schools increased rapidly and improved enormously. After the First World War the post of governess devolved to that of nursery governess or mother's help. Even before 1914 the benefits of being a school mistress as opposed to a governess were manifest, but marriage was always considered preferable to becoming a governess.

Though educational and employment opportunities for women had expanded during the period depicted by Conan Doyle in the canon – 1880 to 1914 – nonetheless he portrayed a rather old-fashioned view of a women's lot more typical of the mid-nineteenth century. There is no mention of university education for women, even in 'The Creeping Man' set in 'Camford', nor of their entry into the professions, except as governesses. Three governesses in his fiction are destined for marriage – Morstan, Smith and probably Dunbar – and one is already a widow – Burnet (Durando). The resourceful Violet Hunter becomes a successful headmistress. Holmes appears quite well informed about governesses' salaries, claiming the going rate to be about £50 per annum, or half of the overly generous salary Violet Smith earned and one third of that offered to Violet Hunter.

Employment

The increase of female employment was deterred by the development of the separate spheres of home and work, since women confined at home could do little to earn money.[112] Because of the cult of the Angel in the House, upper- and middle-class women were discouraged from working. It was felt that employment outside the home was likely to erode and/or corrode female sensibility. Working was not genteel and was considered socially déclassé. This attitude adversely affected single women with limited incomes or divorced women who needed to earn money to support themselves and their children. Gentlewomen who remained unmarried were regarded as social failures. 'They often had to live on a small pension from their families in obscure and lonely lodgings' or become a lady's companion, catering to the whims of a demanding mistress.[113] It was not only spinsters who needed to work to support themselves: deserted wives and those who left their husbands voluntarily had to find means to support themselves, as did impecunious widows. How was the recently divorced woman without much property of her own to live?

There was considerable prejudice against women working. Many people believed that women could never master any profession because their minds and health would break down.[114] Nevertheless, lack of opportunities for unmarried single women stimulated many of the reform crusades. In 1851 the census reported that there were 2.765 million unmarried women; by 1861 the number had increased to 2.959 million; and in 1871 the figure had risen to 3.228 million.[115] There were few options for educated women besides teaching and needlework, which yielded low wages. Thanks to Florence Nightingale, careers in nursing were slowly opening up, but women were not hired to serve as shop assistants or do secretarial work. Women writers assumed male noms des plume and female painters could not exhibit unless their male relations were artists. Aspiring female journalists could not find places, and no women could act as civil servants.[116] Working-class women frequently laboured in deplorably overcrowded and unhygienic premises. In London sweatshops dressmakers and milliners worked eighteen to twenty hours a day for months at a time, producing clothing for retail markets.[117]

In 1857, after the defeat of the Married Women's Property Bill, Mrs Barbara Bodichon started *The Englishwoman's Journal* to advocate expanding the opportunities for women to work. She not only endorsed employing women as clerks and nurses, but also advocated that women be allowed to qualify in the professions of medicine, law or architecture.[118] Mrs Bodichon and her friends were cognizant of the vital link between education and employment, so they set up a training centre, employment bureau and reading room in central London. They strove to gain entrance for middle-class women in respectable occupations like office and clerical work, as well as printing, telegraphy and hairdressing.[119]

Their success is reflected in Holmes' teasing remark to Watson in 1898 in 'The Retired Colourman', while chiding him for unsatisfactory reconnaissance: 'With your natural advantages ... every lady is your helper and accomplice. What about the girl at the post office?'[120]

In 1888 Mary Sutherland tells Holmes she earns two pence a page typewriting between twelve to fifteen pages per day. When he contends that a single woman could live comfortably on £60 per annum, she agrees.

Suffrage

Overarching the issues of education and employment in the struggle for the empowerment of women was the question of suffrage. No mention is made in Holmes' cases of the decades-long campaign, from the 1830s to 1918, for women to obtain the vote. The suffragist movement might as well not have existed, for no notice is taken. Conan Doyle opposed the women's suffrage campaign because he felt that the violent militancy of the suffragettes would lead to mob violence and the breakdown of social order. In addition, he believed that a woman should only qualify to vote if she paid her own taxes. Although he had no objections to women entering the professions and advocated more liberal terms for divorce, he did not embrace the cause for sexual equality in political terms.[121]

Conan Doyle's representation of female roles in society within Holmes' adventures seems anachronistic, but is false only as a sin of omission. No doubt one could find many examples between 1880 and 1914 of the traditional lifestyle presented in the stories. It must be granted that many of the values and attitudes dictating the status of women survived and continued to generate controversy well into the twentieth century – and even into the twenty-first.

CONCLUSION

It is generally acknowledged that the mystique of Sherlock Holmes is universal, but explaining it is a challenge. To answer the question 'Who is Sherlock, what is he, that all the world commends him?', this book analyses the literary and scientific influences on his character as well as the personal contributions of Arthur Conan Doyle himself – both imaginative and practical, conscious and unconscious. Writing it has been a voyage of discovery based, insofar as was possible, on empirical evidence in which myths, superstitions and factual errors have been examined and judged in order to understand the 'real' character of Sherlock Holmes – where he comes from and who he is. Of course, as Conan Doyle admits, Holmes evolves over time, becoming altogether less neurotic and more genially sociable. For example, despite his frequently articulated antifeminism, ultimately he displays empathy, concern and compassion for a great many women.

The second focus of this study is Holmes' professional world. He epitomises the role of consulting detective in the genre. The chronological scope of his investigations ranges from 1880 to 1914, a span of twenty-five years. The work of the police during this period was greatly enhanced by the introduction of a centralised bureau for the collection of records of habitual offenders, called Bertillon cards, complete with photographs. By the end of the nineteenth century techniques had been perfected for preserving footprints at a crime scene. When fingerprinting, the most infallible technique for identifying criminals, was introduced in 1901 Scotland Yard earned international respect. If this technique had been available to the police in 1888, they might have caught Jack the Ripper. By 1904 a reliable precipitin blood test had been discovered and adopted. In general, Lestrade and his colleagues are depicted as ignorant of these discoveries or hesitant to employ them. This is explicable in large part because forty-seven of Holmes' cases occur prior to 1900 and only thirteen afterward. The Murder Squad was not formed until 1907 and only two tales take place after that date. Progress is slow and institutional change is snail-like in pace. Moreover, want of proper internal coordination and lack of qualifications coupled with low retention rates also resulted in a mediocre police force.

Although it was a period of exciting developments in technology and forensic science, and although much is made of Holmes' scientific interests, he does not actually utilise many of the new instruments and techniques available to his counterparts at Scotland Yard at the turn of the century. He studies but does not attempt to take casts of footprints. He is not interested in fingerprints, the chief British contribution to criminal investigation at the time. He does not rely on his much-vaunted skill at chemistry to solve cases. He never even applies his own blood test to catch a villain. Nor does he avail himself of photography to record a crime scene, instead using his memory to register details.

Holmes relies principally on the intense observation of crime scenes, standard practice for CSIs today, from which he links details of trace evidence to form patterns of action, that is, sequences of events. He reconstructs the past and then draws logical inferences to form a hypothesis explaining means, opportunity and motive for the crime. Holmes' method of observation may be more 'scientific', but the essential process can be traced back to Poe's Dupin. However, Holmes applies it more broadly, to include human beings and their behaviour, thanks to Joe Bell. Holmes' great gift of intuitive insight into character, only partly attributable to Bell, enables him to imagine how an individual would behave, to anticipate his actions in certain circumstances, and thereby to entrap a villain. But the zeal for the chase and moral commitment to thwart crime, prevent injustice and protect innocence originate with Conan Doyle, who shared Holmes' vocation – the *real* Sherlock Holmes.

NOTES

All references to Sherlock Holmes stories are taken from *The Penguin Complete Sherlock Holmes*. London (2009).

1 Edgar Allan Poe: Generic Conventions

1. James O'Brien, *Scientific Sherlock Holmes*, p. 6; Martin Booth, *The Doctor and the Detective*, p. 104.
2. R. M. Morris, 'Crime Does Not Pay', *Police Detectives in History, 1750–1950*, Clive Emsley ed., p. 79; Martin Booth, p. 104.
3. Mathew Pearl, 'Introduction', *Murders in the Rue Morgue* (2006), p. x.
4. Arthur Conan Doyle, *Memories and Adventures*, Hodder, p. 69, Cambridge, p. 51.
5. W. J. Young, 'Origins of Sherlock Holmes', *British Medical Journal*, Vol. 2, No. 3842 (25 Aug 1934), pp. 374–5.
6. Anon., 'Conan Doyle as He Appears Here', *New York Times* (3 October 1894), p. 4.
7. Poe, 'Rue Morgue' in *Murders in the Rue Morgue* (2006), Pearl ed., p. 19.
8. *Ibid.*, p. 18.
9. *Ibid.*, p. 17.
10. Peter Costello, *Conan Doyle Detective*, p. 24.
11. Poe, 'Rue Morgue', pp. 21–2.
12. *Ibid.*, pp. 6, 29.

13. Poe, 'Marie Rogêt', *Rue Morgue*, p. 48.

14. *Ibid.*, pp. 65, 71–4.

15. Poe, 'Purloined Letter', *Rue Morgue* (2006), p. 90.

16. *Ibid.*, p. 94.

17. Conan Doyle, 'Copper Beeches', *The Penguin Complete Sherlock Holmes* (2009), p. 317.

18. *Ibid.*, 'Five Orange Pips', p. 219.

19. Richard Kopley, *Edgar Allan Poe and the Philadelphia Saturday News* (1991, passim.

20. *Ibid.*, pp. 7–8.

21. *Ibid.*, p. 11.

22. *Ibid.*, pp. 14–15.

23. *Ibid.*, pp. 8–9.

24. Poe, 'Rue Morgue', pp. 10–11.

25. Kopley, *P* III, p. 137.

26. *Ibid.*, *H* X, p. 62; *P* III, p. 16ff.

27. Poe, 'Rue Morgue', p. 17.

28. Costello, ix; cf J. D. Carr, *Life of Arthur Conan Doyle*, 'Bibliographical Sources, Notebooks and Diaries, Scrapbooks', pp. 341–2; R. L. Green, *Uncollected Sherlock Holmes*, p. 128.

29. Carr, pp. 285–95.

30. Joan Lock, *Dreadful Deeds and Awful Murders* (1990), pp. 167–70.

31. Costello, pp. 75, 222–3.

32. *Ibid.*, pp. 133–9; Charles Higham, *Adventures of Conan Doyle*, pp. 204–6.

33. Costello, p. 139.

34. *Ibid.*, pp. 133–8.

35. O'Brien, p. 6; cf Higham, pp. 41–3.

36. Poe, 'Rue Morgue', 'Marie Rogêt', 'Purloined Letter' passim.

37. Conan Doyle, 'Six Napoleons', p. 591.

38. *Ibid.*, 'Study in Scarlet', p. 41; 'Sign of Four', pp. 126, 128.

39. *Ibid.*, 'Red-Headed League', p. 184; 'Dying Detective', p. 941; 'Illustrious Client', p. 984; 'The Devil's Foot', p. 955 ff.

40. *Ibid.*, 'Five Orange Pips', p. 218; 'Stock-Broker's Clerk', p. 362.

41. Poe, 'Rue Morgue', p. 7.

42. *Ibid.*, 'Rue Morgue', pp. 6–7.

43. *Complete Poetry of John Milton*, John T. Shawcross, ed., pp. 79–80.

44. Poe, 'Rue Morgue', p. 7.

45. Conan Doyle, 'Resident Patient', p. 424.

46. *Ibid*., 'Study in Scarlet' p. 20; 'Sign of Four' (1891), pp. 89, 158; 'Scandal in Bohemia' (1888), p. 162; 'Yellow Face' (1884), p. 351; 'Missing Three-Quarter' (1897), p. 622.

47. Edward Brecher, *Consumer Reports*, ch. 35, p. 3.

48. J. Alexander Bell, 'The Use of Coca', *British Medical Journal*, Vol. I, No. 688 (7 March 1874), p. 305.

49. Robert Christison, 'Observations On The Effects Of Cuca, Or Coca, The Leaves Of Erythroxylon Coca', *British Medical Journal*, Vol. I, No. 800 (29 April 1876), pp. 527–31.

50. Conan Doyle, 'Yellow Face', p. 351.

51. *Ibid*., 'Missing Three-Quarter', p. 622.

52. *Ibid*., 'Musgrave Ritual', p. 386; 'Mazarin Stone', p. 1012.

53. *Ibid*., 'Case of Identity', p. 198; 'Copper Beeches', p. 322; 'Dancing Men', p. 511; 'Dying Detective', p. 932; 'Naval Treaty', p. 448; 'Shoscombe Old Place', p. 1102).

54. *Ibid*., 'Dying Detective, p. 934.

55. *Ibid*., 'Study in Scarlet', pp. 36; 'Red Circle', p. 913; 'Hound of the Baskervilles', p. 766.

56. *Ibid*., 'Musgrave Ritual', pp. 386; 'Red Circle', p. 901; 'Sussex Vampire', p. 1034; 'Veiled Lodger', p. 1095.

57. *Ibid*., 'Greek Interpreter', p. 435; Carr, p. 64. (cf Costello, Higham, Liebow re name of Sherrinford)

58. *Ibid*., 'Gloria Scott, p. 374; 'Greek Interpreter', p. 435; 'Musgrave Ritual', p. 388; 'Naval Treaty', p. 467; p. 'Solitary Cyclist', p. 532; 'Yellow Face', p. 351.

59. *Ibid*., 'Study in Scarlet', p. 22; 'Illustrious Client', p. 993; 'Empty House', p. 486.

60. *Ibid*., 'Musgrave Ritual', p. 387.

61. Poe, 'Rue Morgue', p. 6; 'Purloined Letter', p. 81 passim 87.

62. *Ibid*., 'Marie Rogêt', p. 36.

63. Conan Doyle, 'Study in Scarlet', pp. 16–7.

64. *Ibid*., 'Study in Scarlet', p. 15; 'Sign of Four', p. 90; cf 'Three Garridebs', p. 1053.

65. *Ibid*., 'Golden Pince Nez', p. 607; 'Cardbox Box', p. 888.

66. *Ibid*., 'Reigate Problem', 405–6; 'Black Peter', p. 569; 'Devil's Foot', p. 965.

67. *Ibid.*, 'Veiled Lodger', p. 1095.

68. Green quotes Conan Doyle from *Tit-Bits*, Vol. XXXIX, No. 1000 (15 December 1900), p. 287.

69. O'Brien, p. xiv.

70. Conan Doyle, 'Study in Scarlet', p. 21.

71. *Ibid.*, 'Study in Scarlet', p. 33; 'Sign of Four', p. 91.

72. *Ibid.*, 'Dancing Men', p. 522.

73. *Ibid.*, 'Case of Identity', p. 199.

74. *Ibid.*, 'Sign of Four', p. 91.

75. *Ibid.*, 'Cardboard Box', p. 896.

76. *Ibid.*, 'Sign of Four', p. 91; 'Creeping Man', p. 1080.

77. *Ibid.*, 'Bruce Partington Plans', p. 929.

78. *Ibid.*, 'Devil's Foot', pp. 955, 970.

79. *Ibid.*, 'Last Bow', p. 978.

80. Poe, 'Rue Morgue', pp. 7, 18, 19.

81. *Ibid.*, p. 7.

82. *Ibid.*, 'Marie Rogêt', p. 36; O'Brien, p. 7.

83. Conan Doyle, 'Study in Scarlet', p. 27; 'Sign of Four', pp. 89–90; 'Red-headed League', p. 185; 'Musgrave Ritual', p. 386; 'Bruce Partington Plans', pp. 920, 1071.

84. Poe, 'Purloined Letter', p. 81.

85. *Ibid.*, 'Purloined Letter', p. 84.

86. Conan Doyle, 'Red-headed League', p. 184.

87. *Ibid.*, 'Copper Beeches', p. 317.

88. *Ibid.*, 'Twisted Lip', p. 240; 'Devil's Foot', p. 960.

89. *Ibid.*, 'Devil's Foot', pp. 961, 970; 'Bruce Partington Plans', pp. 929, 931; 'Cardboard Box', p. 894.

90. *Ibid.*, 'Bruce Partington Plans', pp. 929, 931.

91. Poe, 'Rue Morgue', pp. 7, 9.

92. Conan Doyle, 'Cardboard Box, p. 889; 'Dancing Men', p. 511.

93. *Ibid.*, 'Mazarin Stone', p. 1017.

94. *Ibid.*, 'Sign of Four', pp. 96, 157; cf 'Greek Interpreter', p. 435.

95. *Ibid.*, pp. 96, 157.

96. Library Royal College of Surgeons of Edinburgh, Stisted Collection, GD 16/1/2/1/4.

97. Green, *Uncollected Sherlock Holmes*, p. 131.

98. Poe, 'Rue Morgue', pp. 3, 7; 'Sign of Four', pp. 89–90; 'Bruce Partington Plans', p. 917.

2 Joseph Bell: Investigator of Disease and Crime

1. Arthur Conan Doyle, *Memories and Adventures*, Hodder, p. 69, Cambridge, p. 51.
2. Ely Liebow, *Dr Joe Bell*, pp. 48–9.
3. *Ibid.*, p. 49.
4. *Ibid.*, p. 50.
5. *Ibid.*, p. 54.
6. *Ibid.*, pp. 53, 58, 76.
7. *Ibid.*, p. 68.
8. *Ibid.*, p. 79.
9. *Ibid.*, pp. 74, 166.
10. *Ibid.*, p. 88.
11. *Ibid.*, p. 101.
12. *Ibid.*, pp. 42, 119.
13. *Ibid.*, p. 125, cf. 140.
14. *Ibid.*, pp. 152–3, p. 157.
15. *Ibid.*, p. 152
16. *Ibid.*, pp. 118, 152.
17. *Ibid.*, p. 170.
18. *Ibid.*, p. 79.
19. *Ibid.*, p. 119; Irving Wallace, 'Real Sherlock Holmes', *Fabulous Originals*, pp. 35–42; E. J. Wagner, *Science of Sherlock Holmes*, p. 5.
20. Sydney Smith, *Mostly Murder*, pp. 38–9.
21. Liebow, *Dr Joe Bell*, p. 119.
22. *Ibid.*, p. 119, fn 43, 165 (December 1911), 584.
23. Anon., 'Interview with Joseph Bell', *Pall Mall Gazette*, LVII, No. 8900 (3 September 1893); Jessie M. E. Saxby, *Joseph Bell, An Appreciation by an Old Friend*, pp. 18–19.
24. [Lincoln Springfield], 'The Original Sherlock Holmes: An Interview with Dr Joseph Bell', *Pall Mall Gazette*, LVII, No. 8975 (28 December 1893), pp. 1–2.

25. Anon., *The Times*, No. 39708 (5 October 1911), p. 9; *The Times*, No. 39714 (12 October 1911), p. 11; Liebow, 119, fn. 110.
26. Wagner, p. 55.
27. Liebow, pp. 119–22; Wallace pp. 37–8; Costello pp. 26–8; Z. M. Hamilton, *Boston Medical and Surgical Journal*, No. 165 (December 1911), p. 584.
28. Wagner, p. 55.
29. Liebow, pp. 185–9; Costello, p. 26; Wallace, pp. 39–40.
30. Liebow, pp. 187–8.
31. *Ibid.* pp. 125–6.
32. *Ibid.*, p. 127.
33. Clement Gunn, *Leaves from the Life of a Country Doctor*, Edinburgh (1935); Liebow, p. 128.
34. Liebow, pp. 128–9.
35. Conan Doyle, *Memories and Adventures*, Hodder, p. 20, Cambridge, p. 15.
36. Liebow, p. 130, cf. fn 47.
37. [Lincoln Springfield], pp. 1–2.
38. Raymond Blathwayt, *The Bookman* (May 1892), pp. 50–51.
39. Library of the Royal College of Surgeons in Edinburgh, Stisted Bell Collection, correspondence GD 16/1/2/1–6, RSL1, Box B.
40. Harry How, 'A Day with Dr Conan Doyle', *The Strand Magazine*, IV (August 1892), pp. 182–7.
41. Conan Doyle, 'Study in Scarlet', p. 20.
42. Conan Doyle, *Memories and Adventures*, Hodder, p. 20, Cambridge, p. 15.
43. Liebow, p. 10.
44. Library of the Royal College of Surgeons in Edinburgh, Stisted Bell Collection, correspondence GD 16/1/2/1–5, RSL1, Box B; Wallace, pp. 34–5; Liebow, p. 174.
45. How, pp. 182–7.
46. [Lincoln Springfield], pp. 1–2.
47. Douglas Guthrie, 'Medicine and Detection: Dr Joseph Bell and Others', *Medicine Illustrated* III, No. 5 (May 1949), p. 225.
48. Handasyde (Emily Handasyde Buchanen), 'The Real Sherlock Holmes', *Good Words and Sunday Magazine*, XLIII (June 1902), pp. 159–63.

49. Library of the Royal College of Surgeons in Edinburgh, Stisted Bell Collection, correspondence GD 16/1/2/1–6, RSL1, Box B.
50. Green, *Uncollected Sherlock Holmes*, p. 23.
51. Library of the Royal College of Surgeons in Edinburgh, Stisted Bell Collection, correspondence GD 16/1/2/1–6, RSL 1, Box B.
52. *Ibid.*
53. [Lincoln Springfield], pp. 1–2; Henry Mills Aldis, 'The Original of Sherlock Holmes', *Harper's Weekly Magazine* (3 February 1894), p. 114.
54. Conan Doyle, *Memories and Adventures*, Hodder, p. 21, Cambridge, p. 16.
55. Joseph Bell, Review of *Adventures of Sherlock Holmes*, *Bookman* Vol. 32 (December 1892), pp. 79–80.
56. Aldis, p. 114.
57. Liebow, p. 10.
58. *Ibid.*, pp. 125, 211.
59. Saxby, pp. 13–14.
60. *Ibid.*, p. 24; Liebow, p. 180.
61. Conan Doyle, 'Study in Scarlet', pp. 31–2.
62. *Ibid.*, p. 32.

3 Arthur Conan Doyle: Sherlock Holmes Detects in the Real World

1. Green, 'Introduction', *Uncollected Sherlock Holmes*, pp. 10–13.
2. Adrian Conan Doyle, *The True Conan Doyle*, p. 16.
3. *Ibid.*, p. 14.
4. *Ibid.*, p. 16.
5. Jean Conan Doyle, 'Conan Doyle *Was* Sherlock Holmes', p. 575.
6. Conan Doyle, *Memories and Adventures*, Hodder, p. 112, Cambridge, p. 79; Costello, pp. 147–9.
7. Hamilton, p. 584; Young, pp. 374–5; Costello, p. 24.
8. Anon., 'Conan Doyle as He Appears Here', *New York Times* (3 October 1894), p. 4.

9. Conan Doyle, *Memories and Adventures*, Hodder, p. 74, Cambridge, p. 51.

10. *Ibid.*, *Memories and Adventures*, Hodder p. 4, Cambridge, p. 51; Conan Doyle, 'Study in Scarlet', pp. 24–5; 'Cardboard Box', pp. 888–9.

11. Blathwayt, p. 50; How, pp. 182–7; Conan Doyle, 'The Truth about Sherlock Holmes', *Collier's Weekly*, New York, LXXII (29 December 1923), p. 28.

12. Conan Doyle, 'Conan Doyle Tells the True Story of Sherlock Holmes', *Tit-Bits*, Vol. XXXIX (5 December 1900), p. 287.

13. *Ibid.*, *Memories and Adventures*, Hodder, p. 26, Cambridge, 16.

14. Adrian Conan Doyle, p. 15.

15. Arthur Conan Doyle, *Memories and Adventures*, Hodder, p. 100, Cambridge, p. 69.

16. *Ibid.*, Hodder, pp. 100–01, Cambridge, p. 70.

17. Costello, p. 13.

18. Conan Doyle, 'Gelseminum as a Poison', *British Medical Journal* (20 September 1879), p. 14.

19. Costello, pp. 13–14; Conan Doyle, 'Study in Scarlet', p. 137.

20. Costello, pp. 19–20.

21. *Ibid.*, p. 21.

22. *Ibid.*, pp. 22, 50–54, 58–63.

23. *Ibid.*, p. 21, *Centenary Banquet of Madame Tussaud's*, London (1903).

24. Green, *Uncollected Sherlock Holmes*, p. 30; Costello, p. 23.

25. *Ibid.*, p. 128; Carr, pp. 341–2.

26. Ingleby Oddie, *Inquest: A Coroner Looks Back*, pp. 57–62; Costello, pp. 80–81.

27. Green, *Uncollected Sherlock Holmes*, p. 116, cites '"Jack the Ripper", How "Sherlock Holmes" would have tracked him', *Evening News*, Portsmouth (4 July 1894).

28. Oddie, pp. 43–57; Costello, p. 71; Stephen Wade, *Conan Doyle and the Crimes Club*, pp. 9–10.

29. *Ibid.*, 44; *Ibid.* p. 73.

30. *Ibid.*, p. 73; *Ibid.*, p. 45; Andrew Rose, *Lethal Witness*, pp. 23–4.

31. Oddie, pp. 58–62; Costello, pp. 79, 84; Green, *Uncollected Sherlock Holmes*, p. 117.

32. Costello, p. 84, cf p. 87.

33. *Ibid.*, p. 150; Carr, p. 252.

34. Costello, p. 152.

35. *Ibid.*, pp. 150–53.

36. Blathwayt, p. 50; How, pp. 182–7; Library of the Royal College of Surgeons in Edinburgh, Stisted Bell Collection, correspondence GD 16/1/2/1–6, RSL 1, Box B.

37. Anon., 'Dr Conan Doyle: A Character Sketch', *Cassell's Saturday Journal*, XI (15 February 1893), p. 422; Green, *Uncollected Sherlock Holmes*, p. 68; Costello, pp. 33–6.

38. Anon., 'The Conan Doyle Banquet at the Authors Club', *Queen* (4 July 1896), C 19.

39. *Ibid.*, p. 37; Green, *Uncollected Sherlock Holmes*, p. 114.

40. Anon., 'Theatres', *Candid Friend* (9 November 1901), p. 74; Anon., 'Concerning Conan Doyle', *Collier's Weekly*, XLI (15 August 1908), p. 2.

41. Costello, pp. 42–3, cf Charles Higham, p. 173.

42. John Saxon, 'The Mystery of the Stolen Jewels', *Great Stories from Real Life*, Max Pemberton ed., Vol. II, pp. 294–6.

43. Michael Gibson and Richard Lancelyn Green, *Unknown Conan Doyle: Letters to the Press*, pp. 50, 352; Costello, pp. 39–41.

44. Pierre Nordan, *Conan Doyle*, pp. 104–14; Costello, pp. 197–20; Daniel Stashower, *The Teller of Tales: The Life of Arthur Conan Doyle*, pp. 317–9, 322–31; Andrew Lycett, *Conan Doyle: The Man Who Created Sherlock Holmes*, pp. 340–41).

45. Costello, pp. 250–3; Helen Normanton, 'The Crowborough Murders', *Great Unsolved Murders*, pp. 27–34.

46. Conan Doyle, 'Sir Arthur Conan Doyle and the Thorne Case', *Morning Post* (21 April 1925), p. 9.

47. Costello, pp. 49–51.

48. Conan Doyle, *Memories and Adventures*, Hodder, pp. 215–22, Cambridge, pp. 154–8; Booth, pp. 263–4; Lycett, p. 303; Stashower, p. 254.

49. Conan Doyle, *Memories and Adventures*, Hodder, 216–7; Cambridge, p. 154.

50. Booth, p. 263; Costello, p. 100; Stashower, pp. 255–60.

51. Conan Doyle, *Memories and Adventures*, Hodder, p. 218, Cambridge, p. 155.

52. Booth, p. 265.

53. Stashower, p. 259.

54. *Ibid.,* pp. 258–9.

55. Conan Doyle, 'Study in Scarlet', p. 27; 'Scandal in Bohemia', p. 163.

56. Costello, p. 99; Lycett, p. 302; Stashower, p. 255.

57. Conan Doyle, *Memories and Adventures*, Hodder, p. 217, Cambridge, p. 154.

58. Costello, p. 99.

59. *Ibid.,* pp. 108–9.

60. Booth, p. 264; Carr, p. 180; Costello, pp. 109–11; Nordon, p. 117; Ronald Pearsall, *Conan Doyle: A Biographical Solution,* p. 112.

61. Carr, p. 180; Costello, pp. 109–10; Higham, p. 100.

62. Costello, pp. 110–11 quotes text.

63. Carr, p. 180.

64. Costello, p. 111.

65. *Ibid.,* p. 111; Booth, p. 264; Carr, p. 180; Pearsall, p. 112; Stashower, pp. 255–6.

66. Costello, pp. 97–8; Carr, pp. 179, 181.

67. *Ibid.,* pp. 101, 105; *Ibid.,* p. 181.

68. Conan Doyle, *Memories and Adventures*, Cambridge, p. 155; Carr, p. 179; Costello, p. 100; Lycett, pp. 302–4.

69. Carr, pp. 179–81; Costello, p. 101.

70. *Ibid.,* pp. 179–80; *Ibid.* , pp. 99–100; Booth, p. 264; Conan Doyle, *Memories and Adventures*, Hodder, p. 216, Cambridge, pp. 154–5; Stashower, p. 255.

71. Lycett, p. 303

72. Carr, pp. 181–3; Costello, pp. 102–4.

73. *Ibid.* p. 183; *Ibid.,* p. 105.

74. *Ibid.,* p. 183; *Ibid.,* p. 105.

75. Carr, p. 184; Costello, p. 105; Richard and Molly Whittington-Egan, *The Story of Mr George Edalji,* p. 24.

76. Carr, pp. 182–3; Costello, p. 103.

77. *Ibid.,* p. 184; *Ibid.,* p. 103.

78. *Ibid.,* p. 184; *Ibid.,* pp. 105–6, cf. 73–4; Stashower, p. 256.

79. *Ibid.,* p. 184; *Ibid.,* p. 105; *Ibid.,* 256.

80. *Ibid.*, pp. 184–6; *Ibid.*, p. 106; Whittington-Egan, Introduction, p. 15.

81. Booth, p. 264; Costello, pp. 104, 106.

82. *Ibid.*, pp. 264–5; *Ibid.*, p. 107; Green, *Uncollected Sherlock Holmes*, p. 118.

83. Costello, p 107.

84. Booth, p. 265; Costello, p. 107; Carr, p. 18; Green, *Uncollected Sherlock Holmes*, pp. 118–19; Gibson and Green, p. 130.

85. Carr, p. 18; Costello, p. 96; Stashower, p. 257.

86. Costello, pp. 96, 106–7.

87. Lycett, pp. 302–4.

88. Carr, p. 187; Whittington-Egan, Introduction, p. 17.

89. Carr, pp. 185–6; Costello, pp. 107–8; Conan Doyle, *Memories and Adventures*, Hodder, pp. 216–17, Cambridge, pp. 154–6; Stashower, p. 257.

90. Conan Doyle, *Memories and Adventures*, Hodder, p. 217, Cambridge, p. 155; Carr, p. 186; Costello, pp. 107–8.

91. Costello, p. 112.

92. Conan Doyle, *Memories and Adventures*, Hodder, p. 218, Cambridge, p. 155.

93. Booth, p. 265; Carr, pp. 186–7; Costello, pp. 112–13; Stashower, p. 258.

94. Whittington-Egan, p. 35–78; Green, *Uncollected Sherlock Holmes*, pp. 118–19.

95. Whitington-Egan, p. 75; Carr, p. 187; Costello, p. 113; Lycett, p. 302.

96. Booth, p. 265.

97. Green, *Uncollected Sherlock Holmes*, p. 119.

98. Costello, p. 112.

99. *Ibid.*, 112; Green, *Uncollected Sherlock Holmes*, p. 119; Booth, p. 266; Carr, p. 229; Nordon, p. 123.

100. Booth, p. 266; Costello, p. 113; Conan Doyle, *Memories and Adventures*, Hodder, p. 219, Cambridge, p. 156.

101. *Ibid.*, Hodder, pp. 219–21, Cambridge, p. 157; Costello, pp. 114–15.

102. Carr, p. 188; Costello, p. 120.

103. Costello, p. 115, cf. p. 120.

104. Carr, p. 188; Costello, p. 120.

105. Carr calls the perpetrators 'Hudson' to avoid libel charges, pp. 188–90; cf Costello, p. 122.

106. Costello, p. 116.

107. *Ibid.*, p. 118.

108. *Ibid.*, p. 118.

109. Carr, pp. 232–3; Conan Doyle, *Memories and Adventures*, Hodder, pp. 200–21, Cambridge, p. 157.

110. Costello, 120.

111. *Ibid.*, p. 119.

112. Green, *Uncollected Sherlock Holmes*, p. 120; Whittington-Egan, p. 111.

113. *Ibid.*, p. 119; *Ibid*, p. 19; Booth, p. 266; Carr, pp. 191–2; Costello, p. 114.

114. Costello, p. 112; Conan Doyle, *Memories and Adventures*, Hodder, p. 219, Cambridge, p. 156; Carr, p. 234; Nordon, p. 126.

115. Gibson and Green, p. 136; Lycett, p. 304.

116. Carr, p. 219 ff.; Costello, p. 114; Conan Doyle, *Memories and Adventures*, Hodder, p. 219, Cambridge, p. 156.

117. Carr, p. 234.

118. Whittington-Egan, pp. 19–20, 83–4.

119. *Ibid.*, pp. 82–90.

120. *Ibid.*, pp. 90–100.

121. *Ibid.*, pp. 100–08.

122. *Ibid.*, pp. 110–24; Carr, p. 234; Conan Doyle, *Memories and Adventures*, Hodder, p. 221, Cambridge, p. 157; Green, *Uncollected Sherlock Holmes*, p. 119; Nordon, pp. 125–6.

123. Costello, p. 121.

124. Green, *Uncollected Sherlock Holmes*, p. 119.

125. Nordon, p. 126.

126. Carr, pp. 232–3; Costello, p. 122.

127. *Ibid.*, p. 122; Conan Doyle, *Memories and Adventures*, Hodder, p. 221, Cambridge, pp. 157–8.

128. *Ibid.*, Hodder, p. 221, Cambridge, p. 157.

129. Green, *Uncollected Sherlock Holmes*, p. 120.

130. Conan Doyle, *Memories and Adventures*, Hodder, p. 220; Cambridge, p. 156.

131. *Ibid.*, Hodder, p. 220, Cambridge, p. 156; Green, *Uncollected Sherlock Holmes*, p. 120, fn. 245; Stashower, p. 259.

132. Costello, pp. 126–8.

133. *Ibid.*, pp. 129–30.

134. *Ibid.*, pp. 156–8; Nordon, p. 129; Carr, pp. 261–3.

135. *Ibid.*, pp. 158–60 passim; *Ibid.*, pp. 263–4; *Ibid.*, pp. 130–31.

136. Carr, p. 264; Nordon, p. 130.

137. Green, *Uncollected Sherlock Holmes*, p. 122; Carr, p. 265; Nordon, p. 132.

138. Carr, p. 266.

139. *Ibid.*, p. 266; Nordon, p. 133.

140. Carr, pp. 266–7.

141. Costello, p. 160.

142. *Ibid.*, p. 160.

143. Green, *Uncollected Sherlock Holmes*, p. 122.

144. *Ibid.*, pp. 122–3; Costello, p. 161; Carr, pp. 290–91.

145. Conan Doyle, 'The Oscar Slater Case', Letter to the Editor, *The Spectator* (25 July 1914), p. 127; Costello, pp. 160–61.

146. Booth, p. 343.

147. Nordon, pp. 134–5; Costello, p. 161.

148. Costello, p. 161; Green, *Uncollected Sherlock Holmes*, p. 123; Booth, p. 344.

149. Costello, p. 161.

150. Green, *Uncollected Sherlock Holmes*, p. 123; Costello, pp. 161–2; Nordon, p. 135.

151. Costello, p. 162.

152. Booth, pp. 346–7.

153. Green, *Uncollected Sherlock Holmes*, p. 123.

154. *Ibid.*, pp. 123–4; Costello, p. 162.

155. *Ibid.*, p. 124; *Ibid.*, p. 162; Nordon, p. 137; Carr, pp. 332–3; Booth pp. 345–6.

156. Costello, p. 162.

157. *Ibid.*, p. 169.

158. Nordon, p. 138.

159. Costello, p. 292.

4 Sherlock Holmes and the Metropolitan Police

1. Conan Doyle, 'A Study in Scarlet', p. 24.

2. *Ibid.* 'Sign of Four', p. 90.

3. *Ibid.*, 'Bruce Partington Plans', p. 928.

4. *Ibid.*, 'Three Gables', pp. 1029–30.

5. *Ibid.*, 'Retired Colourman', p. 1119.

6. *Ibid.*, 'Three Garridebs', p. 1051.

7. Vincent Starrett, *Private Life of Sherlock Holmes*, p. 87.

8. Brad Keefauver, 'A Basic Timeline of Terra 221b' (2001),
cf. William S. Baring-Gould, *Sherlock Holmes of Baker Street*
(1962).

9. George Dilnot, *Scotland Yard: Its History and Organization
1829–1929* (1929), p. 15, cf. pp. 164–6.

10. Martin Fido and Keith Skinner, *Official Encyclopedia of
Scotland Yard* (1999), p. 49.

11. Dilnot (1929), pp. 166–7.

12. Dilnot, *Scotland Yard: The Methods and Organisation of
the Metropolitan Police* (1915), p. 111, cf. Dilnot, *Scotland Yard*
(1929), pp. 167–8.

13. Dilnot (1915), pp. 112–4; Dilnot (1929), p. 168.

14. Dilnot (1929), p. 168; Friends of the Metropolitan Police
Historical Collection, Met Police Timeline 1829–1899.

15. Conan Doyle, 'Sign of Four', p. 124.

16. Dilnot (1929), p. 30.

17. Dilnot (1929), pp. 12–14, 32–3; Morris, pp. 79, 81–3.

18. Dilnot (1929), p. 10.

19. *Ibid.*, p. 10.

20. *Ibid.*, p. 12–4.

21. J. M. Beattie, 'Early Detection: The Bow Street Runners in
Late Eighteenth Century London', pp. 21–2; Jerry White, *London
in the Nineteenth Century* (2007), pp. 383–4; Alan Moss &
Keith Skinner, *Victorian Detective* (2013), pp. 6–7; 'Bow Street
Runners', Wikipedia, passim.

22. Dilnot (1929), pp. 14–15.

23. *Ibid.*, p. 14.

24. White, p. 384; Proceedings of the Old Baily 1674–1913,
London 1800–1913; Dilnot (1929), p. 16.

25. Beattie, pp. 28–30; Dilnot (1929), p. 18; White, pp. 384–5; P. T. Smith, *Policing Victorian London*, p. 64.

26. Dilnot (1929), pp. 16–18; P. T. Smith, p. 64; White, p. 389.

27. Dilnot (1929), p. 30; Belton Cobb, *The First Detectives*, p. 30.

28. Dilnot (1929), p. 25; White, p. 389.

29. Dilnot (1929), pp. 29–30.

30. Dilnot (1915), p. 17, cf. Dilnot (1929), pp. 29–30.

31. Dilnot (1929), pp. vi, 39; Petrow, p. 91; Douglas Gordon Browne, *The Rise of Scotland Yard*, p. 85.

32. Dilnot (1929), p. 17.

33. Morris, p. 79; Beattie, p. 31.

34. Morris, pp. 82–3.

35. Dilnot (1929), pp. 31–2; Cobb, pp. 12, 38–40.

36. Cobb, p. 88.

37. Fido and Skinner, pp. 226–7; Dilnot (1929), pp. 32–4, 41; Cobb, p. 40; Browne, pp. 81, 86–7.

38. Dilnot (1929), p. 41; Moss and Skinner, *Scotland Yard Files* (2006), pp. 14–15.

39. Fido and Skinner, p. 227; Cobb, pp. 38–40.

40. Moss and Skinner (2006), p. 14, cf. Fido and Skinner, p. 71; Dilnot (1929), pp. 40–41.

41. Dilnot (1929), pp. 40–42.

42. Cobb, p. 56; Moss and Skinner (2006), p. 15.

43. Morris, pp. 79–80; Browne, pp. 12–3, 204; Stephen Wade, *Plain Clothes & Sleuths*, p. 50.

44. Morris, p. 81; Moss & Skinner (2013), pp. 16–17.

45. Wade, p. 38; Joan Lock, *Dreadful Deeds and Awful Murders* (1990), pp. 51–9, cf. *Scotland Yard's First Cases* (2011), pp. 41–7; Browne, pp. 160–9; Moss and Skinner (2006). p. 21.

46. Morris, p. 80.

47. Cobb, pp. 185–203; Wade, p. 39; Lock (1990), pp. 64–8, cf. Lock (2011), pp. 48–50; Browne, pp. 183–203; Morris, pp. 80–81; Moss & Skinner (2013), pp. 14–15.

48. Wade, pp. 36–8.

49. *Ibid.*, pp. 40, 38.

50. P. T. Smith, *Policing Victorian London*, pp. 65–6; Stefan Petrow, 'The Rise of the Detective in London 1869–1914', p. 92; Dilnot (1929), p. 44.

51. P. T. Smith, pp. 65–6, 70–71; Lock (2011), pp. 21–2; Dilnot (1929), pp. 44–8; Browne, pp. 104–7; Cobb, pp. 91–2.

52. P. T. Smith., pp. 62, 65, 67.

53. *Ibid.*, p. 67; Petrow, p. 92.

54. Morris, p. 81; Moss & Skinner (2013), p. 17.

55. Dilnot (1929), p. 44; Wade, p. 40; Lock (1990), p. 69; Moss & Skinner (2013), pp. 16–17; Petrow, p. 92; P. T. Smith, p. 61; Morris, pp. 81–2.

56. P. T. Smith, p. 62.

57. Morris, pp. 81–2; Moss & Skinner (2013), p. 21; P. T. Smith, p. 63; Browne, p. 123; Wade, pp. 40–41.

58. Moss & Skinner (2013), p. 29; P. T. Smith, p. 63; Morris, pp. 84–5.

59. Conan Doyle, 'Empty House', p. 490; P. T. Smith, p. 67.

60. Petrow, p. 102.

61. Kate Colquhoun, *Mr Briggs' Hat*, passim; 'First Railway Murder in Britain', *British Transport Police History Group*, [www.btphg.org.uk/?page_id=3108].

62. P. T. Smith, pp. 71–3; Moss & Skinner (2013), pp. 33–4, 36; Wade, pp. 86–9; re. conflict between prison governor and Mayne, cf. Lock (1990), pp. 177–9; Browne, pp. 141–3.

63. Morris, p. 83; Browne, pp. 142–3.

64. Petrow, pp. 92–3; P. T. Smith, pp. 62, 68.

65. Morris, p. 83.

66. Petrow, p. 93.

67. *Ibid.*, pp. 93–4.

68. Moss & Skinner (2013), pp. 29–31; Browne, pp. 183–90; Dilnot, *Trial of the Detectives* (1929), pp. 11–56, cf. Dilnot (1929), pp. 233–43; Lock (1990), pp. 185–6, cf. Lock, *Scotland Yard Casebook* (1993), pp. 71–4, 75–8.

69. Petrow, pp. 93–4; Morris, p. 83.

70. *Ibid.*, pp. 94–5; *Ibid.*, p. 83.

71. *Ibid.*, pp. 83–4.

72. Haia Shpayer-Makov, 'Explaining the Rise and Success of Detective Memoirs in Britain', p. 103.

73. Friends of the Metropolitan Police Collection, Met Police Timeline 1829–1899.

74. Morris, pp. 84–5; Moss & Skinner (2013), p. 29.

75. Morris, pp. 84–5; P. T. Smith, p. 69.

76. Morris, p. 86.

77. *Ibid.*, pp. 85–6.

78. Petrow, p. 95.

79. *Ibid.*, pp. 94–5.

80. *Ibid.*, pp. 95–6; cf. P. T. Smith, p. 69; Morris, p. 87.

81. P. T. Smith, p. 69; cf. Petrow, p. 95; Fido and Skinner, p. 273; Moss & Skinner (2006), p. 273; Moss & Skinner (2013), p. 29.

82. Morris, pp. 87–8; Fido and Skinner, p. 274; Dilnot (1929), p. 250; Moss & Skinner (2013), p. 29.

83. Petrow, p. 95; Fido and Skinner, p. 274.

84. Friends of the Metropolitan Police Historical Collection, Met Police Timeline 1829–1899.

85. P. T. Smith, p. 69; Petrow, p. 98.

86. Shpayer-Makov, p. 118.

87. *Ibid.*

88. Lock (1993), pp. 188–93.

89. Dilnot (1915), p. 32 ff.

90. Friends of the Metropolitan Police Historical Collection, Met Police Timeline 1829–1899.

91. Lock (1993), p. 164; Moss & Skinner (2006), pp. 64–9.

92. Dilnot (1929), pp. 188–90; Moss & Skinner (2006), p.69; Stephen Wade, *Conan Doyle and the Crimes Club* (2013), p.5.

93. Moss and Skinner (2006), pp. 83–105.

94. J. H. H. Gaute and Robin O'Dell, *The Murderers' Who's Who*, passim.

95. Ibid.

96. Lock (1993), pp. 191–3; (see Chapter 4).

97. Dilnot (1915), p. 42.

98. Ibid., p. 24.

99. Basil Thomson, Queer People, pp. 1–2.

100. Frederick Porter Wensley, *Forty Years at Scotland Yard*, p. 68.

101. Shpayer-Makov, p. 125.

102. James Berrett, *When I Was at Scotland Yard*, p. 102.

5 Advances in Detection: Technology and Forensic Science

1. 'Forensic Science', Wikipedia, p. 1.
2. *Ibid.*
3. Costello, pp. 227, 231.
4. *Ibid.*, 227, 231.
5. Wagner, p. 149.
6. Costello, p. 231.
7. Harry Ashton-Wolfe, 'The Debt of the Police to Detective Fiction', *Illustrated News* (27 February 1932), pp. 320, 328.
8. Moss & Skinner, p. 29; Petrow, p. 93.
9. Wagner, p. 99.
10. 'Fingerprinting', Wikipedia, p. 1.
11. Wagner, p. 101; O'Brien, pp. 51–2.
12. *Ibid.*, pp. 102; 'Fingerprinting', Wikipedia', p. 15.
13. *Ibid.*, pp. 103–4.
14. *Ibid.*, p. 104.
15. 'Henry Classification System', Wikipedia, p. 2.
16. Wagner, pp. 105–6; 'Fingerprints', Wikipedia, pp. 5, 16; O'Brien, p. 52; Lock, *Scotland Yard Casebook*, pp. 167.
17. Lock (1993), p. 168.
18. *Ibid.*, pp. 168–71.
19. Wagner, pp. 106–7.
20. *Ibid.*, p. 107.
21. *Ibid.*, pp. 141–2.
22. *Ibid.*, p. 144.
23. 'Bertillon', Wikipedia, p. 2.
24. 'Forensic Pathology', Wikipedia, pp. 1–2.
25. Wagner, p. 5.
26. *Ibid.*, pp. 6–7.
27. *Ibid.*, p. 8.
28. 'Charles Meymott Tidy', Wikipedia, p. 1.
29. Rose, pp. 23–4.
30. Douglas Gordon Browne and Tom Tullet, *Bernard Spilsbury: Famous Cases of the Great Pathologist*, pp. 38–54.
31. Rose, p. 24.
32. *Ibid.*, p. 24.

33. Rose, pp. 43–9; Browne and Tullet, pp. 89–91.

34. Conan Doyle, 'Study in Scarlet', p. 18.

35. Christine Huber, 'The Sherlock Holmes Blood Test: The Solution to a Century-Old Mystery', *Baker Street Journal*, Vol. 37, No. 4 (December 1987), p. 216.

36. *Ibid.*, pp. 214–20.

37. Kate Colquhoun, *Mr Briggs Hat*, pp. 47, 204, 208.

38. Raymond McGowan, 'Sherlock Holmes and Forensic Chemistry', *Baker Street Journal*, Vol. 37, No. 1 (March 1987), pp. 10–14.

39. *Ibid.*, pp. 13–14.

40. *Ibid.*, pp. 13–14.

41. Huber, pp. 214–20.

42. *Ibid.*, pp. 218–19.

43. *Ibid.*, p. 220.

44. Wagner, pp. 186–7, 189; Sue Bell, ed., *Oxford Dictionary of Forensic Science*, p. 272.

45. Wagner, pp. 200–01.

46. *Ibid.*, p. 147–8.

47. *Ibid.*, p. 149.

48. *Ibid.*, p. 158.

49. *Ibid.*, pp. 159–62.

50. 'Questioned Document Examination', Wikipedia, p. 2.

51. Wagner, pp. 162–4.

52. *Ibid.*, p. 167.

6 Sherlock Holmes and the Fair Sex

1. 'Greek Interpreter', p. 435.

2. 'The Five Orange Pips', p. 218.

3. 'The Sign of Four', p. 157.

4. Library Royal College of Surgeons of Edinburgh, Stisted Collection, GD 16/1/2/14.

5. 'The Sign of Four', p. 96.

6. Green, *Uncollected Sherlock Holmes*, pp. 330–1.

7. 'The Sign of Four', p. 96.

8. 'The Lion's Mane', p. 1088.
9. 'The Sign of Four', p. 90.
10. 'The Copper Beeches', pp. 316–17.
11. *Ibid.*, p. 317.
12. 'The Solitary Cyclist', p. 531.
13. 'Disappearance of Lady Frances Carfax', p. 946.
14. 'The Hound of the Baskervilles', p. 741.
15. 'Illustrious Client', p. 984.
16. 'The Devil's Foot', p. 965.
17. 'The Three Garidebbs', p. 1053.
18. 'His Last Bow', p. 980.
19. 'The Sign of Four', p. 129.
20. 'The Illustrious Client', p. 988.
21. 'The Second Stain', p. 657.
22. 'The Disappearance of Lady Frances Carfax', pp. 942–3.
23. 'The Case of Identity', p. 196.
24. 'The Speckled Band', p. 259.
25. *Ibid.*, p. 263.
26. 'The Abbey Grange', pp. 637–8.
27. 'The Problem of Thor Bridge', p. 1068.
28. 'The Red Circle', p. 902.
29. 'The Priory School', p. 558.
30. 'The Second Stain', p. 664.
31. *Ibid.*, p. 663.
32. *Ibid.*, p. 664.
33. 'Charles Augustus Milverton, p. 574.
34. *Ibid.*, p. 582.
35. 'The Speckled Band', pp. 268–9.
36. 'The Copper Beeches', p. 329.
37. 'The Naval Treaty', p. 462.
38. *Ibid.*, pp. 462–3.
39. *Ibid.*, pp. 366, 468.
40. 'The Dying Detective', p. 932.
41. 'The Abbey Grange', p. 645.
42. 'The Copper Beeches', p. 322.
43. 'The Illustrious Client', p. 990.
44. *Ibid.*, p. 992.
45. 'The Golden Pince-Nez', p. 617.

46. 'The Sign of Four', p. 124.

47. 'Charles Augustus Milverton', p. 576.

48. 'The Dying Detective', p. 932.

49. *The Bible*, Mark 10:9.

50. 'The Second Stain', p. 659.

51. 'The Three Gables', p. 1031.

52. 'The Hound of the Baskervilles', pp. 709, 713.

53. *Ibid.*, p. 766.

54. *Ibid.*, p. 759.

55. 'The Problem of Thor Bridge', p. 1060.

56. *Ibid.*, p. 1057.

57. *Ibid.*, pp. 1061–2.

58. 'The Sussex Vampire', p. 1038.

59. Susan Rice, 'Doyle's Women', *Baker Street Journal*, Vol. 59, No. 4 (Winter 2009) pp. 10–17.

60. All further references to the fictional timeline will be taken from Brad Kefauver's electronic 'A Basic Timeline of Terra 221B', 2001.)

61. Melissa Phillips, *The Ascent of Woman*, p. 64.

62. *Ibid.*, pp. 4–5, 23.

63. *Ibid.*, pp. 23, 99.

64. *Ibid.*, pp. 5, 22–5.

65. *Ibid.*, pp. 5, 25.

66. *Ibid.*, pp. 25–6.

67. *Ibid.*, p. 64.

68. 'The Copper Beeches', p. 327.

69. 'The Beryl Coronet', p. 309.

70. 'The Lion's Mane', p. 1088.

71. 'The Sign of Four', p. 115.

72. *Ibid.*, p. 116.

73. Phillips, p. 69.

74. *Ibid.*, p. 24.

75. *Ibid.*, p. 57.

76. *Ibid.*, pp. 55, 69.

77. *Ibid.*, p. 57.

78. 'The Lion's Mane', p. 1088.

79. 'The Dancing Men', p. 524.

80. Phillips, p. 99.

81. *Ibid.*, pp. 27–8, 93.

82. *Ibid.*, p. 28.

83. 'Black Peter', p. 560.

84. 'The Hound of the Baskervilles', p. 759.

85. Phillips, p. 27.

86. *Ibid.*, p. 29.

87. William Blackstone's *Commentaries on the Laws of England* (1847) cited in Phillips, pp. 28–9.

88. John Stuart Mill's *The Subjugation of Women* (1869) cited in Phillips, p. 99.

89. Phillips, pp. 106, 141, 210.

90. *Ibid.*, pp. 30, 211.

91. *Ibid.*, pp. 69–70, 211.

92. *Ibid.*, p. 92.

93. *Ibid.*, p. 30.

94. 'Divorce Law' in Wikipedia.

95. *The Bible*, Mark 10:9.

96. Phillips, pp. 30–2.

97. *Ibid.*, p. 42.

98. *Ibid.*, pp. 42–3, 210.

99. *Ibid.*, pp. 210–11.

100. *Ibid.*, p. 309.

101. Lycett, p. 210; Stashower, p. 341.

102. 'The Hound of the Baskervilles', p. 119.

103. 'The Abbey Grange', p. 275.

104. Phillips, pp. 3, 22–3.

105. Katherine West's *Chapter of Governesses: A Study of the Governess in English Fiction from 1800 to 1949*; B. J. Rahn's 'A Gaggle of Literary Governesses' passim; *A Gaggle of Governesses*, Pam Bruxner and Bob Ellis eds, London: Sherlock Holmes Society of London (7 September 1997), pp. 59–63.

106. Phillips, p. 105.

107. *Ibid.*, p. 44.

108. *Ibid.*, p. 44; Rahn, p. 60.

109. Phillips, p. 105.

110. *Ibid.*, p. 195.

111. *Ibid.*, p. 105.

112. *Ibid.*, p. 21.

113. *Ibid.*, p. 20.
114. *Ibid.*, pp. 20–21.
115. *Ibid.*, p. 20.
116. *Ibid.*, p. 43.
117. *Ibid.*, p. 21.
118. *Ibid.*, p. 43.
119. *Ibid.*, pp. 43–4.
120. *Ibid.*, p. 244.
121. Stashower, p. 294.

BIBLIOGRAPHY

General Bibliography

Adam, H[argrave] L[ee]. *C.I.D. Behind the Scenes at Scotland Yard*. London: Sampson, Low, Marston & Co. (n.d.) [Chp. 10, 1905 Stratton brothers case]

Baring-Gould, William S. *Sherlock Holmes of Baker Street*. New York: Bramhall House (1962).

Beattie, J. M. 'Early Detection: The Bow Street Runners in Late Eighteenth Century London', *Police Detectives in History, 1750–1950*. Clive Emsley ed. Aldershot, Hants.: Ashgate (2006).

Beckson, Karl. *London in the 1890s: A Cultural History*. New York: W. W. Norton (1992).

Bell, Susan. *Dictionary of Forensic Medicine*. Oxford: Oxford University Press (2012).

Berrett, James. *When I Was at Scotland Yard*. London: Sampson, Low, Marston & Co. (n.d.)

Booth, Martin. *The Doctor and the Detective*. New York: Thomas Dunne Books, 1997.

Browne, Douglas Gordon. *The Rise of Scotland Yard: A History of the Metropolitan Police*. London: George G. Harrap (1956).

_____ and Tom Tullet. *Bernard Spilsbury: Famous Cases of the Great Pathologist*. New York: Dorset Press (1988).

Caminada, Jerome. *Caminada the Crime Buster*. London: True Crime Library, Forum Press (1996).

Carlin, Francis. *Reminiscences of a Detective 1690–1926*. London: Hutchinson & Co. (1927). [Gutenberg]

Carr, John Dickson. *The Life of Arthur Conan Doyle*. London: John Murray (1949); New York: Harper and Brothers (1949).

Cobb, Belton. *The First Detectives*. London: Faber (1957).

Colquhoun, Kate. *Mr Briggs' Hat: A Sensational Account of Britain's First Railway Murder*. London: Abacus (2012).

Conan Doyle, Adrian. *The True Conan Doyle*. London: John Murray (1945).

Conan Doyle, Arthur. *The Case of Mr George Edalji. A Special Investigation*. Reprinted from *The Daily Telegraph*. London: Blake & Co. (1907).

_____ *The Story of Mr George Edalji*. 20 January 1907. Introduction by Richard and Molly Whittington-Egan eds. London: Grey House Books (1985).

_____ *The Case of Oscar Slater*. London: Hodder and Stoughton (1912).

_____ *Memories and Adventures*. London: Hodder & Stoughton (1924); Newcastle upon Tyne: Cambridge Scholars Publishing (2009).

_____ *The Penguin Complete Sherlock Holmes*. Introduction by Ruth Rendell. London: Penguin Books (2009).

Costello, Peter. *Conan Doyle Detective*. London: Constable & Robinson (2006).

Craigshill, S. *The Influence of Duality and Poe's Notion of the Bi-Part Soul on the Genesis of Detective Fiction in the Nineteenth Century*. Thesis. Edinburgh: Napier University (2010).

Dew, Walter. *I Caught Crippen*. Edinburgh: Blackie and Son (1938). [Marquess of Anglsey's jewels]

Dilnot, George. *Great Detectives and Their Methods*. London: Geoffrey Bles (1927).

_____ *Scotland Yard: Its History and Organisation 1829–1929*. London: Geoffrey Bles (1929).

_____ *Scotland Yard: The Methods and Organisation of the Metropolitan Police*. London: Percivall Marshall & Co. (1915).

_____ *Trial of the Detectives*. London: Geoffrey Bles (1928).

Doyle, Arthur Conan *see* Conan Doyle, Arthur.

Doyle, S. and D. A. Crowder. *Sherlock Holmes for Dummies*. New Jersey: Wiley (2010).

Dudley Edwards, Owen. *The Quest for Sherlock Holmes: A Biographical Study of Sir Arthur Conan Doyle*. Edinburgh: Mainstream Publishing (1983).

Emsley, Clive. *Crime and Society in England*. London: Longmans (1996).

_____ and Haia Shpayer-Makov, ed. *Police Detectives in History, 1750–1950*. Aldershot, Hants.: Ashgate (2006).

Evans, Colin. *The Father of Forensics: The Groundbreaking Cases of Sir Bernard Spilsbury*. New York: Berkley Books (2006); Thriplow, Cambridge: Icon (2007).

Fido, M[artin]. *The World of Sherlock Holmes*. London: Carlton Books (1998); Avon, MA: Adam Media Co. (1998).

_____ and Keith Skinner. *The Official Encyclopedia of Scotland Yard*. London: Virgin Books (1999).

Gaboriau, Emile. *Monsieur Le Coq*. New York: Dover Publications (1975).

Gaute, J. H. H. and Robin O'Dell. *The Murderers' Who's Who*. London: G. Harrap (1979).

Gibson, Michael and Richard Lancelyn Green eds. 'The Case of Mrs Castle', *Letters to the Press: The Unknown Conan Doyle*. London: Secker & Warburg (1986).

Green, Richard Lancelyn ed. *Letters to Sherlock Holmes*. London: Penguin Books (1985).

_____ *The Uncollected Sherlock Holmes*. London: Penguin (1983).

Gunn, Clement Bryce. *Leaves from the Life of a Country Doctor*. Rutherford Crockett ed. Edinburgh: The Ettrick Press (1935); rptd. Edinburgh: Berlinn (2002).

Hall, Trevor. *Sherlock Holmes and His Creator*. London: Gerald Duckworth (1978).

_____ *Sherlock Holmes: Ten Studies*. London: Gerald Duckworth (1969).

Harrison, Brian. *Separate Spheres: The Opposition to Women's Suffrage in Britain*. London: Routledge (2013).

Higham, Charles. *The Adventures of Conan Doyle*. London: Hamish Hamilton (1976).

Himmelfarb, Hildegarde. *Marriage and Morals among the Victorians*. London: I. B. Tauris (1989).

Hines, Stephen, ed. *The True Crimes Files of Sir Arthur Conan Doyle*. Introduction by Steven Womack (New York: Berkley Prime Crime (2001). [Edalji and Slater only]

Hyde, H. Montgomery. *Famous Trials 9: Roger Casement*. Ninth Series. Harmondsworth: Penguin (1964).

Jeffreys, S. *The Spinster and Her Enemies: Feminism and Sexuality 1880–1930*. London: Pandora (1985).

Jones, H. E. 'The Origin of Sherlock Holmes', *The Game Is Afoot*. M. Kaye, ed. New York: St. Martin's Press (1994). [pastiches, parodies]

Kopley, Richard. *Edgar Allan Poe and the Philadelphia Saturday News*. Baltimore, MD: Enoch Pratt Free Library (1991).

Lancelyn Green, Richard *see* Green, Richard Lancelyn.

Lansdowne, Andrew. *Life's Reminiscences of Scotland Yard*. London: Simpkin, Marshall, Hamilton, Rent & Co. (n.d.)

Lellenberg, Jon et al. *Arthur Conan Doyle: A Life in Letters*. New York: Penguin (2007).

Liebow, Ely. *Dr Joe Bell*. Bowling Green, OH: Bowling Green University Popular Press (1982).

Lock, Joan. *Dreadful Deeds and Awful Murders: Scotland Yard's First Detectives 1829–1878*. Taunton: Barn Owl Books (1990).

_____ *Scotland Yard Casebook: The Making of the CID 1865–1935*. London: Robert Hale Ltd. (1993).

_____ *Scotland Yard's First Cases*. London: Robert Hale (2011).

Lycett, Andrew. *The Man Who Created Sherlock Holmes: The*

Life and Times of Sir Arthur Conan Doyle. New York: Free Press (2007).

Marlow, Joyce, ed. *Votes for Women*. London: Virago Press (2013).

McIntyre, Brian. *The Napoleon of Crime: The Life and Times of Adam Worth, Master Thief*. New York: Broadway Paperbacks (1997).

Miller, R[ussell]. *The Adventures of Arthur Conan Doyle*. London: Harvill Secker (2008); New York: St. Martin's Press (2008).

Morris, R. M. 'Crime Does Not Pay', *Police Detectives in History, 1750–1950*. Clive Emsley ed., Aldershot, Hants.: Ashgate (2006).

Moscucci, Ornella. *The Science of Women: Gynaecolgy and Gender in England, 1800–1929*. Cambridge: Cambridge University Press (1990).

Moss, Alan and Keith Skinner. *The Scotland Yard Files: Milestones in Crime*. National Archives (2006).

_____ *The Victorian Detective*. Oxford: Shire Publications (2013).

Newman, Gerald. 'Bow Street Runners', *Britain in the Hanoverian Age, 1714–1837: an Encyclopedia*. New York: Garland Publishers (1997).

Nordon, Pierre. *Conan Doyle A Biography*. London: John Murray (1966); New York: Holt, Rinehart & Winston (1967).

Normanton, Helen. 'The Crowborough Murder Case', *Great Unsolved Crimes*. London: Hutchinson (1935).

O'Brien, James. *The Scientific Sherlock Holmes*. Oxford: Oxford University Press (2013).

Oddie, S[amuel] Ingleby. *Inquest: A Coroner Looks Back*. London: Hutchinson (1938). [Crippen]

Park, William. *The Truth about Oscar Slater. With a Statement by Sir Arthur Conan Doyle*. London: Psychic Press (1927).

Pearl, Matthew ed. *The Murders in the Rue Morgue [The Dupin Tales]* New York: Vintage Books (2006).

Pearsall, Ronald. *Conan Doyle: A Biographical Solution*. New York: St. Martin's Press (1977).

Pearson, Hesketh. *Conan Doyle, His Life and Art*. London: Methuen (1943).

Petrow, Stefan. 'The Rise of the Detective in London 1869–1914', *Criminal Justice History,* Vol.14 (1993), pp. 91–108.

Phillips, Melanie. *The Ascent of Women*. London: Abacus (2003).

Rose, Andrew. *Lethal Witness*. Kent, Ohio: Kent State University Press (2009).

Roughead, W[illiam] N[icol], ed. *Classic Crimes*. London: Cassell (1951); London: Panther (1966); New York: Vintage Books (1977). [Slater case]

Saxby, Jessie M. E. *Joseph Bell: An Appreciation by an Old Friend*. Edinburgh: Oliphant, Anderson & Ferrier (1913).

Saxon, John. 'The Mystery of the Stolen Jewels', *The Great Stories of Real Life: Famous Crimes, Mysteries & Romances*. Vol. II, Max Pemberton ed. London: George Newnes (1924).

Shawcross, John T. *The Complete Poetry of John Milton*. New York: Anchor Press (1971).

Shpayer-Makov, Haia. *The Ascent of the Detective: Police Sleuths in Victorian and Edwardian England*. Oxford: Oxford University Press (2011).

_____ 'Explaining the Rise and Success of Detective Memoirs in Britain', *Police Detectives in History, 1750–1950*, Clive Emsley ed. Aldershot, Hants: Ashgate (2006).

Sifakis, Carl. *The Catalogue of Crime*. New York: New American Library (1979).

Smith, A. Duncan, ed. *Famous Scottish and British Trials: The Trial of A. J. Monson*. Edinburgh: W. Hodge (1906).

Smith, D. *Sherlock Holmes Companion*. New York: Castle Books (2009).

Smith, P[hilip] T[hurmond]. *Policing Victorian London*. Westport, CT: Greenwood (1985).

Smith, Sydney. *Mostly Murder*. New York: Dorset Press (1988). [Bell's forensic work]

Starrett, Vincent. *The Private Life of Sherlock Holmes*. London: Ivor Nicholson & Watson (1934).

Stashower, Daniel. *The Teller of Tales: The Life of Arthur Conan Doyle*. New York: Henry Holt and Company (1999).

Suszynski, Jim. (1988 13, 15) [photocopies of press clippings re Sherlock Holmes and drug addiction; located on internet; held in a distant location]

Thomas, Ronald. *Detective Fiction and the Rise of Forensic Science*. Cambridge: Cambridge University Press (1999).

Thomson, Basil. *Queer People*. London: Hodder and Stoughton (1922).

Thompson, F. M. L. *The Rise of Respectable Society: A Social History of Victorian Britain: 1830–1900*. London: Fontana (1988).

Tobias, J. J. *Crime and Police in England 1700–1900*. Dublin: Gill and Macmillan (1979).

Toughill, Thomas. *Oscar Slater: The Immortal Case of Sir Arthur Conan Doyle*. Stroud: Sutton Publishing (2006).

_____ *Oscar Slater: The Mystery Solved*. Edinburgh: Canongate Books (1993).

Trow, M. J. *The Thames Torso Murders*. Barnsley: Wharncliffe Books of Ren & Sword Books (2011).

Wade, Stephen. *Conan Doyle and His Crime Club*. UK: Fonthill Media Limited.

_____ *Plain Clothes & Sleuths: A History of the Detective in Britain*. Stroud: Tempus (2007).

Wagner, E. J. *The Science of Sherlock Holmes*. Hoboken: John Wiley (2006).

Walkowitz, Judith R. *Prostitution and Victorian Society*. Cambridge: Cambridge University Press (1980).

Wallace, Irving. 'The Real Sherlock Holmes', *The Fabulous Originals*. New York: Alfred A. Knopf (1956).

Weaver, Gordon. *Conan Doyle and the Parson's Son: the George Edalji Case*. Cambridge: Vanguard (2006).

Wensley, Frederick Porter. *Forty Years at Scotland Yard*. Garden City, New York: Garden City Publishing Co. (n.d.)

White, Jerry. *London in the Nineteenth Century*. London: Cape (2007).

Wilson, Colin and Patricia Pitman. *Encyclopedia of Murder*. London: Arthur Booker (1961).

Periodicals

Anon. 'Conan Doyle as He Appears Here', *New York Times* (3 October 1894) p. 4.

Anon. 'The Conan Doyle Banquet at the Authors Club', *Queen* (4 July 1896) C 19.

Anon. 'Concerning Conan Doyle', *Collier's Weekly* XLI (15 August 1908) p. 2.

Anon. 'Dr Conan Doyle: A Character Sketch', *Cassell's Saturday Journal*, XI (15 February 1893), p. 422.

Anon, 'Dr Joseph Bell', *The Times* (12 October 1911).

Anon. 'Interview with Joseph Bell', *Pall Mall Gazette*, No. 8900 (3 September 1893).

Anon. '"Jack the Ripper", How "Sherlock Holmes" Would Have Tracked Him', *Evening News*, Portsmouth (4 July 1894).

Anon. [Lincoln Springfield] 'The Original Sherlock Holmes: An Interview with Dr Joseph Bell', *Pall Mall Gazette*, LVII, No. 8975 (28 December 1893) pp. 1–2.

Anon. 'The Real Sherlock Holmes', *Tit-Bits* LXI, No.1,566 (21 October 1911) 127.

Anon. 'Sir Arthur Conan Doyle and the Thorne Case', *Morning Post* (21 April 1925) p. 9.

Anon. 'Theatres', *Candid Friend* (9 November 1901) 74.

Aldis, Henry Mills. 'The Original of Sherlock Holmes', *Harper's Weekly Magazine*, XXXVIII, No. 1937 (3 February 1894) p. 114.

Ashton-Wolfe, Harry. 'The Debt of the Police to Detective Fiction', *Illustrated News* (27 February 1932), pp. 320, 328.

Bell, J. Alexander. 'The Use of Coca', *British Medical Journal*, Vol. 1, No. 688 (7 March 1874) p. 305.

Bell, Joe. Review of *The Adventures of Sherlock Holmes*, *The Bookman*, Vol. 3 (December 1892) pp. 79–81.

Blathwayt, Raymond. 'A Talk with Dr. Conan Doyle', *The Bookman* (May 1892) pp. 50–1.

Brecher, Edward. 'The Consumers Union Report on Licit and Illicit Drugs', *Consumer Reports Magazine* (1972) Chp. 35, Cocaine, p. 351.

Christison, Robert. 'Observations on the Effects of Cuca, Or Coca, the Leaves of Erythroxylon Coca', *British Medical Journal*, Vol. 1, No. 800 (29 April 1876) pp. 527–531.

Conan Doyle, Arthur. 'Conan Doyle Tells the True Story of Sherlock Holmes', *Tit-Bits* XXXIX, No. 1000 (15 December 1900) p. 287.

_____ 'Gelseminum as a Poison', *British Medical Journal* (20 September 1879) p. 14.

_____ 'The Oscar Slater Case', Letter to the Editor, *The Spectator*. No. 4,491, (1914) pp. 127–8.

_____ 'The Truth about Sherlock Holmes', *Collier's Weekly*, LXXII (29 December 1923) p. 28.

Conan Doyle, Jean. 'Conan Doyle *Was* Sherlock Holmes', *Pearson's Magazine*, Vol. LXXVIII, No. 468 (December 1934) pp. 574–7.

Guthrie, Douglas. 'Medicine and Detection: Dr Joseph Bell and Others', *Medicine Illustrated* III, No. 5 (May 1949) pp. 223–6.

Hamilton, Z. M. 'Origins of Sherlock Holmes', *Boston Medical and Surgical Journal*, No. 165 (December 1911) p. 584.

Handasyde, [Emily Handasyde Buchanen] 'The Real Sherlock Holmes, *Good Words, and Sunday Magazine*, Vol. XLIII (June 1902) pp. 159–63.

How, Harry. 'A Day with Dr Conan Doyle', *The Strand Magazine*, IV (August 1892) pp. 182–7.

Huber, Christine L. 'The Sherlock Holmes Blood Test: Solution to a Century-Old Mystery', *Baker Street Journal*, 4 (1), pp. 44–49.

Jones, Harold Emory. 'The Original of Sherlock Holmes', *Collier's Weekly*, XXXII, No. 15 (9 January 1904) pp. 14–15, 20.

McGown, Raymond J. 'Sherlock Holmes and Forensic Chemistry', *Baker Street Journal*, 37 (1) pp. 10–14.

Thomas, Keith. 'The Double Standard', *Journal of the History of Ideas*, Vol. 20, No. 2, (1959), pp. 196–216.

Wallace, Irving. 'The Incredible Dr Bell', *Saturday Review of Literature* XXXI, No. 18 (May 1, 1948) pp. 7–8, 28.

Young, W. J. 'Origins of Sherlock Holmes', *British Medical Journal*, Vol. 2, No. 3842 (25 August 1934) pp. 374–5. [reference to Hamilton]

Internet Sources

'Bow Street Runners', Wikipedia
'Fingerprinting', Wikipedia
'First Railway Murder in Britain', *British Transport Police History Group*, www.btphg,org.uk/?page_id=3108
'Forensic Pathology, Wikipedia
'Forensic Science', Wikipedia
Friends of the Metropolitan Police Historical Collection, Met Police Timeline 1829–1899
'Henry Classification System', Wikipedia
Keefauver, Brad. 'A Basic Timeline of Terra 221B' (2001).
'Questioned Document Examination', Wikipedia

Unpublished Letters

Library of Royal College of Surgeons of Edinburgh, Stisted Collection, GD 16/1/2/1/4, RSL Box B

INDEX